Marcus
&
Lyric

Corinna M. Dominy

D1418179

Copyright © 2014 Corinna M. Dominy

All rights reserved.

ISBN:1497300304
ISBN-13:9781497300309

For my Mommy

Corinna M. Dominy

ACKNOWLEDGMENTS

God has blessed me immensely and allowed another 'novel' idea to take shape and grow characters! I am constantly and incredibly humbled by Him. The fact that He uses me to help spread His message of love is sometimes more than my little heart can bear! My passion for writing has nothing on my passion for my Creator and I joyfully use the gift He has given me for His good.

Many thanks go to my mom. Even when times were hard, while I was growing up and she had her hands full (up to her elbows, at least!) with me, she never gave up and never gave in, even to my teenaged demands. Now, as an adult, I also consider her a mentor and a friend. From baby advice and how to be a mother, to financial advice when my husband and I bought our first house, and everything in between, my mom is my go-to person. Thanks, Mom! I love you.

Once again, I'd be remiss not to thank my grandma. She did such a diligent job proof reading my first manuscript, it was a no-brainer to ask for her help again. Thank you, grandma!

Thank you, David, for your help and listening ear. And especially for taking an entire afternoon to create the cover! I am so lucky to have you as my supporter and encourager. Most importantly, God blessed me the most when He gave me you!

Dear reader, thank you for wanting to read what I've written. I hope you enjoy the characters, Marcus and Lyric, as much as I've enjoyed writing them.

Chapter 1

Security is not the absence of danger, but the presence of God,
no matter what the danger
Author unknown

A decision had been made, although he was still puzzled as to how he had reached it. According to the paper in front of him, the bruised, frightened, vulnerable and forlorn girl sitting across the table was named Lyric Bell.

With a name like that, he vaguely wondered if her parents had been hippies or merely creative in their naming.

When Marcus Coulter had decided to put in an ad for a roommate, he hadn't thought to specify gender. Frankly, he hadn't thought he needed to. He had been honest in saying he was a Christian and assumed from that, he wouldn't have any female applicants. And really, what woman in her right mind would want to live with a male stranger in New York City a mere eight months after the 9/11 attacks?

But, on the day of walk-in interviews, Lyric Bell had surprised him. Not merely because she was a woman, but because of her appearance as well.

Since she had sat down, he'd covertly been studying her. Not only her appearance, but he was trying to piece together her history, too.

Lyric wore a black hoodie pulled over her head, with faded, almost raggedy, light blue jeans, and scuffed white sneakers. Only a fringe of wavy, strawberry blonde peeked out from beneath her dark hood. Her thin face enhanced her wide eyes that matched the color of the faded denim she wore.

What had surprised Marcus were the bruises along her jawline and the black eye. The purpose for her hideout inside her sweatshirt, he deduced, being that it was a late-May spring day. The bruises and black eye looked a few days old, but did nothing to lessen the impact of anger Marcus suddenly felt toward the unknown stranger who was responsible.

Even all that combined couldn't have prepared Marcus for the shock of what he did next.

As soon as Lyric had sat down, Marcus silently prayed, *'Lord, what on earth is she doing here? She obviously needs help, but I don't have any to give her! What do I do with her?'*

Out loud, Marcus began introductions. "Hi, I'm Marcus. I see from your application that you're Lyric."

A mere nod answered his question.

He extended his hand, "Nice to meet you."

Lyric looked uncertain, but finally extended her hand. Marcus grasped it, but immediately loosened his grip, barely holding on. Her hand felt small, frail and clammy.

Lyric jerked her hand back and discreetly wiped it on her jeans.

Marcus already determined he would get her some kind of help before she left. He wouldn't, couldn't with a clear conscience send her back to whoever gave her those bruises. Again, he felt an unexplainable stab of pure anger at whoever that might be.

'Get a grip, Marcus! You don't even know the guy!' He was certain, however, that it was a boyfriend.

Trying to decide what course of action to take, he stalled for time. "So, where are you from? What do you do? Tell me about yourself."

He had posed the same series of questions to all of his applicants. All of whom had seemed normal enough, miraculously.

Lyric suddenly looked like a deer caught in headlights.

"Um…" she began in a tentative, whispery voice.

Why all of the questions, she wondered. She had never interviewed for an apartment before. When she had arrived in New York at the young age of eighteen, she had met another girl at the bar where she was waitressing and ended up moving in with her. A relief at the time because most of the money she had brought with her had gone to pay for the small room in the seedy motel she'd been living in.

"I live in Harlem." That was it. Her only answer.

Marcus carefully controlled his surprise and horror. She shouldn't be living in such a rough neighborhood without someone properly looking after her! And obviously no one was. Another flash of anger.

Indicated on her application, Lyric was twenty-two, but she barely looked eighteen!

Marcus couldn't seem to fight the protective feeling. He didn't know why. He didn't know Lyric. All he knew was that, had he a younger sister in the same situation that Lyric seemed to be in, he'd want someone to help her.

'God, I can't have her live here…can I? That would be – wrong…wouldn't it? How do I help her?'

He suddenly felt compelled to get some answers and, in so doing, he would have the answer to his own question.

Clearing his throat, Marcus looked Lyric directly in the eye and gently asked, "Why did you choose to come here for an interview? I mean, in this day and age especially, you don't know who you can trust. And I'm a strange guy." He flashed a crooked smile, hoping to put her at ease.

Lyric answered with a small, tight smile. In her same quiet tone, she said, "Your ad said you are a Christian."

The reply caught Marcus off guard. "Yes?" he questioned uncertainly.

'This does not make things any clearer, Lord!'

"I know I can trust Christians," was her only simple reply.

'Okay.' Marcus was still puzzling.

"Are you a Christian?" popped out before Marcus had time to think.

With a slightly wistful sigh, Lyric said, "Not anymore."

Seemingly without thought, he heard the most puzzling words come out of his mouth. He was quite certain God was running it. "Lyric, would you like to move in here with me?"

Silently Marcus protested, *'This will not look good, God.'*

To which he was given the reply, *'Sometimes helping people is more important than appearances.'*

Hope seemed to light up her eyes. "Are – are, uh, your interviews over?" She told herself to calm down and not get her hopes up.

Marcus had slated the day for interviews. Lyric had been his sixth. Apparently his last.

"They are now," he smiled warmly.

ˏˏ

In hindsight, Marcus knew he should have started the conversation with his mom over the phone differently. Instead of, "Hi, Mom. So...I found this girl..."

Of course his mom pounced on that and it took him a good five minutes to explain the real circumstances.

Lynne Coulter had always wanted her second-born, and youngest, to find "a nice girl that we can meet."

So, after Marcus was finally allowed to explain, he found he was holding his breath to hear what his mom would say. He knew she wasn't one to pass judgment, but he also wasn't sure how she'd feel about him sharing his apartment with a strange girl.

There were a few moments of silence only broken by quiet sniffles. Finally, Lynne told her son, "That's so romantic."

Marcus was a bit thrown. "Mom!" he protested, exasperated. "It's *not* romantic! If it were, she couldn't stay here."

Sighing wistfully, Lynne answered, "Oh, I know...I only want you to find someone."

"I'm not really looking," he reminded gently. It wasn't that he was averse to the idea, but he was busy with night school and his full-time banking job.

"Well, I'm proud of you, honey. You listened to God on this one and He'll bless you for helping this poor girl, even if it seems like unconventional circumstances."

Marcus let out his breath in a *whoosh!* He'd had his doubts about whether or not he had done the right thing. He'd feared it might have been a bit rash, but as he kept thinking over his decision, he wondered if it had been his decision at all. Hearing his mom's words, he was finally reassured.

"Thanks, Mom," he replied softly.

"When she's all settled, can we meet her?" Lynne suddenly asked brightly.

Marcus rolled his eyes to the ceiling, seeking divine guidance. "Sure, Mom, I'll have you and Dad over for dinner, okay?"

"We'll look forward to it."

Marcus hung up and set his phone down. Poor Lyric, she had no idea what she had just gotten herself into.

Chapter 2
Fear makes strangers of people who would be friends
Shirley MacLaine

By Friday evening, Lyric was all moved in. She had a double bed and a small dresser, besides her clothes and a few personal items. Although her new lodgings weren't big, her room looked sparse with only the bed pushed against the window and the dresser occupying the opposite wall.

Marcus had offered to go with her to get her things, but she'd declined. She hadn't told Austin, her boyfriend and the cause of her anxiety, she was moving out. If he knew, of course he'd be furious. That's why she'd chosen a time when she knew he was gone. She'd actually dared a prayer of mercy to the God she'd forsaken long ago. Besides, she would have felt ridiculous asking Marcus to help her move her two big items. And the less he knew, even about where she lived, the better. The place was a dump anyway and she was ashamed of it.

She ended up feeling a bit ridiculous. She'd had to call a mover because she couldn't very well haul a bed and dresser across the city on her own. The mover had mercifully kept a straight face when he loaded her two lonely items into the back of his truck. On the other hand, she had very much felt like laughing, but refrained from making herself appear even more crazy than she most assuredly already had.

Lyric had told the mover to unload her pathetic cargo on the sidewalk and did elicit Marcus' help from there.

The dresser was small enough to be carried into the elevator and Marcus was also able to get the bedframe in as well. The mattress, on the other hand, was a different story. With much squishing and squashing along the narrow stairwell and plastering themselves against the wall, the mattress finally made it up to the eighth floor.

Now, the two sat, watching television. Other than that, the apartment was silent. Feeling more than a bit awkward, she cast furtive glances in Marcus' direction. He seemed completely at ease. Yes, it was his apartment, but a stranger lived there now. To look at him, one would think it was an everyday occurrence to have strangers moving in. She had the uncomfortable thought that Marcus probably wouldn't allow them to remain strangers for long. Lyric wrestled with how much of herself she would want to reveal to him. She had to admit surprise that he hadn't pressed further about her background, being that he knew next to nothing about her. That was just fine with her. Except…she knew she'd eventually be forced to reveal one little thing.

As Marcus continued to flip through channels, she risked another glance in his direction. She wondered if, maybe, Marcus wasn't inclined to open up to her, either. That would suit her just fine. No pressure to get to know each other, they could simply be roommates in the strictest sense of the term.

Lyric let out a sigh of serenity as she became engulfed in the relative quiet. She hadn't experienced that in a very long time. With Austin, there was always someone knocking at the door for a deal, or yelling and arguing, usually because of a deal gone wrong, or the phone was ringing, and almost always the TV was loudly on to distract the neighbors from the other noises, like gunshots. Usually from Austin or one of his sidekicks that did Austin's dirty work. In the midst of it all, whenever Austin got mad, no matter what had set him off, he would take it out on Lyric. Only once had she dared call the ambulance. Austin made sure she never did that again. Suddenly breaking from the gloomy thoughts of her past life, Lyric shivered.

Marcus broke the silence then. "How 'bout I order us a pizza?"

"Uh, sure…I'm not sure I have any cash on me, though."

Giving her a puzzled look, Marcus answered, "Uh, ok. What do you like on it?"

"I mean, I can't pay for my share."

"It's okay, Lyric, I got it." He smiled, showing that he had dimples. "What do you like on your pizza?"

"I'm not particular except I'm afraid I don't like the standard bachelor favorite. Pepperoni."

Marcus chuckled, "Duly noted," then picked up the phone.

After the pizza was delivered and they were dishing out their first slices, Lyric heard the dreaded words.

"So, Lyric, tell me about yourself." He thought he was being friendly, but saw panic clearly written on her face. It almost immediately disappeared, but it stuck with him.

"Um, there's not much to tell," Lyric mumbled, as she sucked a string of cheese into her mouth.

"Where did you live before gracing my humble abode?" It was a dangerous question he knew, but he suddenly found himself desperate for any and all information about Lyric. All he knew was that it had been in Harlem.

She stuck to being vague. "Uh, not too far."

Marcus could clearly see she'd been hesitant to answer and wondered why. Still, he couldn't help but press this mystery known as Lyric. "Did you move out of your parents' house? Do you have any siblings?" He figured she'd moved out of her boyfriend's place, but was hoping she would give more information. The desire to know what she had run from was nearly overwhelming.

Great, just great. So much for being vague. Lyric did not like where this line of questioning was leading. Still, she could try to remain vague. "Nope, and I'm an only child."

Lyric wished he'd tell her a little about himself and get the focus off of her.

"Do you have a job?" According to her application, she did. He was hoping to get her to open up about *something*!

Lyric was relieved that this question was less personal. She answered promptly, "Butterman's Health Food." Letting out an unconscious little giggle, she continued, "I know, it sounds quite contradictory. I do stocking and checkout. There are only a few employees."

Quickly deciding this was her chance, Lyric took it and turned the tables. "What about you? Where do you work? What about your family and all that?" She flashed a quick smile to hopefully calm any choppy waters she may have caused in getting personal with him. This was new territory for Lyric, talking about personal things. She'd never had personal conversations with Austin…she doubted he even knew she was an only child nor what the story was with her parents. And although she didn't know Marcus, something told her he wasn't anything like Austin.

Marcus disarmingly returned her smile. It made the corners of his green eyes crinkle.

Lyric was pleased to note that his smiles always reached his eyes. Austin's smiles didn't do that. His tight smiles had kept his brown eyes cool and guarded.

"I work as a bank teller and will be starting night classes on Monday. I'm trying to get my accounting degree. I want to start my own accounting firm someday. As for family, I have an older brother, Levi; a sister-in-law, Rachel; two nieces, Hailey and Sydney; and two nephews, Zachary and Logan; and two parents." Another quick, grinning flash. "Oh, and Sydney and Logan are twins."

For some reason, Lyric found it comforting that Marcus seemed to smile a lot.

Marcus couldn't be distracted for long, however. Trying to keep things light, he tried for a teasing tone. "So do you have a boyfriend?" He saw the deer-in-the-headlights look come across her face.

Alright, enough with the probing. Lyric shut down. "I don't want to talk about this." Scrambling up, she escaped to her room.

Landing with a thud in the center of her bed, Lyric tucked her knees under her chin, wrapping her arms around them. Calming herself, she took a few deep breaths. Retreating was her means for escaping anything. She'd learned that had been the only option open to her. Unless Austin wanted her badly enough. Then no means of escape was possible. The thought made her shake and tremble all over. She had to deep breathe again to gain back a modicum of control. Somehow Lyric knew deep within her gut that Marcus would never lay a hand on her and the thought was soothing. She vaguely wondered if she would actually get a full-night's sleep without fear of being woke up by the door or phone or Austin wanting to beat his frustration out of her or…other things. She sighed and looked toward the door. She supposed she had been rather rude.

In the living room, Marcus was giving himself a lecture. '*Well done, Coulter,*' he reproached sarcastically. *Why* had he pushed her so much?

Yes, he'd wanted to find out more, more, more, but he should have known better than to actually voice it! She clearly had been in an abusive situation, but it was none of his business and he shouldn't have tried to make it be. She clearly hadn't wanted to answer his questions. He had to earn that kind of trust! Yet he'd allowed this weird sense of protectiveness he'd developed to rule his actions. It was ludicrous! He really needed to apologize.

Of course he still wanted to know about the black eye. Where it had come from. If she had any other injuries. He was realizing that he was kind of obsessed with finding out all of the information. It was more than idle curiosity to him. If he'd had a sister, he suspected this would have been the reaction he'd've had if something similar had happened to her. But, for the time being, he determined he would have to let the matter rest. If she never felt like talking about it, he'd have to accept that. It wasn't about him, anyway, it was about Lyric feeling safe and secure in her new home.

Over an hour later, he could stand the guilt no longer. Marcus decided to chance the risk and check on Lyric.

'*Help me find the right words, Lord*,' Marcus silently pleaded as he knocked on Lyric's bedroom door. "Lyric, are you awake? Can I please talk to you?"

Lyric's heart leaped into her throat, momentarily frightened he had come for her after all. As usual when Lyric tensed up, waiting for Austin's wrath, she began to cower on her bed. The voice and the fact that he had actually knocked finally penetrated her thoughts. This wasn't Austin, this was Marcus. He was nice. She headed for the door.

As she silently opened the door and then retreated back to her bed and sat on the edge, Marcus noted how her strawberry blond hair hung down her back in soft waves.

Standing in the doorway, Marcus leaned against the frame and folded his arms, crossing his ankles in a casual stance.

Lyric finally looked at him and, straightening, he took the opportunity to say what he needed to say. "Lyric, I'm really sorry. Your personal life is none of my business. I sincerely hope you can forgive me."

She had to will her mouth not to gape open. Austin never would have admitted wrong doing, much less apologize for it! As Marcus pushed off the doorframe and turned to go, Lyric sat up straighter and cleared her throat. "Marcus," he turned. Feeling self-conscious, she simply stated, "You're forgiven."

"If you ever do want to talk about…anything, I'm here." Again, he turned to go.

Stunned by his obvious caring, Lyric could only stutter. "Th-th-thank you."

"You're welcome." He smiled and then shut the door behind him.

She was ashamed of herself that a simple apology from a man could bring such emotion. The only other man she had ever been close to was her father, and he had never done anything to her to apologize for. Thinking of

her father hurt and she automatically pushed away any thoughts of him or her mother. She was good at that.

Crawling into bed, Lyric lay there and let her mind wander to the obvious differences between Austin and Marcus. After only one day, she already knew she'd lucked out in the roommate department. Even though his green eyes had pierced through her as he'd fired his questions, as if he could see deep down into her soul. It was a disconcerting feeling. Yet, when he'd apologized, they'd turned to a liquid sea of green, full of regret, sorrow…but also warmth and sincerity. She'd known instinctively that she could trust what he said.

Lyric regarded the whole package of Marcus Coulter. His black hair, artfully mussed, was a nice contrast to his bright, emerald green eyes. He was tall and broad shouldered, solid. He lent an air of strength, stability, security…all things she yearned to feel. And she had a hunch, women's intuition, perhaps, that he would not hesitate to defend her, if needed. She didn't know why she felt it so strongly, but she did. She felt safe. Genuinely safe. She hadn't felt that way in a long time and it was nice.

As Lyric started to drift off to sleep, she reflected that maybe God had taken pity on her and led her here. Whatever it was, she was grateful.

ˌˌˌ

The next morning, Lyric stepped into a fragrant kitchen. Marcus was cooking fluffy omelets filled with diced ham, peppers, and onions.

"I hope you're hungry."

"Are you sure you shouldn't be trying to become a chef instead of an accountant?"

Smiling, Marcus set a plate down in front of her as she took a chair. "I only dabble."

Lyric took a bite and savored it. "Mmm! These are yummy!"

Surreptitiously, Lyric glanced at Marcus. Did he want something? Shaking herself, she chided. *'Of course not! He is just a nice guy! Sheesh, Lyric'*

Marcus cocked his eyebrow. "Yummy?" he teased.

Smiling and catching herself, Lyric blushed and amended. "Good. They're good."

"I'm glad you approve, but don't get used to it." He winked. "I'll be too busy playing college boy to cook on the weekends."

Marcus set his own plate down across from Lyric.

"My own schedule isn't exactly conducive to routine, either," she found herself telling him.

Marcus finished half his omelet before making a suggestion. "It might be helpful to both of us if we knew each other's schedules. So, you know, we can be considerate of each other's space and everything. You basically know mine. I'm outta here by 7:30 in the morning on weekdays. I work 9 to 5 at the bank. Mondays, Wednesdays, and Fridays, I have classes until nine at night. My classes on Tuesdays and Thursdays end at ten. I'm sure Saturdays will be dedicated to studying and Sundays I leave for church at 9:00 a.m."

A little wary what the 'church talk' will lead to, Lyric asks anyway, "You go to church, huh?"

"You're welcome to come."

She *knew* he'd been too good to be true. '*He's one of* those *people*,' Lyric thought cynically. '*Uh, no thanks!*'

Seeing that he'd get no response, and vowing, again, not to push, he simply invited, "So, what's your schedule like?"

"Actually, I don't have set hours. I work full time, but my days change often. I actually had taken yesterday and today off to apartment hunt, but the store's closed on Sundays. I do work this Monday, eleven to seven. That's when we close. As I get my schedule each week, I can post it on the fridge...or something." She sounded as if this were her apartment! "Will that be okay?" she finished uncertainly.

Nonchalant, Marcus commented, "Whatever works. I don't pry anymore, remember?" Then he grinned.

Lyric returned the smile.

As it appeared neither had plans, they simply hung out at the apartment for the day and vegged in front of the T.V.

Lyric couldn't remember the last time she'd done that. In fact, she didn't think she ever had since she was a teenager. It felt good. She'd kinda forgotten how it felt to relax.

Marcus actually handed her the remote! It was ridiculous how empowering it felt to control that remote! They took turns tossing each other the remote after a show or movie was over, flipping through the channels.

After one such time, she got ready to toss the remote back to Marcus from her place in the recliner. Her aim was off and she ended up clocking him in the chest. She froze in instinctive fear and her face turned pale. "I'm so sorry, Marcus! I didn't mean to hit you!" Lyric tensed herself to get ready for a physical attack, covering her head with her arms.

Marcus, seeing her reaction, froze, too.

'*What do I do?*' he panicked. Forcing himself to calm down, he realized she was reacting on instinct.

After Lyric realized Marcus wasn't attacking, she poked her head up and sheepishly looked around.

A slow grin spread over Marcus' face. "Ow! You've got a good arm on ya. Watching the ball game earlier must've taught you to pitch through osmosis or something."

Lyric tried to smile through stiff lips as her erratic breathing began to smooth back out. Discreetly, she swiped at the cold sweat that had beaded on her upper lip.

Marcus had noticed Lyric's reaction, but didn't give it away. Skittish...no, it was more than that. Scared. Scared and skittish and it made him heartsick to know what had caused it. She'd never told him, but he knew. No one acted like that without a reason. He watched as her color returned, as she seemed to understand he wasn't going to lay a hand on her.

Lyric could only openly stare at Marcus now, conscious of how she must have looked. Surely he couldn't have missed that!

She swallowed convulsively. If that had been Austin, he'd have pummeled her for her careless throw. Lyric's stare of what could only be described as awe wasn't lost on him.

Marcus threw her what he hoped to be a casual glance. "Ya okay?"

Shaking herself, Lyric managed, "Yeah, yeah, I'm fine."

He wouldn't pry, he reminded himself fiercely. Now, especially, was not the time to make that mistake again.

With forced nonchalance, he turned his attention back to the screen. "Hey, do you like this movie?"

Lyric saw the beginning credits of 'Groundhog Day.' In disbelief, she realized Marcus was not going to comment. A bit distracted with relief by this, she managed to answer, "Yeah, sure. It's a good movie."

The rest of the evening passed in easy companionship. As they turned their separate ways, Marcus commented, "That was fun. Too bad we couldn't make a routine of it, huh?"

Lyric smiled her agreement. "Goodnight, Marcus."

"Goodnight, Lyric."

Lyric had half expected an invitation to church. To her relief, he didn't mention it except to remind her he would be leaving at 9:00, if he left before she woke up.

Lyric decided she rather liked Marcus Coulter. He definitely beat out Austin Wood – by a long shot!

Chapter 3

*I am afraid to show you who I really am, because if I show you
who I really am, you might not like it...and that's all I got*
Sabrina Ward Harrison

"Marcus, I have something to tell you." The dramatic face Lyric made in
the mirror stared back at her. The expression looked faked.

"That won't work," Lyric muttered to herself.

It was late-June and she'd been living with Marcus for about a month
now and still he knew nothing of her secret. They'd shared bits of
information, even delving into family. A taboo subject for her, but she'd
shared what she thought was just enough. She knew way more about his
family than he did about hers. And still, this secret hung over her. What
she had gotten to know of Marcus had impressed her and she felt she could
trust him with the secret. Yet, she couldn't really know how he'd react
until she told him. Would he think she'd been lying and kick her out? He'd
have every right. She was tired of carrying the weight alone and needed to
tell him and be done with it. Whatever happened, happened. Simply put,
Marcus, as her roommate, deserved to know.

Lyric could still faintly hear Marcus in the other room talking on the
phone to his best friend, Andrew. He talked more than most girls she
knew! The thought made her giggle. It seemed he was always either
talking with Andrew or his older brother, Levi, or his mom.

Andrew lived in Boston, but Levi lived somewhere in upstate New York.
Lyric couldn't remember where, exactly.

'*As soon as he's off the phone, as soon as he's off the phone,*' she
chanted the promise to herself.

Restless, she wandered into the living room where Marcus was and
planted herself on the couch. Now all she had to do was wait...for Marcus
to get off the phone...and for her confidence to catch up with her actions.

Glancing at her from his place on the recliner, Marcus smiled, although
still on the phone. Definitely different than Austin. Austin had only noticed
her when it was convenient for him. Quickly she banished the thought,
suddenly feeling disloyal to Austin and afraid he'd somehow find out.

"Yeah, man, that sounds like a plan. I'll see if I can squeeze it into my
schedule." As Marcus talked, he got Lyric's attention and tossed her the
remote.

Lyric idly flipped through channels as she kept an ear on the conversation. It sounded like it was nearing the end.

"Alright." Pause. "Of course!" Pause. "We'd love to meet her." Pause.

"Okay, man, take care. Bye."

The 'we'd love to meet her,' hadn't escaped Lyric's notice. Did Marcus
have a girlfriend? How come he hadn't said anything? How come she

hadn't met her yet? Did he not feel comfortable bringing her by? Did she know Marcus had a girl roommate?

'Lyric, your insecurity is showing,' she warned herself.

Caught up in her own thoughts, Lyric didn't notice that her thumb was mindlessly hitting the channel button at top speed.

"Ahem…found anything good yet?" Marcus asked, noticing Lyric's preoccupied state and trying not to grin.

Not realizing he was off the phone, Lyric nearly jumped a mile and practically threw the remote when he addressed her. "Ahhhh!" Taking in a deep breath of air, Lyric calmed herself. "You scared me! Sorry."

"You've been flipping through the channels like your life depended on it since I tossed you the remote."

Lyric's cheeks pinked. "Oh."

"You know I'm not going to ask. There's no need to be jumpy." Marcus smiled reassuringly. Easily getting up, Marcus declared, "I'm going to the kitchen for a drink. Want something?"

Lyric still wasn't used to these little niceties. Austin had never asked if she wanted anything, even if he was on his way to get something himself. Of course, if she'd done that…well, there was a reason she'd earned all her bruises and black eyes. That's why it always surprised her a little when Marcus asked. Deep down, she knew it was a basic human courtesy, but Austin hadn't trifled with things like that.

She heard her own voice squeak in pathetic weakness as she mustered, "Orange juice? I mean, if you happen to have any."

Marcus knew Lyric had a past. She'd shared a bit. Even without the information, he knew enough in her behavior alone to deduce she'd had a rough one. Still, it grated on him when she reverted into her weak, subservient role. He'd gotten glimpses of what was underneath and it was far from weak. If only she'd see her own potential and let him help her! He'd learned his lesson in that area, though, and would concentrate on trying to gain her trust.

Marcus came back in with the drinks, handed her the orange juice and then plopped back in the recliner.

'Now! Go! Tell him!' her mind screamed. Quickly, before losing her nerve, she muted the T.V. and simultaneously announced, "Marcus, there's something I need to tell you." Should she just blurt it out?

Marcus eyed her as he nonchalantly sipped his Pepsi, waiting for her to go on.

Buying time, Lyric took a gulp of orange juice. Clearing her throat, she forged ahead. "I…uh, I have a boyfriend. Sorta. His name's Austin."

Silence.

Marcus knew there must be more. He could sense it. And he suspected she knew he already knew as much. "Okay," he encouraged.

"And he doesn't know I'm here."

'Liar! Liar! That's not really what you wanted to tell him. He probably already knows you have a boyfriend, you coward. How else would you explain the black eye you had?'

Lyric suddenly found herself spewing out all of the things she had kept inside while living with Austin. How he'd suffocated her, abused her, controlled her. How she had no friends she could talk to because Austin wouldn't have allowed it. How she finally decided she simply had to get out of there for her own safety. When she told Marcus of how she'd finally left, it wasn't without a note of pride in her voice and Marcus noticed.

"And one day, I finally decided I had to leave. And I did. I finally left him!" To hear herself say it aloud still shocked her. "I'd lived with Austin for a year-and-a-half. In the beginning, like the way most things are, I imagine, things were great. I thought I had found someone I could be happy with. He'd treated me well and gave me nice things."

Sighing in resignation, Lyric added, almost to herself, "I should have known better, meeting him in a bar the way I did." Shaking her head as if to clear it, she continued. "I left my home about a year before meeting Austin. I had felt smothered at home. My parents…well, it's safe to say they'd doted on me. At the time, I didn't quite grasp just how lucky I was. Especially now after seeing all the homelessness and poverty in the city. I had it so good." Lyric grew silent for a time, trying to collect herself. As usual, when she thought of her parents, she wanted to cry. That's why she rarely allowed herself to think of them. She could never go home to them. Not after hurting them the way she had.

Marcus patiently waited, sipping on his Pepsi and occasionally glancing at the moving pictures on the T.V. Seemingly, he didn't notice her brush her finger under her eye. But he had.

Finally, Lyric continued. "I still love Austin. I think. Anyway, at first, we took things slow, getting to know each other. I was so naïve then. He acted so charming and kept telling me he loved me. Before I knew it, I was moving in with him. We'd only been dating six months. And that's when things changed. He started being controlling, wanting to know where I was at all times and who I was with. Then he started acting jealous when I would go out with friends. None of them were even male! I can't even imagine what he'd think right now, me living with you." Lyric shook her head and continued. "Then all these people started coming by. Mostly, Austin would just keep them at the door and not let them in. I had no idea who they were, but eventually I figured out that Austin was into drugs and was a dealer. I didn't really see anything, but I just somehow knew. I started being able to recognize the signs of him being high and learned quickly to stay away when he was high. Then it got worse and he started drinking a lot more than usual. That was when I tried being as invisible as possible. It seemed nothing I did was right…and I paid for that mistake. He hit me so bad once that both my eyes were swollen shut and I couldn't go to work at my job at the bar…the very bar where we'd met. I got fired for missing work because I didn't tell my boss the real reason. If I had,

Austin would've just hit me again all the sooner. I slowly began to realize I wasn't who I used to be. I'd let Austin take away my identity. The last time…well, you saw the evidence of that."

Marcus couldn't speak. He'd felt the cold hands of rage choking him. And he felt a little sick. He'd been mad enough, seeing Lyric for the first time, wondering who had done it to her. Now he had a name and Marcus wanted to get *his* hands on Austin. And then Lyric uttered the words that further shocked him.

"You must understand, Marcus, I still love him. When he's Austin, himself, unaltered by drugs or alcohol, he's a good man. He's always so sorry he hurt me when he sobered up or came down off of his high. He just makes bad choices sometimes, that's all. He's the only man I've ever loved and who has loved me back and pays any kind of attention to me."

Marcus had a hard time swallowing the absurdity of Lyric's words. How? How could someone so good and pure be attracted to, even love, someone so vile? *'Don't interfere!'* he warned himself. *'And stay quiet!'*

"I left him, though. And he doesn't know where I am, for now. He's probably really mad and when he finds me, I'll have to pay the consequences." Marcus noticed Lyric went pale as she said that, but had put on a false bravado. "For now, I can't worry about that. I'm safe. For the time being, anyway. He has ways of finding people if he wants to bad enough. He'll want to find me, if for no other reason than to teach me a lesson for leaving. I know what that feels like. I was dumb enough to threaten to leave him once. He was drunk, but he still beat me pretty good. I know now that it was my fault for staying, so I simply decided to leave."

'Please, God, don't strike me for not being completely honest,' Lyric offered to the God she rarely talked to anymore.

Marcus was staggered at the unemotional tone Lyric used when speaking of Austin. It belied the deep trauma she most certainly had experienced while living with Austin. She was obviously in so much denial, her mind was protecting itself.

Using all of his self-possessed willpower to remain calm and not show his fury, Marcus asked, "What will you do if Austin finds you?"

Back to her inner, fragile shell, she practically whispered, "I'm hoping you'll be here when he does."

"You can hope. I'm gonna pray."

˄˄

Since telling Marcus all about Austin, Lyric felt as though a load had been lifted from her shoulders. She felt safe with Marcus and hoped every day that Austin wouldn't show up while Marcus was gone. And although she wasn't sure what to make of God, she felt comforted knowing Marcus somehow had the right connection to properly pray to Him.

Although Lyric had told Marcus the majority of her background, there was still something she was keeping back. Something that, had Marcus known, he might not have chosen her as a roommate.

On the other hand, Marcus had surprised her. He was much more understanding about things than she thought he'd be. Of course, she didn't have much to compare him to. Just Austin. He wasn't much to compare anyone to. Austin had taken care of her, though – sorta. When he was sober, which was rare, he did.

Truth be told, Lyric was scared to admit that no one else would accept her. Under different circumstances, she doubted even Marcus would've taken her in. If she hadn't been with Austin, she wouldn't have found herself in the situation she was now in.

Lyric didn't miss Austin, but there were times when she longed for the familiar again. Marcus was very nice, but she didn't know him well and sometimes felt as though she was intruding in his home. He'd never made her feel that way, however. That feeling was put upon herself by herself. It had only been about a week since she spilled her guts. Besides, they were still adjusting. She knew she wouldn't have felt settled in right away. And, for all intents and purposes, Marcus was a virtual stranger still. That, in and of itself, was odd. How did she *really* know Marcus was safe? She'd left one man's home for another. How did she know Marcus wouldn't end up being like Austin? Yet, somehow, she knew. She'd call it instinct…but she'd never trusted hers fully. It always seemed to lead her astray.

She remembered well the day she came to Marcus for her interview. Walking into the room, her first impression of him was that he was a man of confidence. One who could, and would, easily take control if the situation warranted it. Recalling the memory reminded her that she'd had an odd sense of security. Like she belonged there with him because she'd be safe. It'd been a long time since she'd felt genuinely safe.

Being such a short time, Lyric wasn't sure how she felt about Marcus…past his protector image, anyway. In a way, she supposed it might be akin to a big brother of some sort. She didn't know his age, but figured he was older than her twenty-two years.

Some days, Lyric was glad Austin was out of her life. But that was also when the fear would set in. Austin was looking for her, of that she was certain. And she dreaded the day she would be found.

Then there were the days she almost hoped to be found, if for no other reason than the dread and waiting would be over. She did admit that there were aspects of Austin she missed, she supposed, but mostly, it was the mere familiarity of her old life.

Taking a deep breath, Lyric rolled to her side in bed. Right that moment, she was leaning toward hoping she'd never see Austin again. And she hoped Marcus was still praying about the same thing.

Marcus. She still had something to tell him.

Marcus lay in his bed in the next room letting his own thoughts roam. He hadn't analyzed all of his feelings yet, but anger stood out the most. Not usually a violent person, but he had dreams and visions of merrily wringing Austin's neck.

"Lord, help me," he whispered, disconcerted by the foreign feelings.

What was this hold that Lyric had on him that made him want to inflict bodily harm on a stranger? He didn't even really know Lyric herself! Lyric had obviously brought some baggage with her. That didn't particularly bother him, however. Lots of people had an unfortunate past. What bothered him was the rage he felt toward a man who would treat a woman in such an abhorrent way.

Marcus could admit that he was quite proud of Lyric. Perhaps he should tell her that. Change was unsettling, at the least. Despite her circumstances and fear of repercussion, Lyric had decided she'd had enough, stood up for herself and left. That took courage.

It was hard for him to define his relationship with Lyric, having known her only about a month.

He would have found it amusing had he known Lyric was pondering the same thing at that moment. He would've also been surprised to know that she viewed him as an older brother. He was, in fact, twenty-four.

Marcus shook himself and decided to have a little pep talk. As odd as his protective feelings were toward Lyric, he knew he couldn't interfere with her life. Yet, she almost seemed to count on the fact that he'd be there for her. She'd pretty much said so. Obviously she was scared and needed someone to look after her. It was a task he knew he'd be performing from the very first time he'd laid eyes on her.

Before drifting off to sleep, Marcus lifted up a plea. *'God, you brought her to me. Help me to know what I'm supposed to do with her.'*

Chapter 4

If you can't get rid of the skeleton in your closet,
you'd best teach it to dance
George Bernard Shaw

In the morning, Marcus went to work at the bank and Lyric left for her job at the health food store.

All morning while he worked, Marcus couldn't get what Lyric had told him about Austin out of his head.

He had to admit, the thought of Austin made him a little apprehensive. Not that he couldn't take care of himself. At a little over six feet with broad shoulders, he was impressive to look at, to say the least. He lifted weights and had a workout regime four times a week. Despite all that, he still worried about Lyric. She'd only ever known men like Austin. Literally, she had only ever known Austin. And Austin wanted her. She was his possession and he'd want it back. Sure, Lyric hadn't said so in so many words, but from what Marcus could gather, that would be how Austin operated.

'*Lyric, Lyric, always Lyric,*' Marcus chided himself. He still couldn't explain the strange hold she had on him. He'd felt it from day one. One thing was for certain, it was most certainly a God thing.

```````````````````````````````````````````````````````````````````````````````

Lyric wasn't much of a worrier by nature. She was used to flying by the seat of her pants. By her own admittance, however, that's what had gotten her in all this mess in the first place.

However, this morning, she was worried. She worried about what she'd told Marcus last night. He hadn't said much that morning. Although she was beginning to realize that Marcus didn't say much, anyway. He was pretty quiet and kept to himself. She didn't know how he felt about all that she had told him. It had seemed, however, by the set of his jaw, that he might have been upset. And the fact that he'd been clenching and unclenching his fist. And she now found herself wondering what she had done or said to make him mad at her. She thought he had wanted more information about her past. Perhaps he would want to kick her out. The thought had knots forming in her stomach.

If not, then the fact that she knew she hadn't told Marcus all of the truth still gnawed at her. However, knowing what she did of Marcus, she hoped it wouldn't make a difference…he was already mad at her, obviously. It was good to know he wouldn't express it with his fists. And, perhaps, she could summon the courage to ask him what she had done to make him mad. Even if he chose not to answer, at least she knew Marcus wouldn't degrade her for asking, the way Austin would.
```````````````````````````````````````````````````````````````````````````````

A small stab of disloyalty pierced her then. She needed to stop comparing Marcus to Austin. Austin wouldn't like it. And, deep down, she knew the inevitable to be that she would have to go back to Austin. He'd force her to. And even if he never found her, which was doubtful – he had ways – there was still the fear that Marcus would kick her out once he knew the full truth. Austin was the only place she could go back to – it was all she had known.

"Earth to Lyric!" Camilla, a co-worker and friend of Lyric's, waved a caramel-colored hand in front of Lyric's face.

Snapped out of her reverie, Lyric looked at Camilla, blinking.

"We're supposed to be stocking shelves, remember? You don't want Mr. Butterman to find you not working, do you?"

Despite her serious thoughts, Lyric couldn't help a chuckle. "I still find it ironic that someone named *Butter*man owns a health food store."

The two girls shared a giggle as they continued stocking shelves.

Lyric was enjoying the simple pleasure of flipping through channels. She'd had to walk on eggshells living with Austin. When Marcus walked in the door a little after ten that night, Lyric knew he wouldn't be drunk – and he wouldn't demand full control of the remote. Small thing, the remote, she knew, but Austin had to control *everything* – every aspect of her life had been his. Lyric cringed at the thought that one day, sooner than she'd like, she would have to return home. That's why she had deferred telling Marcus her secret for so long.

"Hey, Lyric," Marcus greeted. He loosened his tie as he passed through the living room on his way to his bedroom.

She hadn't heard him come in, but no longer jumped or flinched at his unexpected presence. Instead, she returned his smile and greeting. "Hey, Marcus."

Pausing by his bedroom door, which opened to the living room, just as Lyric's did, Marcus asked, "Anything good on? I'm gonna change and would love to relax in front of the TV."

"Just news, mostly, right now."

Marcus made a comically disappointed face, then disappeared into his bedroom.

Lyric smiled and mused that she'd definitely have loved to have an older brother like Marcus. Thinking along those lines naturally led her to think of her parents and, out of habit, she immediately dismissed those thoughts.

Marcus came back into the room.

"I made some spaghetti. There are leftovers in the fridge."

"Thanks, Lyric!"

Lyric turned back to the TV and the uninteresting news.

After a few minutes, Marcus came back in with a bowl of reheated spaghetti.

Marcus hadn't realized how much he liked having Lyric there, on her own merit, not merely because he wanted to protect her. She'd usually have some sort of meal cooked when he got home, always enough for two and she always offered him some. Even though he didn't expect it, it was something nice to come home to. A lot better than the frozen TV dinners that had constituted his fare. And, confirmed bachelor as he was, he noticed he liked coming home to someone. He figured that was a leftover sentiment from when Andrew lived there.

Lyric noticed when Marcus was done eating and forced herself to mute the TV. Holding her breath and breaking out in a sweat, she turned to Marcus and blurted out, "Can I ask you something?"

"Sure," came his easy reply.

Licking her lips, she asked the question that had been on her mind all day. "Why are you mad at me?"

Marcus was completely caught off guard. "What? What made you think I'm mad at you?"

"Last night, I noticed you kept clenching and unclenching your fists and your jaw was locked tight. I've noticed you do that when you're mad." Sadly, Lyric added, "You've done that a lot since I've been here. If I anger you that much, I won't hold it against you if you want me to move out."

Marcus laughed once, but it had an edge to it. "Lyric, please be assured, I am not mad at you." He paused, not sure how much she would want to hear.

"What, then?" she prompted.

Looking sideways, he puffed his cheeks out with air, then swiftly expelled it all. Looking back at Lyric, he hesitantly said, "Ok…it's like this…Austin…you see, well…he makes me so mad! Irate, actually. No, more like furious! Livid, even!" His words spilled out more forcefully than he'd meant to.

"Austin?" Lyric was dumbfounded. Marcus didn't even know Austin!

"Yes. Violence of any kind toward a woman makes me extremely angry, Lyric. You deserve much better than him. Yet, I sense a pretty strong hold he has on you."

Lyric knew he was right. Except for deserving better. She reaped what she sowed. Having no defense, she said nothing.

Marcus decided to tell Lyric the truth. Part of it, anyway. "Lyric, I feel immensely responsible for you. I know you don't go to church or anything, but I believe God brought you here so I could protect you." He wasn't about to tell her he'd felt that way since the first time he'd laid eyes on her. That'd surely frighten her and make him sound like some religious fanatic…perhaps she already thought so.

Lyric was sure every bit of shock she felt registered on her face. "I know I haven't painted a very good picture of Austin," she began slowly, "but he does have his good points. Without him, I don't know where I'd be. I would've been homeless before I'd even started my new life."

Marcus' stomach churned and bile rose in his throat as he heard Lyric's martyred words defend Austin. "It sounded like you'd had a good life before Austin came along." He'd meant it to sound encouraging, but it came out sounding accusatory.

Seeing he'd hurt Lyric, he quickly amended, "Ok, so what are Austin's finer points?"

Despite herself, Lyric gave Marcus a crooked smile. "I can't remember right now."

A few moments of contemplative silence followed. Lyric broke it quietly, speculatively, and almost to herself, murmured, "I think Austin's such a draw for me because no one else will have me."

"What do you mean?"

"I don't have the best past, Marcus. I've already told you most of it. I left home at eighteen, on my eighteenth birthday, in fact."

"Can I ask you a personal question, Lyric?"

Lyric hesitated. "Ok…"

"How old are you?"

Lyric laughed. "Didn't your mother ever tell you it's rude to ask a woman her age?" She teasingly winked at him then answered, "I'm twenty-two."

Marcus was surprised. She wasn't much younger than he was. "Why, Lyric, I'm stunned. I'm only twenty-four, but I can guarantee you've experienced more in life than I have."

Lyric ruefully waved her hand as if to nonchalantly dismiss the statement. "Yeah, well, that's probably why only someone like Austin would accept me. He's the only guy I've ever loved and who's ever loved me."

Marcus frowned. "I don't think he does love you, though." He said it so softly, Lyric almost missed it.

"You're wrong, Marcus, he does." Lyric vehemently championed for Austin. She didn't quite understand why. "Besides, it doesn't matter if *he* does or doesn't; I love *him*. He's the only one who accepted me for who I am."

"But does he really *know* you, Lyric?"

"Does it matter? He accepted me!"

Marcus was taken aback at Lyric's bitter tone. "You haven't met anyone else besides Austin. How do you know no one else would have?"

"Come on, Marcus! Even you should know enough about life to know that a girl like me – especially at that time, waitressing at a *bar* – wouldn't find someone, well, like you. A nice guy who'd actually notice her. You – guys like you – don't date questionable waitresses – you don't even frequent bars!"

If Lyric hadn't been so serious, Marcus would've laughed. He knew that he had someone before him who didn't realize her own worth. She had no self-esteem and he was afraid that if Austin did find her, she'd go back to him without hesitation. If, for no other reason, than it was comfortable. He was bound and determined that wouldn't happen.

As if reading his mind, Lyric confessed aloud, "I've already accepted the fact that I'll eventually have to go back to him." There was a wistfulness that told the truth – she didn't really want to.

Despite the knowledge, Marcus couldn't help but be shocked at the spoken words. "Why?" he had to know.

"He's all I've got."

"That's not true. You have me now." Puffing his chest in mock arrogance, he announced, "I'm your protector, remember?"

Lyric smiled sadly. "I appreciate that, but you're too good for me." A bit impudently, she insisted, "I'll eventually have to go back to my own kind."

Turning serious again, Marcus answered, "No, you don't, Lyric. You can stay here as long as you want."

'*I know something you don't know,*' sang in Lyric's head. As soon as he knew, he'd tell her to leave.

Marcus saw the stubborn set of her jaw and knew the discussion was over.

Lyric flipped the channel and brightly announced, "*Letterman*'s on."

ˆˆˆ

The weeks turned to deeper summer and August was just around the corner.

Their routine was established now. If Lyric worked, she was usually home by eight o'clock. Marcus usually came home soon after nine or ten, depending on the classes he had that night.

Lyric made dinner when she got home and always made enough for Marcus, too. It made her feel good knowing she could help him out in some small way, after all he had done for her – just letting her stay was enough! And it helped alleviate the guilt that she was still hiding a secret. A secret that was practically killing her to keep! She felt as though she'd burst with it and needed to tell him soon…but she was afraid of the repercussions.

After dinner, they'd watch TV…sometimes she'd share the remote.

On the weekends, Marcus worked on homework and Lyric did errands or grocery shopped, if she didn't have to work.

Sundays Marcus went to church. Lyric stayed home and cleaned. They were the loneliest days because Marcus drove an hour to his parents' house for Sunday dinner and wouldn't get back until late afternoon. Usually he had homework to finish up when he got home, so Lyric didn't see much of him on Sundays.

One Sunday, she was especially lonely and thought about seeing Austin. First, she went on a walk to clear her head. She knew it'd be a bad idea to go see Austin, but nonetheless, she found herself going down his street. Instinctively, she knew she was driven by loneliness rather than by a real desire to see Austin. Especially considering she had taken the subway for part of her "walk." In fact, she discovered she really hoped she didn't run into him. Quickly, she walked by her old apartment building and felt an overwhelming sense of despair. That apartment building held nothing but bad memories for her.

As she turned down another street, walking swiftly toward home, she realized she missed what Austin represented. Home. Familiarity – such as it had been. Security. Yet, Austin wasn't her home any longer. Reflecting, perhaps he never had been. And she had her own familiarity now that she was growing accustomed to – Marcus. As for security – well, she supposed Austin never truly was that. Really, all she longed for that she'd had with Austin, was a place. As sick as it was, at least she knew where she belonged in Austin's world. In Marcus', she still felt out of step, somehow. She didn't belong in Marcus' world. He was too good. He was a *good* person!

Overwhelming sadness enveloped her then and she began to cry. She didn't know why, exactly.

All that would be lost when she finished telling Marcus the truth. She simply didn't want it to end! But where was her life headed? Nowhere and back to Austin, all at the same time. Austin was a dead end, but that was the path she had chosen and it'd always suck her back in. She had no way out! She knew that eventually Marcus would have to reject her. Good and bad simply couldn't exist together for long, and then she'd have nowhere to go except back to Austin.

She could hardly contain her emotions by the time she got home. She was making a beeline for her bedroom, blinded by tears, before she realized Marcus was home.

"Hey, Lyr –" the words died on his lips as he took in her face. In alarm, he asked, "What's wrong?" He stood up and reached out to grab her arm.

Shaking it off, Lyric continued on her path to solace. "Nothing that I didn't already create for myself. Leave me alone."

Helplessly, Marcus watched her go, determined to fulfill his promise that he wouldn't pry. Long into the night, he could still hear Lyric's sobs and wished he had made no such promise. Barely being able to stand it, he left her alone.

Lyric couldn't remember the last time she had cried, but was sure it hadn't been so much or for so long! The tears seemed to keep coming. Startled, she realized she hadn't cried once like this while living with Austin. She'd cried, on occasion, when he beat her, but it didn't take long for her to figure out that it gave him pleasure to see her tears of pain, causing him to prolong the torment. And so, she had learned to shut off her feelings and emotions while he whaled on her. Austin never would have allowed her to express her feelings, much less cry like this. Grudgingly, she had to chalk yet another one up for Marcus. It would be so hard to have to leave Marcus. He left her alone and didn't belittle or demean her for having feelings.

Her tears were from years of pent up emotions; of sadness, of loneliness, of a life she'd never intended for herself. When those were finally spent, a fresh batch sprang up at the thought of one day having to leave Marcus. She forgot how calm life could be until she'd moved in there. Alas, leaving was inevitable. Although she still had no real direction to her life, this time with Marcus had been a much better life than the one she'd had with Austin.

Shockingly, Lyric found she was, bit by bit, starting to resent Austin quite a lot. Especially now that she had someone to compare him to.

Chapter 5

Be polite; write diplomatically; even in a declaration of war
one observes the rules of politeness
Otto von Bismarck

It was Saturday again. Lyric didn't have to be at work until three that afternoon. They only needed the four hours until closing. She'd tentatively approached Mr. Butterman to ask for one light shift a week. She'd had to explain why, but besides him and herself, no one else knew "why."

"Lyric," Marcus interrupted her secret worrying over breakfast.

Still coming back to reality, she gave him a listless "Hm?"

"I need to talk to you about Austin," he began abruptly.

Lyric's stomach clenched. "Ok."

What Marcus really wanted to ask about was her crying last week, but stuck to his vow not to pry. Instead, he voiced, "More so, I want to establish some ground rules."

Dubiously, Lyric eyed him.

Marcus couldn't help but notice the dark circles under her eyes. And he couldn't tell if the puffiness was from lack of sleep, or from crying.

"I don't want him here if I'm not here. If he shows up, don't answer the door. If I'm here, I'll answer the door. You told me it was basically inevitable he'd show up here, so I'm establishing rules before that happens. He is not welcome in our home."

At first, with his beginning words, Lyric thought she'd be angry. She always got angry when Austin put restrictions on her. Surprisingly, she felt relief. And, oddly, cared for. No one, much less a man, had ever done anything in her best interest, since coming to the City on her own. It warmed her. Touched, she could feel tears sting her eyes.

Silently, she rebuked, *'Stop being so emotional!'*

Aloud, she agreed, "Ok." Swallowing, she dared continue on. "Thank you, Marcus. Honestly, I don't know if I'd be able to stand up to him alone. If I had to, I'd probably go home with him. He'd make sure of it."

Sick at the thought, Marcus' words came out unintentionally harsh. "Your home's here now. With me."

At Lyric's taken aback look, he amended. "I mean, you don't need to find another home," he explained lamely. "You have one."

Confused at his own awkwardness, Marcus abruptly stood up from the table. Grabbing his dirty dishes, he stalked to the sink and dropped them in. And then he skulked to his room and closed the door with more force than necessary.

At first uncomfortable, Lyric froze in place out of habit. After Marcus strode by, a smile slowly spread across her face. She recognized the actions as mere concern for her. And it felt pretty good. Actually, it felt great!

Having nothing else to do at present, Lyric stood up and tidied the kitchen.

```````````````````````````````````````````````````````````````````````````

At work, Lyric threw herself into her duties. She didn't want to think about Marcus or Austin or any of it anymore. Thinking of Marcus confused her. Thinking of Austin shamed her. And since the two were worlds apart, she decided they both couldn't occupy space in her mind at the same time. So, she decided to give neither any space. Since they didn't, however, something else did. The Secret, as she called it. The Secret that she hadn't told Marcus, or anyone, about.

Camilla sidled over.

Camilla, Lyric's co-worker and friend, had gorgeous, thick black hair that hung to the middle of her back in kinky curls. Brown eyes complemented her smooth, caramel-colored skin. At 5'8", her thin frame nearly towered over Lyric's 5'4" form.

Lyric was grateful for the break from the mental exercise she'd been experiencing.

"How goes it?" Camilla asked, smiling.

"Fine," came Lyric's reply.

"Still living with what's-his-name?" Camilla nudged Lyric knowingly.

Lyric had told Camilla about Marcus. As Camilla was pretty much the only friend she had, she'd confided most of her deep, dark secrets—except The Secret.

"Marcus? Yeah."

"He hasn't tried anything, has he?" Camilla felt absurdly protective of her friend. Lyric had shared all the sordid details about Austin.

"Camilla, I told you, he's nothing but a gentleman. It's actually been weird to get used to, but I think I'm doing exceptionally well."

"He may not beat you, but don't let him talk you into – other things. You're a pretty girl, Lyric."

Camilla was divorced from a cheating husband so she didn't trust men. Period.

Laughing at the absurdity, Lyric merely said, "You'll have to meet him. He's the sweetest guy! He'd like you for sure. You both have something in common already."

Curiosity piqued, Camilla bit. "Okay, what's that?"

"You both have an insane need to be all protective of me."

"Have you told him about Austin?"

Lyric rolled her eyes. "What do you think his protectiveness is all about?"

"Alright...he *does* sound like a good guy."
```````````````````````````````````````````````````````````````````````````

"It was even before he really knew about Austin, though. Marcus actually told me God told him to protect me – or something equally unbelievable."

Camilla let out a low whistle. "Whoa, Lyric. Hold on to that boy!"

Rolling her eyes yet again, Lyric reminded her, "We're just roommates! And don't you find that weird?" she continued on in one breath. "God *told* him to take care of me?"

"Oh, no, honey. I don't. I believe in God."

Incredulous, Lyric vocalized, "You do?"

"Oh yes, I do. I was born Catholic and not quite sure what I am now, but I do believe the Lord works in mysterious ways."

Camilla and Lyric hadn't gotten around to spiritual matters but, looking back, Lyric had always sensed a peace, a serenity, something, about Camilla. Until that moment, she'd had no idea what it was.

Looking up, Camilla said, with regret, "I've got customers coming to the counter. Gotta go. We'll have to continue this discussion another time."

Lyric watched the golden-toned, exotic woman – she'd guess nearer thirty than twenty, based solely on wisdom – gracefully glide away. Her naturally curly black hair bounced slightly as she walked. Lyric watched as her full lips stretched into a warm, welcoming smile.

Lyric looked down at her drab appearance and let the familiar feeling of inadequacy envelop her.

ᴧᴧ

Lyric had left for work an hour before. Marcus had heard her leave. He hadn't come out of his room since breakfast.

Needing a friend's input more than he needed studying, Marcus reached for his cell phone. He hadn't been able to fully concentrate on his homework, anyway.

On the third ring, Andrew picked up. "Hey, Marcus!" Caller I.D. sure was handy.

"Hey, Andrew, how's life in Boston?"

"Same ol', same ol'. You and your mysterious roommate have yet to join Elizabeth and me down here for dinner."

Marcus remembered a conversation a month or so ago about that. Elizabeth was a girl Andrew had met at his new job. They'd seemed to have really hit it off from the first.

"Kind of a long drive for one dinner," Marcus jokingly scoffed.

"Actually, man, I'm glad you called. I would've called soon, anyway. I'm going on a business trip with some of the guys and Elizabeth and we're headed to the City. The four of us should hook up while we're there."

"Great! I'll see if Lyric wants to come and we can finally meet Elizabeth."

Marcus and Andrew talked at least once every couple of weeks, so Marcus had talked to Andrew several times since Lyric moved in.

"I'm dying to meet your mysterious new roommate who has deigned to take my place," Andrew teased. "Seriously, though, how's she doing?"

Marcus filled Andrew in on the latest with Lyric and what he found out about Austin.

Andrew gave a low whistle when Marcus finished. "If you ever hunt that guy down and need help taking him on, call me." Andrew was only half serious.

Marcus gave a dark chuckle. That was saying something for Andrew. He was even less prone to violence than Marcus! It was usually Marcus' temper that got the better of him and it only put in an appearance when Marcus witnessed injustice done to others. Lyric's case was a prime example.

The two chatted for another good forty-five minutes, hammered out details to meet up during Andrew's business trip, then said their good-byes.

Marcus contemplated Lyric's answer. Would she want to meet two strangers? One was a stranger to him, too. As for the other, it suddenly seemed extremely important to him to have Lyric meet his best friend.

In the middle of his contemplating, he heard Lyric come in the door.

Stepping out of his room, he caught her unloading groceries from bags on the kitchen counter.

"How's the big, bad world of health food treating you?" he greeted as he helped put things away.

Lyric smiled. "Pretty good. I detoured on my way home and got big, juicy, artery-clogging steaks. Don't tell my boss, Mr. Butterman, though."

Trying to find *some* way to introduce the subject of Andrew and meeting him for dinner, Marcus lamely blurted out, "How would you feel about steaks with Andrew…and Elizabeth…on Friday?"

Lyric momentarily froze, snatches of her and Camilla's conversation in her head.

'*Don't panic,*' she told herself.

Seeing her panic-stricken expression, Marcus began rambling. "I've told you about my best friend, Andrew. I've told him about you, too. Anyway, he'll be in the City on a business trip. And Elizabeth is part of the team being sent in for business. He wants us to meet her. And, well, he really wants to meet you, as well. You up for it?"

Lyric heard herself responding, "Uh, okay." In truth, her curiosity was piqued. What would Andrew, Marcus' best friend, be like? It was very nice of him to want to meet her. And she also wondered about Elizabeth, whom she knew was Andrew's girlfriend. Would she like her?

Marcus felt a flood of relief and answered with an enthusiastic, "Great!"

Marcus and Andrew had agreed to meet at 7:00 at Angelo's, a restaurant with a light and friendly atmosphere and, incidentally, great burgers and steaks. It had been a favorite hangout of theirs when Andrew lived in the City.

Marcus entered the restaurant closely behind Lyric. Almost immediately, he spotted his best friend sitting in a booth with a pretty redhead that had to be Elizabeth.

As Marcus and Lyric approached, Andrew rose and greeted Marcus with the customary guy handshake-fist bump-hug.

Marcus turned to Lyric then and introduced her. "Andrew Mitchell, this is Lyric Bell. Lyric, Andrew."

Lyric proffered her hand for a shake, but Andrew took it and gallantly kissed it, causing his girlfriend to rise and giggle.

"Alright, you," Elizabeth teasingly scolded in a sweet, southern accent, "leave the poor girl alone."

Indeed, Lyric's face had flamed at the unexpected greeting.

Elizabeth addressed Lyric. "You'll have to excuse him. He takes vulgar pleasure in shocking people – especially when meeting them for the first time." She gave him a fond look.

"I betcha don't forget me," Andrew grinned as he sat back down.

"Since Andrew's gallantry has apparently disappeared, I suppose it's up to me to introduce myself." Laughing at Andrew's guilty schoolboy look, she told Marcus and Lyric, "I'm Elizabeth Thomas." She greeted first Lyric, then Marcus, with a warm, friendly hug.

"Marcus Coulter and this is Lyric Bell," Marcus supplied. He then guided Lyric into the booth by lightly placing his hand on the small of her back.

He thought nothing of the touch; Lyric, however, tried very hard not to.

The four settled down to chat and made small talk as they ordered and waited for their food.

As the night wore on, Lyric reflected on Marcus and Andrew. She hadn't realized two such decent guys could even exist at the same time! Or, rather, she had forgotten, given her most recent experience with guys: Austin and his cronies.

And Elizabeth had turned out to be warm and genuine, as well. Lyric found it was fairly easy to sense whether or not someone was being real. Most likely, she possessed the knack due to her shady past. It had led her down some rocky paths and to meet some less than savory people.

At the end of the night, Elizabeth startled Lyric by asking, "Do you wanna exchange numbers, e-mails? I'd really like to get to know you better – and I have a feeling I'll need a girlfriend to rescue me when these two get together." She conspiratorially indicated Marcus and Andrew.

Lyric felt a rush of warmth for Elizabeth and readily agreed.

"I had a really lovely time," Elizabeth told both Marcus and Lyric in her sweet, southern accent as she and Andrew stood by the curb trying to hail a cab.

"We'll have to do this again when Levi and Rachel can join us," Marcus said.

Although Lyric had never met either, she knew Levi to be Marcus' older brother and only sibling. Rachel was Levi's wife. Marcus talked of, and to, Levi quite often. Lyric was fairly certain she would like to meet both, but knew it probably wouldn't happen. Even there, outside of a New York City restaurant, she felt too far removed from Marcus' life. He was, simply, too good for her and circumstances such as those didn't usually change. Suddenly, Lyric felt a sweep of melancholy and was grateful when they could finally be on their way home.

ˏˏ

On their walk up the street to the apartment after the dinner with Andrew and Elizabeth, Lyric ventured, "I liked your friends. Elizabeth reminds me a little bit of Camilla from work."

After short reflection, Lyric boldly asked the question that she had been pondering and would lead, hopefully, to some answers she had wondered about for a while. "Is she a Christian?"

Surprised at the question, Marcus answered honestly. "Andrew wouldn't date anyone who wasn't."

Without giving herself a chance to chicken out, Lyric quickly asked, "And what about you?"

Lyric did not have any special feelings toward Marcus, per se. She was only curious as far as her assumptions were concerned. They were that she, not being a Christian, really had no business in Marcus's life. He had said nothing of the sort. It was her own conclusion.

"Me?" Marcus' incredulity was hardly disguised. Lyric's shock value was scoring a ten-out-of-ten for surprising questions.

"No," he answered simply.

Lyric had figured as much. And, really, Marcus deserved his own Elizabeth. Or even someone like Camilla. Lyric had a feeling Camilla would probably turn into a Christian. She laughed to herself. Okay, that wasn't the right phrasing, as if POOF! Camilla would transform into a Christian. Camilla certainly had the qualities to be one and probably didn't have the marred past, like she did.

Struck by their past conversation, Lyric added, "You'd like her. You're both insanely overprotective of me, so that's something you have in common already!"

Marcus laughed. "Well, then, I like her already."

Feeling buoyed and free from her earlier dark mood, Lyric happily pranced ahead to the apartment building. Slowing his pace, Marcus watched her. He didn't know if he'd ever seen Lyric look so happy or carefree. Usually, she always seemed to be looking over her shoulder for Austin, causing her to be stressed and anxious all of the time.

The unhappy thought that Austin would eventually find her– his kind usually showed up to claim what they thought was theirs – caused Marcus
to pause. Bolstered by determination to guard Lyric, Marcus muttered to himself. "Bring it on, Austin, bring it on." Then he caught up to Lyric.

' '

The following morning was Sunday. Lyric was aware when Marcus got up for church. She inwardly cringed at the thought of Marcus asking her to go. She was half afraid he would, based on the subject of their conversation the previous evening.

Sure enough, Marcus casually asked. She declined. Even so, Marcus predicted, "One of these times you'll give in and come. Besides, you still have to meet my family. We have the ultimate family dinners after church and the food alone is worth it." He smiled teasingly.

Smiling, Lyric declared, "I don't think your family is ready for the likes of me yet."

"Don't be silly. They'd love you! Actually, my mom is dying to meet you. I had promised to invite her and my dad over after you got settled in. Now, it's two months later, and I have yet to make good on my promise."

Leaning down, he gave her the now-familiar kiss on her forehead. "Alright, since I'm apparently lacking in persuasion, I'll be off – alone."

As much as he didn't want to admit it, his disappointment that she didn't go with him to church went deep.

After the door clicked shut behind Marcus, Lyric irritated herself by allowing a few tears to fall. "You're too good for me, Marcus– and so's your family."

Chapter 6
It takes a long time to bring the past up to the present
Franklin D. Roosevelt

A few days later, it happened. Thankfully, it was evening and Marcus' last class had been cancelled.

A knock sounded at the door.

Marcus had been flipping channels as Lyric dozed on the couch. She did that a lot in the evenings, Marcus had noticed, and secretly worried about it.

Confused by the visitor, Marcus got up to answer the door.

A greasy brown-haired stranger, with matching eyes, stood on the other side of the door.

"Can I help you?" Marcus inquired politely.

"Yeah, I believe you took my girl."

Marcus felt rage shoot through him as he realized this was Austin. He checked himself just in time, before he lashed out and punched the guy in the face.

Austin looked beyond Marcus and spotted Lyric in the living room. He took a step forward and Marcus instinctively put a hand on Austin's chest to stop him.

"Excuse me, you're not going to barge into my home."

"You have something that's *mine!*" Austin's loud, angry voice snapped.

"Funny, last time I checked, this was America and no one owns anybody else. You need to leave."

Behind him, Marcus heard Lyric's groggy voice. "What's going on? Is someone here?"

Forcing his tone to be even, calm, Marcus answered. "Just stay there." Leveling a steely glare on Austin, he said, "It's no one." Anger and hostility welled up in Marcus with surprisingly strong ferocity for this virtual stranger.

Austin went ballistic. "Lyric! Lyric!" he screamed. "You come here now, wench! You're mine!"

Lyric had hastened to the door by this time, habit forcing her to obey Austin.

Pointing his finger in her face, he leered as he practically yelled at her. "You belong to me! Why'd you run out on me for this loser, huh?"

Fear and dread settled heavy in her stomach, making her feel physically sick. She slumped against the door, grabbing the edge of it to steady herself and keep from falling. Tears of defeat pricked her eyes. He had found her. He had won. Weakly, she tried to rally and barely audible, she told him, "Go away, Austin."

"I will not. Not without you! You're mine!" Austin made the mistake of trying to push past the door then.

Marcus had had quite enough of Austin Wood. As Austin tried grabbing for Lyric to force her backwards and into the room, Marcus intervened on instinct with a quick and effective punch to his face. Marcus' fist connected squarely with Austin's nose and Austin reeled backwards in pain, grabbing his nose and screeching.

"My nose! My nose! You broke it, you punk!"

Face dark with rage, in a deadly quiet voice, Marcus commanded, "Leave. My. Home. *Now.*"

Austin's voice turned whiny. "Ok, man! You didn't have to go and break my nose."

Watching the events unfold in open-mouthed shock, Lyric began to tremble. As Austin began to stagger away, she found the courage to hiss, "Don't come near me again!" She had the sudden urge to spit at his feet, but refrained.

Marcus issued a parting warning to Austin's retreating back, "If you ever come back, I will have you arrested for trespassing."

Closing the door, Marcus realized he was shaking and his hand was beginning to throb.

Lyric had retreated to the living room and Marcus saw her curled up on the couch, also shaking.

Passing through the kitchen area, Marcus stopped at the freezer to grab some ice and wrap it in a towel. Holding it to his hand that was starting to turn a nice shade of purple, Marcus went to Lyric and knelt beside the couch. Gently, he laid a hand on her back and tried to keep his voice soothing. "It's okay. He's gone now and he's never going to come back."

Marcus hadn't realized Lyric was crying until she turned to face him and he saw the tears running down her face. Her trembling was not only caused by shock, but by her silent sobs, as well.

"Yes, he will!" she wailed. "Men like that…they don't stay away. I'm sure he had Derrick or Johnny or Kroger looking for me. I know that's how he found me. As long as you have something of his – me – he'll keep coming around."

"I'll get the police involved if I have to."

"You think he's scared of the police? There are enough corrupt cops in New York City that would think nothing of taking his drug money to look the other way."

Finding it was pointless to argue, Marcus put his ice towel down on the end table and scooched onto the couch. Lyric moved over so she was huddled in only half the couch, with Marcus settling in on the other end.

Lyric struggled to sit up and Marcus laid an arm across her shoulders. Tentatively, she laid her head against his shoulder.

Trying to sound cheerful, Marcus told her, "Don't worry. Big brother will take care of you, no matter what."

After a few minutes, Lyric hesitantly asked, "So...you don't want me to...uh, move out?"

Looking down into her clear, blue eyes, Marcus was dumbfounded. "Why would you think that?"

Weakly, Lyric shrugged her shoulders. "Oh, you know, unwelcome ex-boyfriend stalking me. Not exactly an anticipated guest. As long as I'm here, he'll try to get me back."

Instinctively, Marcus gathered her closer as if to physically protect her. "Do you want to go back?"

Lyric shuddered. "No, but I may not have a choice." She fixed her blue eyes intently on his green gaze. "If he proves too much of a nuisance, I can't put you through that. I'm guessing this isn't exactly what you signed up for when you were looking for a roommate."

Sighing wearily, suddenly tired of the subject, Marcus reiterated what he had said before. "I know you don't understand this, but I meant what I said before. I told you God brought you to me to protect. So I'm in this for however long He deems necessary."

Strangely comforted, Lyric snuggled deeper. In a few minutes, she was asleep.

Marcus watched her sleep. He could imagine growing up with her as his kid sister. He hadn't realized until that moment how much he viewed her as just that and the thought made him smile.

Gingerly, he picked her up, careful not to jostle her awake, and carried her to her room. She was way too light for his liking, he contemplated as he tucked her into bed.

Quietly, he turned out her light, closed the door and made his way to his own room.

``````````````````````````````````````````````````````````````````````````

Lyric awoke, but stayed in bed for a few minutes more. Remembering the events of the night before made her shudder. Closing her eyes, she tried to block it out. It was simply too painful. Finally sitting up, she hugged her knees to her chest, trying to calm herself.

Comfort was something she had been seeking and found last night with Marcus' strong arms around her. Too bad she hadn't had an older brother growing up. Levi, Marcus' own older brother, must have been some role model. Marcus acted the part to perfection.

Sighing, Lyric got up to start the day.

Padding in to the kitchen in her stocking feet, Lyric saw that Marcus had already left for the day. His backpack, which seemed to have a permanent seat on any one of the dining chairs, was gone, as were his keys, which usually hung on a hook next to the door. There was something new, however. Perched against the door of the microwave was a note that read:
``````````````````````````````````````````````````````````````````````````

Lyric,
Please use extra caution while you're alone in the apartment today. Make sure the door is double-locked with the deadbolt and <u>don't open it for anybody!</u> Since I can't be there physically, I will be praying for extra protection for you.
Love, your big brother,

Marcus

Immediately Lyric went to the door and slid the deadbolt into place. Then she pondered the note. She decided she was touched by the concern Marcus obviously felt for her safety, in light of Austin's visit the previous night, rather than insulted by the note, which could be construed as sounding as if it were meant for a child.

She went to the teakettle to fill it with water and set it to boil on the stove. She could've simply zapped a cup of water in the microwave and added a teabag, but she was a self-proclaimed tea snob and had to properly steep her tea. Once it was done, she poured a cup and took it with her to the bathroom to sip on while she got ready for the day. Really, there was no rush. She still had two hours to kill before she needed to be at work. It gave her just enough time to contemplate her predicament that she had only hinted at to Marcus the previous evening.

The thought of going back to Austin made her physically ill, yet she knew in her gut she couldn't be completely done with Austin, either. Besides, she still had to tell Marcus The Secret, which would most likely result in him making her leave, anyway. And she had nowhere to go but back to Austin. That was the path she had chosen and she had to live with the consequences. She couldn't hide behind Marcus forever. In fact, when she had first left Austin, she knew she'd have to return to him someday. It was inevitable; that's where her path led because that was her getting what she deserved.

The problem was, she hadn't anticipated her someday coming so soon. The thought made her sick and brought tears to her eyes, yet she refused to give in to them. It was her own fault and now she had to lie in the bed she'd made. The enormity of the hold Austin had on her should have shocked her, but it didn't. What did shock her was the immense security she had found with Marcus and her deep unwillingness to let it go. She hadn't realized how much she had craved such security and safety.

Which brought her to her next conundrum. Even if Austin was a non-issue, she didn't belong in Marcus' world. In reality, their lives were so diverse it really had to have been some small miracle that they even met at all. He lived an upstanding life. She, however, most certainly had not. Austin was Marcus' polar opposite. Marcus was the sweetest, kindest guy she'd ever known…and most definitely too good for the likes of her. If only she could find a guy like Marcus to take care of her for…well, forever…but she'd ruined her own chance for that.

She could no longer stave off the tears and they overflowed.

'*This is stupid,*' she chastised herself. '*Stupid! Stupid! Stop it this instant! It's your own dumb fault and having a pity party isn't going to change anything.* You *chose this path, now you have to stay on it.*'

Lyric pulled herself together and dried her eyes. She gave herself a hard look in the mirror as she applied her customary lip gloss and mascara.

Giving herself one final, parting shot, she told her reflection, "Buck up!" Then she turned and left the bathroom.

'''

All day long, Marcus had kept a running prayer for Lyric in his head. He was trying to let God deal with the worry, but it still seemed to plague him. Not only was there the fear that Austin would show up uninvited while Marcus wasn't home, but in talking with Lyric last night, it hadn't been hard for Marcus to deduce that Lyric would go back to Austin if he provoked her further. Marcus had sensed, and seen, Lyric's low self-esteem from the first. Austin's little visit the night before hadn't helped things.

Marcus unconsciously gritted his teeth.

"Excuse me," inquired the white-haired lady who had just come up to his teller window. "Do I annoy you?" She wore a bemused expression.

Marcus snapped his head up and cleared his blurry day dream vision of what he would have liked to do to Austin the night before.

"I'm sorry, ma'am," he immediately apologized.

There was a sparkle in the lady's eye as she knowingly patted his arm. "Must be about a girl."

Marcus chuckled self-consciously. "You're good, but it's not quite what you might think."

"All I know, dearie, is when a man has that look of determination, he's working out how to be the hero to some lucky young woman."

Marcus rarely got embarrassed, but he did then. His cheeks turned bright red. Quickly, he ducked his head as he helped the woman make a withdrawal.

The lady patted his arm again, reassuringly. "Nothing to be embarrassed about, young man. Your young lady is lucky to have you fight for her." She grabbed her purse and, before turning away, parted with, "You have yourself a nice day now."

Marcus managed to mutter, "Thank you, ma'am, you do the same."

'*Good going, Coulter. Keep your mind on your work! You can fantasize about Austin's demise later.*'

Marcus was fairly successful the rest of his workday in focusing on his job.

After work, he made the necessary transfers on the subway as he headed for school.

In school, however, he found it harder to concentrate on the academic without thoughts of Austin and Lyric creeping in.

`` ` `` ` `` ` `` ` `` ` `` ` `` ` `` ` `` ` `` ` `` ` `` ` `` ` `` ` `` ` `` ` `` ` `` ` `` ` ``

Lyric paced, trying to convince herself to do the right thing, all the while being a coward. It was inevitable, really. It had to be done at some point. She'd make sure of it. She'd be forced to, actually, so…the sooner, the better; no time like the present…and all that jazz.

Sighing, Lyric looked longingly toward her bedroom. That was the coward's way. Going to bed and forgetting all about it until morning.

No, waiting up for Marcus was definitely the right thing. The thing she *should* do.

Her emotions toyed with her. But things always looked brighter in the morning. Why not simply wait until then? Besides, he'd be tired tonight. Too tired to talk about such important things.

Yes. Definitely the morning, then. That was the sensible choice. She was merely postponing it for twelve hours. It could keep for that long….

But would she *really* tell him in the morning? Or would she come up with another excuse?

Standing in the middle of the living room, Lyric soon found herself without options as she heard the key in the lock and saw the knob of the door turn.

If she was gonna play the coward and hide out in her room, now was her chance.

With a strength she didn't feel, Lyric turned toward the door and stood her ground with resolve.

Chapter 7

*It is the law of nature that woman should be held under
the dominance of man*
Confucius

Marcus stepped into the apartment. "Lyric!" he greeted in surprise. "What are you still doing awake?"

Lyric was usually either in bed or sacked out on the couch. Either way, she was very rarely awake when he got home.

Marcus put his briefcase and schoolbag down by the door.

"Oh, um," Lyric stammered, "I was just going to bed."

Squinting at her closely, Marcus walked nearer. "Are you alright? You look a little pale." He reached out and felt her forehead. "And your forehead feels a little clammy."

Marcus took Lyric's hand and led her over to the sofa.

"Um," Lyric tried again, licking her lips. She was sweaty and cold at the same time, but wasn't feverish. No, this was caused by anxiety.

'Don't chicken out!' her head screamed.

"You haven't seen Austin again, have you?" Marcus questioned sharply.

"No." Lyric tried for a reassuring smile, but it came off as tight-lipped.

Looking her square in the eye, he seemed convinced she was telling the truth and gave his head a little nod of satisfaction. He had never disliked someone so much in his whole life as he did Austin Wood.

Alarmed that he may have seen Austin made Lyric ask, "Why? Have you seen Austin?"

"No and I'd like to keep it that way."

Rallying for Austin and trying to prepare herself for the inevitable, Lyric spoke up. "You know, Austin's not all bad." Lyric had not expected the look of anger…no, more than that…fury? hatred? that stormed Marcus' face at her words.

"Not all bad?! How can you *say* that, Lyric?" Marcus exploded. "He used you, he abused you, he comes to our home uninvited without so much as an apology to you! He's a coward, not even worth being called a man!" Marcus was breathing heavily, trembling with rage.

Marcus tried forcing himself to calm down. If he wasn't careful, he was going to give himself a heart attack. He wasn't used to these types of outbursts. He was usually such a genial fellow. He'd never had much of a temper problem…until he met Austin Wood.

Lyric was a little frightened by Marcus' reaction. Not that he'd hurt her, but even she knew it was uncharacteristic of Marcus to carry on so. Oddly enough, Marcus' outburst made her feel cared for and, in turn, made her feel safe. She knew Marcus' strong feelings about Austin were only borne out of concern for her.

Marcus gazed at Lyric and noted that the dark circles under her eyes somehow made them appear even lighter blue, almost translucent. Her strawberry blond waves were up in a ponytail with a few wayward strands stubbornly clinging to her neck.

"I know, Marcus, calm down. I know how you feel about Austin. The only thing I can figure is he had his guys, Derrick, Johnny and Kroger looking for me. They are good at their jobs and would be too afraid of Austin to fail. I'd be only too happy to never see any of those four again."

Seeming mollified, Marcus relented. "I know. I'm sorry about the tantrum." He cringed.

What a hypocrite he must seem! Jesus taught to love your enemies–not break their noses! True, Jesus had been speaking more about the world as a whole and those in it as enemies of God, but to love them anyway, as God did, but still…he was sure the rule still applied. He couldn't quite picture God coming down and breaking their noses if they didn't love Him back.

Marcus had never had a true enemy–until now. And he wasn't sure what to do about it. Looking at Lyric, he cringed again. How could he explain what he'd done? He couldn't! Should he apologize to her for punching Austin? How could Marcus demonstrate a loving Christian if he had such an adverse reaction to Austin? And the truth of the matter was, he wasn't sorry for defending Lyric. If Austin got his nose broken in the process…well, Marcus couldn't quite feel sorry for that. Not yet. And then he cringed.

He sighed heavily for he desperately wanted Lyric to know Jesus, and she wasn't going to if he didn't demonstrate it better. After all, it was evident God had put her on his doorstep–quite literally–for just such a reason, presumably. Even his pastor had agreed with him when he'd told him about the living arrangements Marcus had found himself in. This inexplicable rage – for that's the only way he could describe it – he had for Austin had to be curbed.

Lyric saw a host of emotions play across Marcus' face as he appeared to be contemplating something deeply. She laid her hand on his shoulder. "Are you going to be okay?" Her eyes penetrated.

Swallowing forcefully, Marcus took a deep breath. "Yes, I will be." Waiting only a beat, he blurted, "I know I've promised not to pry, but can I ask you something?"

Unsure, Lyric finally relented, "Okaaaay," drawing the word out slowly.

Marcus nearly burst, "Why him? Why'd you choose *him?*" Marcus almost spit the last word out like an epithet.

Momentarily confused, Lyric asked, "I told you the story, didn't I? He sorta chose me, as it were. I was young, naïve…just plain stupid, I guess. What girl wouldn't jump at the chance to be with a man who paid attention to her? Especially when said girl is trying to make it in the big city."

"I wish you'd never met him," Marcus blurted out.

Surprised by this dark Marcus, Lyric tried laughing to lighten the mood. Instead it fell flat, and she became melancholy. She murmured, more to herself, "So do I."

'Almost,' she added to herself.

Inwardly she cringed. The moment had passed for her to tell Marcus. And it was eating her up.

"I wish you would've met someone else who'd taken care of you."

Seeming to be lost in the past, Lyric spoke, "Well, he did take care of me. At first. It wasn't until later that…he didn't."

Lyric started feeling uncomfortable with the direction the conversation was going.

Marcus looked like a suffering man, his green eyes almost black with pain. "He didn't though, Lyric. Don't you see? You deserve better! You've *always* deserved better. Even back then, when you first met Austin. You do know that, don't you?"

And there it was. The discomfort of having her insecurity thrown back at her. It almost seemed to physically knock the wind out of her. The enormity of her pain felt fresh because she had managed to keep it hidden for so long. Marcus Coulter had hit a nerve.

Fresh tears sprang to her eyes and all she could do was whisper, "No, I don't know that, Marcus. And you can't know that, either. You only know what I've told you, and I haven't told you everything."

A spasm of guilt clenched her gut. Now that she'd started, she couldn't seem to stop. With increasing speed and volume, her words tumbled out. "How do you know that I didn't deserve Austin, huh? My past is pretty messed up and I wasn't always a nice person. In life, you have to lie in the bed you've made for yourself. No, I'm not proud of the choices I've made, and I've had to reap the consequences."

Tears were running freely down Lyric's face and snot bubbled out of her nose. Not a pretty picture, she was sure.

Marcus grabbed the Kleenex box off of the end table by his elbow and gave Lyric a handful.

Gently and ever so quietly, Marcus told Lyric, "No one *ever deserves* to go through what you did with Austin. Everyone has value and worth, no matter their past."

Lyric kept her eyes downcast and wouldn't look at him. She was afraid he'd start talking about God and knew that if he did, she'd hate him for it.

Marcus badly wanted to tell her about God and how He saw her. And how much He valued her. But Marcus could see Lyric shut down and listened to the still, small voice telling him, '*Not now, Marcus, don't push her. She'll know about Me soon enough.*'

Lyric finally looked up. And, speaking with venom, spat, "I know you'll never understand, Marcus. You've lived a life not even remotely close to mine. I don't feel like I even deserve to know you."

With that, Lyric stalked to her room, leaving Marcus feeling instantly chilled.

vvvvvvvvvvvvvvvvvvvvvvvvvvvvvvvvvvvvvvvvvvvvvvvvvvvvvvvvvvvvvvvvvvvvvvvvvvvvvvv

'Coward! Chicken!' Lyric taunted herself the next morning. *'You couldn't tell him, could you? Instead, you take the coward's way out and end the night by escaping to bed. But not until you threw the world's biggest pity party in history.'*

Lyric had to think about what day it was. Inwardly she groaned when she realized it was Saturday and she would inevitably be meeting Marcus outside her bedroom door.

Mentally, she prepared herself. *'Suck it up, suck it up.'* Taking a deep breath, Lyric opened her bedroom door and padded to the kitchen.

The coffee was already brewed.

"Good morning," Marcus greeted brightly.

Too brightly? Lyric recognized her over-analyzing tendency rearing its head.

"Morning," she mumbled.

By now Marcus knew she wasn't a morning person. He seemed satisfied with her response. Without further comment, he handed her a mug of coffee.

"Thanks." Was this a peace offering? No. He hadn't done anything wrong.

'Stop it! Stop analyzing!' she scolded herself. *'He's just being Marcus.'*

Marcus took his mug to the table where his laptop looked ready to go. His college books were strewn across the rest of the surface.

Relieved, Lyric realized Marcus wouldn't bring up the previous night's conversation.

Indicating the academic mess on the table, Marcus said, "You know what my agenda is for the day." He smiled a school-boyish smile. "Homework. What's yours? Do you have to work?"

Absentmindedly waving her hand and walking to the sofa beyond the kitchen island, Lyric plopped down with, "Yep. One to seven."

"How you got lucky enough to get afternoon shifts, I'll never understand. You never have to be in to work before noon!"

Lyric turned to the back of the sofa to look at him. Smiling slyly, she told him, "I put on the application that I'm not a morning person."

Marcus, who had just taken a swig of coffee, spluttered and nearly choked. Laughing, he responded with amused incredulity. "You didn't!"

Lyric laughed, too. "Yes, sir, I certainly did. I was young and stupid, remember? In hindsight, I'm surprised Mr. Butterman hired me."

"I'm sure he knows talent when he sees it."

Lyric snorted. "Stocking shelves and checking groceries doesn't exactly require talent."

"You're a good employee, obviously. You've been there how long?"

"Two-and-a-half years – since my obvious theatrical talent was going unnoticed." Lyric gave a feigned dramatic sob.

When she looked up, she caught Marcus' bemused expression as he started clapping in staccatoed sarcasm.

Snickering, Lyric ordered in mock sternness, "Do your homework, Coulter," and promptly stuck her nose in a magazine.

`````````````````````````````````````````````````````````````````````

At work, during their break, Camilla asked, "How's your new living arrangement going?"

Lyric had filled her in on the latest. Camilla knew all of Lyric's history almost as well as Lyric herself.

"Fine, but it's a couple of months now. It's not so new."

"Really? Huh. Seemed not that long ago."

"Hey, I told you he's a Christian, right?"

"Yes." Camilla rolled her eyes. "Why? Is he Bible thumping yet?"

Lyric shook her head. "See, that's the weird part. Anytime I think it might come up, it doesn't. And when I first moved in, he told me when he went to church, but it was only stated for informational purposes, while we were discussing our schedules. Other than that, he hasn't mentioned it."

"Oh," Camilla said with a knowing look. "So, he tries to do it all casual-like."

"Actually, it didn't feel that way. It *really was* more like, 'Here's my school and work schedule and then I go to church on Sundays and to my parents' afterward.' He did invite me to church once, but didn't get all pushy."

Approval touched Camilla's words. "That sounds promising."

"And then we had this really deep talk last night. I felt sure he'd start in on God, but he didn't. Even though I think he wanted to."

Camilla grunted, "Mhm…you gotta respect a man who doesn't force his belief on you."

"I do respect him. A lot."

"What'd you two talk about?"

"Austin. It got weird pretty quick, though. He started talking, actually, telling me, about how I was worth so much more than the likes of Austin, or some such nonsense." Lyric laughed softly so Camilla wouldn't know how deeply the conversation had affected her. She'd never had anyone tell her she was worth anything before. Except her parents. But that was so long ago. Almost a lifetime, it felt like.

Lyric noticed and felt Camilla's silence then. "What?"
`````````````````````````````````````````````````````````````````````

"Not much. It's just that, well, Lyric, he *does* have a point, you know. I remember seeing you come to work, downcast, forlorn." Camilla eyed Lyric carefully. "You remember? You *have* to know Marcus is telling the truth. You *do* know that, don't you? You *are* worth something, Lyric. You matter."

Lyric shrugged noncommittally. "All I know is, I made my bed and I've had to lie in it. And if it weren't for Marcus having pity on me, I'd still be lying in it."

'Liar!' her conscience pricked. *'You're still lying in it!'* She hadn't told Camilla that part, either. Lyric didn't feel ready to lose either Camilla or Marcus yet, but she knew she most likely would soon.

Realizing their break was over, they stood up. As they did so, Camilla nudged Lyric's shoulder and asked, "So, when do I get to meet him?"

`,,,,,,,,,,,,,,,,,,,,,,,,,,,,,,,,,,,,,,,,,,,,,,,,,,,,,,,,,,,,,,,,,,,,,,,,,,,,,,,,,,,,,,,,,,,,`

Lyric worried, fretted, stewed. Having Camilla ask to meet Marcus simply drove even deeper the need to come clean with Marcus. It was only fair he knew all her secrets. If there wasn't going to be a Marcus for Camilla to meet, it was best to find that out sooner rather than later. On that note, it'd be best to find out if she had a Camilla as well. Somehow Lyric knew Camilla wouldn't take her secret as hard as Marcus might. No, as he most assuredly *would.*

All the way home from work, Lyric found herself arguing the same tired argument she'd been having with herself in the weeks since moving in with Marcus.

He'll find out eventually.

The longer you wait, the more mad he'll be.

At this point, Austin will still take you back if Marcus rejects you. Too much longer and Austin might reject you, too.

Lyric's stomach clenched at that. Austin didn't know her secret, either, and would also be furious.

This night, however, Lyric resolved to do the inevitable. She *would* tell Marcus.

As her footsteps took her nearer to home, she unconsciously matched their rhythm to The Little Engine That Could. *'I think I can...I think I can...I think I can....'*

Chapter 8
Secrets are made to be found out with time
Charles Sanford

Lyric stepped into their apartment and glanced around, looking for Marcus. He was where she thought he'd be – at the dining table. Studying, she presumed.

With a boldness and a briskness she didn't feel, Lyric marched to the table and sat herself down. "We need to talk."

Marcus closed his text book and eyed her curiously. "Okay."

'*Don't lose nerve,*' Lyric demanded of herself.

"Shoot," Marcus prompted.

And the words came pouring out.

"I realize I should have told you this sooner. The day we met – or at least the day I moved in, even. And I know you have every right to ask me to leave right now, but I have something to tell you." Lyric paused, gasping for breath.

"I kinda gathered that. Calm down. I honestly can't imagine anything so bad as to make me want you to leave. Just tell me."

Taking a deep breath, Lyric continued. "Okay, here goes." Pause. "I'm pregnant."

Stunned, Marcus didn't know what to say. He needed a minute to process, but it seemed Lyric had more.

"It's Austin's – of course – but he doesn't know."

Marcus blanched at that. "He doesn't know? Who does know? How far along are you?"

Lyric hadn't thought past actually telling Marcus. She hadn't anticipated these questions. Or the embarrassment they brought.

"Um…so here's the thing…I haven't told anyone except Mr. Butterman. Besides him, you're the first. Camilla doesn't even know. I haven't been to see a doctor yet. But I found out just before moving in here, so I'm guessing about eight weeks."

Marcus was clearly concerned. "You haven't been to see a doctor? Why haven't you been to see a doctor? How are you feeling? Are you alright? Is there anything I can do?"

Lyric suddenly felt impatient. Marcus was not reacting the way she'd predicted. She had expected he'd be mad she kept the secret and so kick her out. This whole caring thing threw her off guard. In some weird way, she'd been hoping she'd have an excuse to go back to Austin. Not because she particularly wanted to or cared for him, but…he *was* the baby's father, after all. And, well, she didn't deserve the compassion Marcus was showing her. That was the crux of it. Lyric had screwed up again and instead of the beating she was accustomed to from Austin, the berating she was convinced she deserved, she was getting warmth from Marcus. Of course, she didn't voice any of this.

"Well, to answer your questions, no; I don't have very good insurance; I'm feeling good, actually; fine; and…er, don't throw me out?" She asked the latter with a sheepish grin.

Marcus simply stared. Shaking his head as if to clear cobwebs, he asked, "Why on earth would I throw you out? Also, I'm going to help pay for a doctor – "

"No!" Lyric fiercely interrupted. She certainly couldn't have that. It was enough just knowing Marcus didn't sound like he was going to make her leave. She couldn't let him come in and make her problem easier on her. Yes, she needed to go to a doctor, but *she'd* deal with it; it was her problem.

"Come on, Lyric, please let me help. You need to make sure everything's alright with the baby. And *you* need to be checked, too."

Marcus' tone was so persuasive, Lyric almost gave in, but she couldn't. "It's my problem. My screw-up. I'll make it work somehow."

"Please, Lyric," Marcus tried again. For he knew that even if Austin knew of the baby, he most likely wouldn't help Lyric. "At least let me pay for your first visit. Just so we know – you know – everything's okay."

Marcus' eyes pleaded so convincingly, his genuine concern finally won her over. "Okay, but *only* the first appointment. I'll tell Austin and he'll have to help out with the expenses. He gets enough drug money, I'm sure."

Marcus' complete demeanor changed then. "Lyric, I'm going to break a rule one time. You can have Austin over here so you can tell him. And I want to be here when you do. I don't like the thought of you going over there alone. Can't stand the thought of you being alone with him – "

"Marcus. I'll be fine." Lyric forced a cheerfulness she didn't feel. As nice as it was to have someone look out for her for a change, it didn't mean she wanted him involved. "This isn't your problem."

"Please, Lyric, please promise me. I don't trust Austin."

"I probably wouldn't be alone with him. His men will probably be there." Forced cheerfulness again.

Marcus smirked in spite of himself. "That doesn't help your case, Lyric. I'll make myself available anytime. I'll take time off work. I'll skip classes. Promise me you won't see him alone."

Exasperated, but touched by his continued concern for her well-being, Lyric conceded. "Alright! Gosh! You really know how to wear down a girl's defenses."

Satisfied he got his point across, Marcus relented. "Thank you. I *really* don't trust that guy. But I suppose he needs to know about this baby."

For some unknown reason – hormones? – Lyric found herself defending Austin. "He's not all bad. There's good in him somewhere. He just let himself get out of control right before I left him. But I always have this sense that I'll go back to him – someday."

Marcus found himself feeling enraged by that. "Why? Lyric, he *doesn't* deserve you! You deserve *so much* better than him!"

"Chill out, Marcus! What's your deal? You act as if my life is any of your business. We're just roommates, okay? I told you the important stuff and Austin hasn't been back. I even promised to let you be present when I tell him he's a father, which is highly personal and I didn't have to do. I don't understand you. This isn't your life. Butt out!"

Hurt more than he cared to admit, Marcus tried to explain what he himself didn't fully understand. "Look, all I really know is that *you matter.* And you obviously haven't heard it enough. You are a beautiful person, Lyric and you're worth much more than you give yourself credit for. Austin is not good for you, but for some reason you think he is. He is toxic and will keep sucking the life out of you. He doesn't treat you the way you deserve to be treated. And you've already invited me into your life so now it's my business, too. I believe we are friends, so I am speaking as your friend. I want to help you. I care about you." Marcus stopped himself before he started preaching. Lyric didn't seem ready to hear about God yet, but Marcus sensed she was getting closer. Silently he added, '*And more importantly, Jesus loves you.*' It would have sounded corny aloud.

Marcus longed for the day he could tell Lyric that and have her be receptive. He prayed it would be soon. '*These things take time,*' he reminded himself.

Lyric wasn't used to hearing such a glowing report about herself. Or such hard words about her life. She'd almost have rather had Austin's ugly, belittling words than Marcus' honest, heartfelt ones. Probably because she knew, deep down, that Marcus was right and, also *way* deep down, any words Austin yelled at her were false. Just because she'd believed them on the surface at the time, didn't mean they were true. Besides, how else could she explain why she finally left Austin? Yet, why did she feel the sudden need to go back? Yes, it was comfortable, so to speak, familiar. Was that the only reason?

Moved to tears by Marcus' words, she didn't let him see. Instead, she escaped to her room.

ˏˏˏ

When she got up the next morning, Marcus was gone. Church, she rightly suspected.

Dully, she pulled on the first clothes she found that fit. Mentally, she made a note to go shopping for maternity clothes. She didn't think she needed them quite yet, but would before long.

Usually, the health food store wasn't open on Sundays. Today, however, they had to get ready for their annual anniversary sale. And because they were there anyway, Mr. Butterman opened the store.

At work, Lyric cringed as she walked past Mr. Butterman's office. Her secret was officially out. She supposed she could tell people now. First things first, she headed to the break room to punch in and tell someone else her news.

Walking in, Lyric spotted her. How could she not? Olive skin, shining ebony hair, chocolate brown eyes. Camilla was an exotic vision.

Approaching her, Lyric called out timidly, "Camilla? I need to talk to you."

After Lyric explained everything, Camilla squealed with glee, "A baby?" Then gushed, "We've gotta have a baby shower!"

Lyric was pleased Camilla had taken the news so well.

"And that roommate of yours…I gotta meet him. Is he single?"

Lyric laughed. "Yes, but I have a feeling he doesn't date outside his faith."

Camilla rolled her eyes. "I can change that. If he's as cute and sweet as you say, I wouldn't mind the challenge."

Grinning, Lyric had to agree. "If anyone can, it'd be you!"

When Lyric got home from work, it was to discover Marcus had beat her there.

"You're home early. I don't usually expect you 'til about seven."

"Oh, I cut out early. I have a test tomorrow that I haven't studied for." Marcus indicated the books spread out in their usual place on the table. "How was work? I got your note."

Since Lyric didn't usually work on Sundays, she'd left a note for Marcus, just in case.

"Fine. The usual. Except I told Camilla about the baby."

"That's great!"

"Yeah. She wants to throw me a shower."

"That'd be fun."

Lyric peered at the kitchen counter then, noticing the little white cartons. "Mmmm!"

"Help yourself. Chinese takeout."

"Thanks." Lyric helped herself to a carton of sweet and sour pork that she took with her to her room so she could change.

A few minutes later, she found herself bewildered and in tears. Coming out of her room still dressed in her clothes from work, she cried, "Marcus! I have nothing to wear!"

Startled, Marcus looked up from his books. "What? What do you mean?"

"I mean, *I have nothing to wear!*" Lyric felt herself getting ridiculously panicked. "I went in to throw on some pants or something and nothing fits. I'm too fat! Suddenly, *I'm fat!* This morning, I could barely find something that fit me. Maybe I'm farther along than I thought!" Lyric was overwhelmed. "Maybe I'm ten or twelve weeks instead of eight!" Her huge eyes welled with tears and fear.

Marcus wisely resisted the urge to laugh at her absurd outburst. Getting up, he crossed through the open living room from the dining nook. "Do you think maybe this is one of those mood swings?"

Clearly not the right thing to say.

Looking at him as if he were daft, Lyric cried harder. "No! Why would you ask that?"

Gently, Marcus extricated himself from the obvious faux pas and told her, "Hang on."

He went into his room and came back out with a Dallas Cowboys sweatshirt and navy blue sweat pants.

Incredulous, Lyric squeaked out, between tears, "I have to wear *boy* clothes now?"

Marcus gently led her into her room and sat her on her bed. Sitting next to her and putting his arm around her, he told her, "Only for now. I'm bigger than you so they should fit. You can get some new clothes tomorrow."

"And I'm supposed to wear *your* clothes to go shopping for them?" Lyric wailed.

Trying to get her out of her funk, Marcus joked, "Good thing you told me, huh? It would've been mighty suspicious having you going off about clothes not fitting."

"Uh, yeah." She took a few deep breaths, trying to calm down. She tried giving Marcus a weak smile.

'*Welcome to pregnancy, Lyric,*' she told herself.

```
````````````````````````````````````````````````````````````````````````
```

Marcus had never been shopping for a girl before – at least, not without his mom's or sister-in-law Rachel's help. It was a whole new territory for him.

His last class of the evening had been the one with the test. As soon as he had finished, he was free to leave. He'd gotten out nearly forty-five minutes early from the usually hour-and-a-half class. Knowing he'd have extra time, he'd decided to take a quick shopping trip on his way home before all of the stores closed.

With much help from a sales associate and over an hour later, he headed home with his purchases.

"Lyric!" he called out as he walked in the door. "I have a surprise for you."
```

Setting the bags down, he headed for her room, but she came out, looking bleary-eyed.

"Oh, I'm sorry. Did I wake you?" he asked, perplexed.

'Of course you did, you dolt! It's still the same time you usually get home, thanks to the shopping excursion. She's usually asleep by now, you know that!'

"Nah, I was only dozing. Being pregnant is tiring."

Marcus looked closer. Lyric didn't look tired, she looked exhausted. "Rough day?"

"No more than usual." Lyric let out a big yawn. "Today at work, Mr. Butterman gave me the number to his wife's doctor."

"That was certainly helpful."

"And I made an appointment to see her, the doctor, next week. I suppose I should tell Austin before then."

"You probably should. First, though, go look in the bags I brought in."

Curious, Lyric spotted the bags in the living room. She vaguely recognized the logo on the bags.

"Clothes?" she asked, bewildered.

"Not just any clothes. Maternity clothes."

Lyric squealed in pure delight. She pulled article after article of clothing out of the bags: blouses, tee shirts, pants, jeans, skirts, dresses.

"I got a gift card for you to go back there for, uh, *other* items. Personal, um…er, items."

Like a kid in a candy store, Lyric excitedly went to try on her outfits. She came out in a soft cotton tee shirt in butter yellow and dark blue jeans with buttons on the back pockets and a design around the side pockets.

"How did you know my size? They fit perfectly! And how did you know about the band that expands jeans and pants as my belly grows?"

Blushing crimson, Marcus felt like he was confessing to a crime. Maybe he was. "I, uh, looked at a few of your clothes that were on your floor. The sales lady told me that maternity clothes were the same size. She was very nice and helpful with everything, even making suggestions, like the belly band thing."

Lyric seemed to be ruled by her impulses as of late. She found herself throwing her arms around Marcus in a fierce hug.

Letting go, she suddenly felt awkward. "I'm sorry. No one's ever done anything so nice for me before."

"Are you sure it's okay? The sales lady warned me women like to shop for themselves, but you were so upset yesterday. And I wanted to help. I only got you a few outfits. And I didn't get you any sweat pants or pajamas or…" his voice trailed off in embarrassment. Clearing his throat, he told her, "Anyway, that's what the gift card's for. And you can take anything back you don't like. Or all of it, if it doesn't…if you don't like it."

Lyric reluctantly expected the tears now. "Are you kidding? I'm in heaven! I have more clothes now than I ever did in my pre-pregnancy clothes. You sure know how to spoil a girl, Marcus Coulter!"

Chapter 9

Don't you dare, for one more second, surround yourself with people who are not aware of the greatness that you are
Jo Blackwood Preston

The next week, Lyric got up early on Sunday morning. She wasn't entirely sure of what she was doing or if she would be well-received, but decided she had to try. Marcus had given her such a nice gift with the clothes, she felt she owed him *something.* And she knew what would make him the happiest.

Taking a deep breath, she opened her bedroom door and walked out.

Marcus looked up and nearly choked on his coffee. Lyric was standing there dressed in one of her new outfits, a long black skirt and white blouse that seemed to accentuate her tiny baby bump.

"I thought I'd go to church with you, if that's okay."

Marcus' face lit up. "I'd be delighted to have you accompany me."

⁁⁁⁁

On the hour drive to the church he grew up in, the church he loved, Marcus could scarcely keep the smile off of his face. He'd been shocked when he saw Lyric dressed up and hoped she'd say she wanted to go to church.

He kept silently repeating, ' *Thank you, Jesus.* ' He couldn't seem to comprehend anything else.

Lyric was nervous. She hadn't been to church since leaving home five years before.

Marcus was excited for Lyric to hear about his Lord. He didn't know much about her church history, but from the little he knew, this was a huge step for Lyric.

At the church, he helped Lyric out of the car. He couldn't wait for his family to meet her, either. They'd been dying to, he'd told them so much about her.

Walking to the door of the church, he sensed Lyric's tension.

"Relax. It'll be okay. You'll get to meet my family. They've been dying to meet you."

Momentarily diverted, Lyric thought about that. She'd only had Camilla to confide in; it never occurred to her Marcus had a whole slew of people he talked to. It hadn't crossed her mind he'd even *want* to talk about her to anyone.

"Well, I wasn't worried about that until you mentioned it. What I was *really* worried about was the roof caving in. I'm sure God's ready to smite me the moment I set foot in the door for even daring such a thing."

Marcus gave her a bemused smile. "You're funny." Then he opened the door for her.

"Here goes," she breathed.

The foyer was cool, in direct contrast to the early-August heat they'd stepped out of.

Dutifully Lyric followed Marcus through the milling people as he smiled a greeting to different ones, occasionally stopping to introduce Lyric. If anyone suspected her circumstances, they didn't let on. They all greeted her with surprising warmth.

Entering the sanctuary, they started down the aisle in much the same fashion, when Marcus announced, "Ah, there they are. My family." He led Lyric over to a group of four with two little children running around them, and two chubby infants being held by their parents, Lyric surmised.

"Hi Mom, Dad," Marcus greeted the other two adults. Turning to the mom and dad of the twin babies, Marcus said, "Hey Levi, Rachel."

"Unca Mawcus!" squealed the little girl of the running twosome. Without breaking stride, she ran straight to Marcus and threw her little arms around his legs.

Scooping her up, Marcus planted a kiss on the little girl's plump, rosy cheek.

Her black curls bounced as she struggled in Marcus' arms to turn and get a good look at Lyric. Her blue eyes inquired even as she pointed and asked, "Who's 'at?"

"This is my good friend, Lyric. Lyric, this is one of my nieces, Hailey."

Turning back to his parents and Hailey's parents, he introduced, "This is my dad, Kurt and my mom, Lynne and my brother, Levi and his wife, Rachel. And Levi's holding Sydney and Rachel has her twin brother, Logan. You met Hailey and the little guy that was chasing her is Zachary. They are three and four, respectively, since Hailey just had her birthday at the beginning of last month." He grinned at Lyric's flabbergasted expression. "I know, it's a lot to take in."

Zachary could've been a four-year-old version of Marcus – or Levi – they looked very much alike, except where Marcus was broad-shouldered and tall, Levi was lean and agile.

Both Zachary and Hailey had the definite look of Coulter with their black hair and blue eyes. Their grandpa had the bearing of family patriarch, but not as serious as the title forebode. He had an open, friendly face and his handshake had been firm.

Lynne Coulter looked neat and put together, but not at all the Stepford wife-type that Lyric had expected.

Her hair was a chestnut brown with distinguished threads of gray running through its soft waves. Her brown eyes were warm and inviting, like melted chocolate.

Lyric looked back to the babies. Less than six months old, she wondered if they would take after their blond-haired, blue-eyed mommy.

It only seemed fair, being that their two older siblings took after their daddy.

Lyric liked Rachel instantly who, instead of the standard handshake, had leaned in for a one-armed hug with baby Logan. "I'm so happy to finally meet you!" she'd enthusiastically greeted. And, somehow, Lyric had instinctively known she'd meant it. Rachel reminded Lyric a lot of Marcus.

"Shall we find a seat? Service is about to start," Lynne offered.

As the songs started and Lyric realized she knew some of them, she felt suddenly homesick. She missed her childhood church. Her parents. Her old friends. Once again, her hormones kicked in and she was finding it hard to keep her eyes dry. Embarrassed, she hoped no one noticed, but she caught Marcus looking.

"Are you okay?" he mouthed, face full of concern.

Giving a tiny nod, she turned away, shame heating her face.

Further humiliation came later, after church when Rachel turned to her and gave her a hug. "Don't you hate pregnancy hormones? I always cried at the drop of a hat. In fact, I literally did once! When I was pregnant with Hailey, I had grabbed Zachary's little ball cap and dropped it and burst into tears." Rachel giggled.

Lyric hadn't realized anyone else knew of her condition. She wasn't showing that much yet.

Sidling up to Marcus, she murmured, "Did you tell your family I'm pregnant?"

Glancing sideways at her, Marcus answered, "Yeah, was I not supposed to? They've all been praying for you. I told them last Sunday, the day after you told me, so they could be praying for that, too."

Lyric was irrationally irritated, but she tried being reasonable. So, they were praying for her. What was wrong with that? It'd been a long time since anyone seemed to genuinely care about her, much less a whole handful of people. People she hadn't even met until today! And yet, she couldn't help firing back, "So I'm just a prayer case to them? A little project they get to pray for?"

Grabbing Lyric's arm, Marcus hustled her outside to his car. Eyes flashing, he spoke, "Look, you don't even know my family. They are not like that and it's not fair for you to make judgments. They cared about you before they even knew you. We're a close family. Yes, I tell them things about my life that are happening. You happened into my life so, yes, I told them about you. If you had said, though, that you'd rather keep the baby a secret, I wouldn't have said anything. I was excited and wanted to share. And they are, too, by the way. And they're happy for you. And they want the best for you, so they've been praying because only God can provide the best."

Overwhelming emotion engulfed Lyric then. She bit her trembling lip. "They've really been praying for me?"

"Yes, they have. And they've all really wanted to meet you."

"Well, I sure hope their prayers work. I suppose I could use some."
"It got you here, didn't it?" And Marcus grinned his most disarming smile.

"Can we go home now?"

A look of alarm crossed Marcus' face. "Oh, Lyric, I thought you knew. I go to my parents' for Sunday dinner after church."

Of course! How stupid! How could she have forgotten? And Lyric's heart sank. It wasn't that she doubted they were all nice people, deep down, but honestly, she was kind of waiting for the other shoe to drop. They couldn't possibly be so genuinely and blindly accepting of her. And the thought of spending the day trying to impress them exhausted her.

Eyeing Lyric, Marcus decided, "I'll take you back home to the city, and I'll just be a little late to dinner."

Now Lyric felt enormously guilty.

"Lyric!" Lynne called, actually jogging over with energy.

Any energy impressed Lyric these days.

"I just wanted to make sure you knew you're more than welcome to come for dinner."

"Actually, Mom, she'd rather just go home."

Lynne looked so ridiculously disappointed, Lyric found herself changing her mind.

"No, no, Mrs. Coulter. I'll be glad to come over. Thanks for inviting me."

A beaming smile replaced the disappointment. "Oh, good! And, Lyric, call me Lynne, okay?"

"Okay...Lynne." Lyric forced the most genuine smile she could.

Getting into the car after shutting Lyric's door, Marcus couldn't help but grin at her.

"What?" she whined.

"You just made my mom very happy. And if I had come without you, I'd get an earful. So you've made me very happy."

An ornery streak took hold of Lyric then. "Bully for you," she pretended to grouse. And then couldn't help but adding, "I think I like her better than you, anyway."

She arrogantly tossed her head then and Marcus chuckled.

The drive took about ten minutes from the church. The Coulters, Marcus' parents, lived in a beautiful suburban neighborhood of modern homes. From the outside, it looked just like the other cookie cutter houses surrounding it. Once inside, however, Lyric discovered it was comfortably furnished in Lynne's own, unique eclectic style of shabby chic. She felt instantly at home.

As Marcus' brother Levi's family came in, Lyric felt herself relishing the sounds of family. Of Hailey's squeal of delight as Levi hauled her in like a sack of potatoes.

Unconsciously Lyric patted her small bump of a baby. Would she play with her baby that way? Would she be an affectionate mother, like Lynne seemed to be? Lyric spied her through the doorway to the kitchen, giving Levi a hug.

"Dining room's this way." Marcus came up behind her and walked past toward the doorway Lyric had been looking through.

The house seemed to be spacious without being pretentious. Suddenly, nostalgia overwhelmed her. She was reminded of her own home growing up and how her parents' house was much like the Coulters'.

For the remainder of the day, Lyric stuck close to Marcus, feeling somewhat out of place in their family dynamic. It gave her plenty of time to reflect and she decided, possibly, she should give Austin another chance. She wanted a family for her baby. A family like the Coulters. Once Austin knew about the baby, surely he'd change. He wouldn't hurt his baby, surely. He wouldn't hurt the mother of his baby…surely.

"Oh, Lyric" Rachel intercepted her as she and Marcus were getting ready to leave.

Lynne was close behind Rachel, smiling.

Looking back at her mother-in-law, Lynne urged Rachel on with an excited nod.

"Um, we were wondering if," she paused, biting on her lip. "Can we give you a baby shower?" she blurted out.

Caught off guard, Lyric stuttered and stumbled over her words, finally giving an, "Um, uh, yeah, sure."

Rachel clapped her hands with joy and then threw her arms around Lyric.

Lynne leaned in then and kissed Lyric's cheek. "Thank you!" She seemed just as excited as Rachel.

Giving Marcus a final hug, Lynne sent them on their way.

\\\

"You're awfully quiet," Marcus commented on the way home. "Something on your mind?"

"Not really," Lyric mumbled. She wasn't about to tell Marcus her decision regarding Austin. Marcus hated Austin enough as it was. Her decision to go back and try to make
things work as a family definitely wouldn't endear him to Austin.

Marcus knew enough not to pry. He watched Lyric closely, however, in the following days. She only grew more pensive and quiet but wouldn't budge when he tried to draw her out.

Lyric couldn't seem to shut her mind off. She couldn't quite figure out how to tell Austin about the baby. She had told Marcus she would tell

Austin somewhere public. That way she wouldn't have to invite him back to their apartment and she could also tell Austin semi-privately without the audience of Marcus. Marcus hadn't been thrilled about it, but relented.

Finally, Lyric decided on the coffee shop around the corner from work. That way, she'd have work to take her mind off of whatever unpleasantness that might occur.

With trembling hands, Lyric dialed Austin's number and then crossed her fingers. Part of her wished she'd get his voicemail so she could simply leave the information of where and when to meet her.

No such luck. He answered on the third ring. "Yo."

"Hi, Austin, it's me," Lyric timidly greeted. She willed herself to control her trembling. "It's – it's Lyric."

Lyric could hear the smirk in his voice. "So you finally came to your senses, huh? Couldn't live without me, baby? I knew you'd come crawling back."

Feeling sudden revulsion, Lyric almost hung up. '*I'm not a coward,*' she told herself. Firmly.

"Austin, can I meet you at the Starbucks by my work? I need to talk to you."

"We're talkin' now."

"No, I mean face-to-face."

"Whoa! Must be serious." Austin changed his voice to a purr like he did when he was trying to be persuasive. "Why don't you come by our apartment?"

It almost worked. Weakly, Lyric answered, "Austin…." Closing her eyes, she demanded herself to focus. Snapping them open, she said, "No, Austin. I need to *see* you." Abruptly she realized she'd used the wrong words.

"I miss you, too, baby," Austin's voice was low, purposefully seductive.

Louder, Lyric instructed, "Meet me tomorrow, noon." And hung up.

She sat for a moment trying to sort out what she was feeling. Austin revolted her, if she thought about what he'd done to her. When he talked to her the way he just had, however, and she could imagine his brown eyes going soft as he spoke, she couldn't help longing for him again.

Besides, reality was, she couldn't get anyone better than Austin. She was pregnant and would soon have a child in her arms. The men she deserved were men like Austin and at least they would expect a girl like her to have a kid. And with Austin, she knew what to expect. He *could* be decent. Hopefully finding out he was a father would make him decent for good.

Lyric glanced at her watch again and noted he was only ten minutes late. It seemed like an hour. She tapped her foot impatiently, making her little table jiggle.

Finally, she spotted him. Her heart thumped while her stomach lurched. Interesting reaction.

Striding over, Austin leaned down and planted his lips firmly on hers. She didn't struggle or push him away. She started to kiss him back, but then she stopped and simply stayed still.

"Not gonna admit you still have feelings for me, are you?" Austin all but taunted.

Her heart lurched this time. He was handsome, she had to admit. His brown eyes were his most compelling feature – or weapon – depending on his mood.

'*Don't give in,*' she ordered herself. First she needed to see his reaction.

Austin took a sip of the coffee he'd put in front of him. Lyric followed suit with her green tea, then cleared her throat.

"Austin, I need to tell you something."

Using his second best weapon, Austin smiled disarmingly. "I'm all ears, baby."

"Austin, I'm pregnant."

The smile faltered.

"It's yours. I'm pregnant with your baby."

The smile vanished as Austin stood up and walked away.

Lyric was too stunned for a reaction at first. Slowly, her heart dropped as the hurt set in. Then realization came as she acknowledged that, deep down, she knew Austin wouldn't be happy about a baby. Still, she hadn't counted on complete betrayal. She'd naively thought she could talk him into seeing the positive.

And that's when the anger came, and the tears with it. How *dare* he walk away from their baby? And she was furious with herself for being so stupid.

Laying her hand on her baby, she murmured, "I'm sorry you have such an idiot for a mother."

Chapter 10

*The best way to find out if you can trust somebody
is to trust them*
Ernest Hemingway

Marcus noticed Lyric continued to be quiet all week. Added to that, she'd been jumpy. And when he tried finding out the reason, she all but blew him off, finding a polite way to do it, of course.

He worried more than he knew he had any right to. He was her friend, but they still hadn't known each other very long. It had only been a couple of months since he had first met Lyric sitting across the very table he was supposed to be using for homework. In fact, she had moved in Memorial Day weekend. Still, he wanted to have the right to worry about her. He wanted to show how much he cared, but knew she wouldn't let him. She seemed prickly on that subject.

"How'd work go?" Marcus asked later that evening after she'd gotten home. He'd hoped she would mention going to church again, being that the next day was Sunday, but he doubted it.

"Fine. I'm tired. I know pregnancy's supposed to make you tired, but I feel exhausted." Frowning, she continued, almost to herself. "I don't know as much about this as I should."

Mentioning the pregnancy reminded Marcus of the doctor. "Didn't you have a doctor's appointment yesterday?"

"Yeah, but they just did a test to make sure." She snorted as she gestured to her baby. "I guess they just thought I was fat. Oh, and they gave me some pamphlets."

Marcus raised his eyebrows. "Pamphlets?"

Lyric smiled. "Yep. On what is going to happen to me – to my body. I haven't read them yet, though."

By now, Lyric had made her way to the armchair and draped herself in it, one leg dangling off the arm.

"Did you make another appointment?"

Sighing, Lyric couldn't look at Marcus. She knew he had her best interests at heart, but things came easy for him so how could he possibly understand? She simply didn't have the money for this! Especially without Austin helping. She had paltry insurance coverage. Without meaning to, irritation colored her tone. "Marcus, I don't have the money for this! I barely have insurance! I've started scraping together a semblance of savings for the birth alone, but even at that, I know I won't have enough saved up by the time the baby comes."

"I told you I'd help. I have savings. You need to take care of the baby and yourself."

"You paid for my first visit. And I only went then to make you happy and to get you off my back about it. You don't belong in this part of my life. You're too good for it. It's my mistake. I'll deal."

Before Marcus had time to register any emotion Lyric's little speech had evoked, a rough, hard knock sounded at the door.

"I recognize that knock," Lyric fretted, eyes huge with worry, "It's Austin!"

Instantly on his feet, Marcus threw the door open, all but ripping it from its hinges. Marcus exploded, "What are you doing here, Austin?"

Shocked at his reception, Austin stumbled back, hands instinctively up, shielding his face – or nose, rather. "I just wanna talk to Lyric."

Swinging his head around, Marcus pointed a glare at Lyric. "Do you want to talk to him?" He dealt his words in a clipped tone.

Lyric had had time to settle down some and could now feel only a *little* bad for Austin. Silently, she nodded.

"Fine!" Marcus gestured for Austin to come in. "I'm not leaving and I'll have my bedroom door open in case you try anything, Austin." He leered at him, causing Austin to shrink back.

Marcus stalked to his room. How Austin got under his skin so firmly, Marcus couldn't fathom. He only knew Lyric was at stake when Austin was around and it infuriated him to have to put her at risk. It was her decision, though, so he made himself stay out of it. Since his door was open, he could hear their conversation clearly.

Austin sat on the couch, across from Lyric. Looking in her eyes, he forced a few tears. "I'm sorry, baby. I shouldn't have left. Your news surprised me. That's all. I'm back, now, though and I want in. I want to be a part of its life. Of your life. Please take me back. Please come home."

"Austin, seeing you walk away hurt so much. I couldn't stand to have that happen again."

"It won't, baby, I promise."

Lyric closed her eyes for a moment trying to gain strength. Confusion swept through her. Why did she feel like running and staying at the same time when Austin was around? She acknowledged he'd treated her badly, but she believed he *could* change! So badly *wanted* him to change. *Needed* him to, in fact, because his life was the only life she fit into.

Glancing out the door from his room, Marcus silently willed, *'No, Lyric! Don't go with him! He's lying! Oh, God, Jesus…*please*! Tell her! Don't let her go with him.'*

Out of nowhere, a voice seemed to whisper in Lyric's ear. It sounded strangely like Marcus. *'No it isn't. You deserve better than Austin. You know you do, deep down. You simply haven't seen your true worth yet.'*

Lyric's eyes snapped open and she found herself drowning in Austin's smoldering gaze. Forgetting the eerie-Marcus whisper, Lyric asked, "Will you change, Austin? Will you stop beating me just because you're mad?"

"Aw, baby, you know I'm sorry when my temper gets out of control. Yes, I'll work on it. I love you, baby."

'*Come on, Lyric,*' Marcus silently pleaded from his room. '*He's promised* nothing*! Why can't you realize that?*'

Lyric knew Austin meant it. *Had* to believe it. "Do you really mean it? You want us in your life? You'll take care of us?"

Marcus could scarcely stomach Austin's charade and the false, misplaced hope that it was giving Lyric. She was groveling!

"Yes, of course!" came Austin's reply.

Lyric felt an incredible weight lift off her shoulders. Austin would take care of her! What had she and Marcus been talking about before Austin came? Doctor bills! Now she wouldn't have to worry!

"You'll be with me through all of the doctor visits, cravings, sleepless nights?"

"I will, baby, I will."

Lyric didn't see the wary look in Austin's eyes because she had thrown her arms around him.

Marcus had, however, and his disgust and contempt grew for one Austin Wood.

Austin drew away first as Lyric prattled on about how she'd worried about money and doctor bills, but wouldn't have to anymore.

Austin listened with half an ear as he plotted how to charm her just enough to distract her from what he really wanted with her.

Before he left, Austin even gave her all of the money in his wallet. He could get more, but it seemed that, for her, it sealed his commitment.

After closing the door, Lyric danced a little jig. She had him back!

Marcus came out then, his heart aching for Lyric.

"Lyric, sit down, please." He tone was so gentle, Lyric was immediately on alert.

"We're friends, right?" Marcus asked.

"I suppose."

Deliberately shutting exasperation out of his tone, Marcus softly said, "I don't think mere roommates take each other home to meet their families."

A slight flush of embarrassment crept up Lyric's neck and she smiled shyly. "Okay."

"As your friend, I need to say a few things."

Slowly nodding her head, she encouraged, "Go on."

Fixing a steady gaze on her, Marcus' big brother mode kicked in. "Lyric, Austin isn't good for you. I know he swept in here tonight and told you everything you wanted to hear, but they were just words."

Trying to understand where Marcus was coming from, Lyric patiently explained, "No, Marcus, he wasn't. I know you don't like him, but he's trying to do right by me."

Marcus was growing impatient with Lyric's naivete, but tried reminding himself that it wasn't her fault. "I know that's what you *want* to believe–"

Lyric didn't mean to get riled, but she could feel an anger slowly simmering. She spat, "No, it's the *truth*! And you better get used to seeing more of Austin now that he's in the picture."

Pushing himself up from his seat, he declared, "I can't deal with this."

Lyric had him. How could he deny Lyric? If Austin wanted in her life, and she wanted it, he had no place to stop it.

Not done yet, Lyric continued to Marcus' retreating back. "Fine! I knew this wouldn't be to your liking. I'm gonna move back *home* with Austin."

That stopped Marcus cold. He turned around. "Lyric," he tried desperately once again to change her mind. "*Please* think about it first. I saw the look in his eyes when you hugged him. He doesn't really want this. It makes me think he has another agenda."

"You're spying on me now? I don't need looking after! I'm not a child! Let me decide things for myself. *I choose Austin!*" Smiling harshly, Lyric eyed Marcus as she told him, "He's my answer to prayer."

Bile rose up Marcus' throat. No way that filth could be an answer to anyone's prayer!

"Oh, yeah, how?" he challenged.

"Before he came, we were discussing doctor bills. Remember? I don't have to worry about them now. God answered. Austin said he'd take care of me. He even gave me three hundred bucks before he left. He told me he'll go to the next doctor's visit with me. Last week, the nurse said next time I came in, we could probably hear the baby's heartbeat and maybe even see the baby on the ultra sound." Lyric's eyes had gone dewy.

Marcus simply couldn't stomach it. Instead he told her wearily, "Well, I'm really happy for you, Lyric. Goodnight, I'm going to bed."

''

Lyric had made another doctor's appointment and it was nearing. She couldn't help but feel excited. Now she needed to phone Austin and let him know.

Anticipation welled up inside her as she listened to the phone ring on the other end.

"Yo!" Austin answered.

"Austin, it's me."

Silence for a beat. Then, "Oh, Lyric! Hi!"

Lyric felt the familiar, yet long-absent tug at her heart. She'd missed Austin, she decided. Despite his faults, in that moment, she forgot them.

"So, my next doctor's appointment is Thursday."

"Okay."

"It's at 1:00. Will you be able to make it?"

No hesitation this time. "No, baby, I'm sorry. I can't."

Lyric's disappointment was keen. Trying hard not to whine like a child, she asked, "Why?"

"Just stuff. I have other – stuff – going on."

"Don't you want to hear your baby's heartbeat? I may be far enough along we can see the baby through ultrasound!"

Lyric's dream she'd built up in her head of her and Austin together, in the doctor's office, holding hands, listening to their baby, shattered.

The tears that worked their way down her face did not find a place in her voice. "Ok, Austin. Fine. I'll let you know when the next one is."

"You know, don't bother. I'll probably be too busy for doctor visits and stuff. Just call me with updates. The doctor part of these things is more for the girls, isn't it?"

The tears vanished. "These things?! Austin, we're having a *baby*! I thought you wanted to be involved!"

"Calm down, Lyric." She recognized his annoyed tone, the one time he used her name, followed by light slapping, which could turn instantly to a full-on beating. She shivered at the memory.

"I *do* want to be involved," Austin continued on. "I was planning to be as soon as the little tyke was born. Besides," he made his voice persuasive, "I thought it'd be easier to be involved once you moved back home."

Partly because she was irked and partly because she felt an insane desire to be in control, especially of Austin, she only said, "That is yet to be determined."

It created a reaction. Good. "Look, Lyric, you said you'd come home. What's keeping you? Is it that guy you're living with?"

"No! Leave Marcus out of this! He has nothing to do with any of it. He's just a roommate."

"Sure he is." And then Lyric heard the click in her ear.

On the other side of the city, Austin smiled as he hung up the phone. He was making progress! Ever since Lyric told him about the baby, he knew how he'd get his revenge on her for leaving. Since she left him and he couldn't beat on her anymore, he used hope. He'd seen how hopeful she was, thinking he'd change and want to play happy family. Step one had been making her think he wanted to be involved, go to the doctor visits, and all that nonsense. It'd been fun dashing her hopes just now. It'd felt downright good! Next, he'd act the sorry sap and beg to be included. Heck, maybe he'd buy this baby a blanket or something – only to back out and dash her hopes again. He knew she probably wouldn't move back, but it'd make things easier and she could be his punching bag again. He could've even made her lose this nuisance of a baby. Austin was smart, though, and had already figured out that Marcus would prevent it as much as he possibly could. He could feel his anger start to boil at this and wished Lyric was there for him to take his anger out on. Since she wasn't, he was even angrier and picked up a lamp and smashed it on the wall instead.

,,,

When Marcus walked into the apartment that night, he was welcomed by the sight of Lyric curled up on the couch, crying.

Leaving his stuff by the door, he hurried over to her. "What's wrong?"

Through sobs, hiccups and lots of snot, Lyric relayed her conversation with Austin. "And, sometimes, I don't think he really loves me."

'*Of course he doesn't!*' Marcus wanted to yell.

"I just wanted us to be a family. I think he's so used to having me there, that's the only reason he wants me to come home."

'*No, it's because he wants to beat on you,*' Marcus interjected in his thoughts.

"At least, he calls it that. I'm not so sure anymore. I really have come to think of here as my home."

Marcus barely resisted the urge to wave a victory fist in the air. Instead, aloud he said, "I'm really glad to hear that, Lyric."

Sighing, finally calm, Lyric blew her nose one last time.

"I'm starting to wonder if the only reason I really wanted Austin to come is so I wouldn't be alone. I'm kinda scared. And at the very least, I long for someone to simply share the moment with so I won't feel so alone in all of this."

On impulse, Marcus heard himself offer, "I'll go."

"It's during the day, Marcus, you're at work." Lyric waved it off, afraid she'd made him feel guilted into it. That's all Austin had seemed to live off of – making her feel guilty. Probably so he could beat her some more. Lyric still wasn't used to Marcus saying what he really meant.

"I can take time off. When is it?" Marcus eagerly asked.

Stunned that Marcus was serious, Lyric answered slowly, "Thursday at 1:00."

Excited, Marcus smiled. "I am *so* there!"

Chapter 11
It is not the size of a man but the size of his heart that matters
Evander Holyfield

"Weird day for a baby appointment," Marcus remarked as he drove through the deserted City.

He could tell Lyric was nervous and was trying to take her mind off of it.

She cocked her head. "How do you mean?"

Marcus gestured around him. "There are only about three times a year the City is deserted like this. Memorial Day, the Fourth of July and Labor Day weekend. People tend to like to get out of the City during warmer weather. Why is your doctor open?"

Lyric smiled. "Well, technically, it's the Friday *before* Labor Day, but they do close early, if that makes you feel any better."

"That reminds me, my mom told me to bring you straight over after the doctor appointment for our annual barbecue. Besides, she and Rachel will be chomping at the bit to hear all about your appointment."

Strangely, Lyric found herself *wanting* to see all of the Coulters again. Even more, she was excited to share whatever news the doctor told her.

"Ok," Lyric acquiesced, "but *I* get to tell them about the baby this time."

Marcus grinned. "Deal."

`````````````````````````````````````````````````````````````````````````

Lyric nervously sat on the paper-lined examining table. She heard the knock.

"Come in," she called.

Marcus poked his head around the door. "You decent?"

Lyric gripped the sheet draped over legs and lap tighter in her fist. "Uh-huh."

Marcus took the chair by Lyric and they made small talk. He was still trying to ease Lyric's obviously taught nerves.

Finally, after what seemed like ages, a nurse came in to check Lyric's vitals. After she was done, she cheerfully announced, "The doctor will be here shortly."

Butterflies attacked Lyric's stomach then as panic set in. Glancing at the nurse's name tag, Lyric had the sudden urge to plead, "Rita, please don't go!"

But Rita left the room and Lyric began to shake. "I don't know what I'm doing, Marcus."
`````````````````````````````````````````````````````````````````````````

He grabbed her hand and said, "You're doing an incredibly brave and wonderful thing!"

"I don't know if I can do this! I don't want to be alone – I don't want to do this alone." Lyric felt the prick of tears.

"Look at me, Lyric," Marcus gently prodded, letting go of her hand.

Lyric's eyes reluctantly met his.

Quietly, he reassured her, "I'm here if you need me."

"You're not involved, though! I mean, you shouldn't feel like you have to pick up slack where that *loser* failed just because I'm your roommate. I'm not *your* obligation."

"No, you're not. You're my *friend.* I'm *happy* to be here with you – honored, really, that you'd *let* me in this part of your life. I'm *excited* about your baby – my whole family is! I *want* to help where I'm needed. We've only been roommates a couple of months, but you feel like more of a–a– kid sister."

Swallowing tears, Lyric gave him a tremulous smile. "Thank you, Marcus, I'm glad you feel that way. You are sorta big brother-like." She grasped his hand again. "Thanks for coming."

A quick knock on the door sounded and the doctor came in.

"Miss Bell," the doctor greeted, and then hesitated when he saw Marcus. "Oh, er, Mrs.–"

"Nope. It's Miss. This is Marcus. He's – he's my – uh, brother," Lyric finished giving Marcus a quick smile. "I roped him into coming today."

Dr. Oberman smiled. "Brave man."

With brown hair graying at the temples and kind, brown eyes, Dr. Oberman looked and acted the part of an understanding doctor. He was a different doctor than Lyric had seen her first visit, but she didn't mind.

During the exam, he was gentle and even involved Marcus in the discussion of Lyric's care.

"Prenatal vitamins are extremely important. So is plenty of rest," the doctor admonished.

"I've been taking them. And it seems all I do is sleep!"

"Good. It's important to listen to your body and do what it says. If you're tired, sleep. If you're hungry, eat – you get it."

After more general instructions, Dr. Oberman rubbed his hands together in anticipation. "Now, how 'bout we listen to the heartbeat and take some pictures?"

Marcus saw the immediate delight rush to Lyric's eyes and flush her cheeks.

"Can we?" Lyric asked with girlish excitement.

"Sure." Dr. Oberman rolled over a little cart with a screen attached to a machine on it. He worked his fingers over a keyboard then turned toward Lyric. "Alright, just relax. This is where the fun begins!"

Already lying down from her exam, Lyric willed her body to relax even in spite of her anticipation. She was going to see her baby for the first time!

Dr. Oberman discreetly exposed Lyric's stomach to squirt gel on it, warning that it would be cold. He then put the Doppler on her stomach and a dark image filled the screen.

Lyric grabbed Marcus' hand.

He had unobtrusively moved his chair up towards Lyric's head during her exam.

"Look!" Lyric scarcely breathed, squeezing his hand.

Moving the Doppler, the doctor took measurements then turned the screen toward Lyric. "Here's the head," he pointed out, "and the beginnings of little arms…and here are the legs. You're measuring great! Based on these, you are about ten weeks gestation."

Confused, Lyric asked, "But how can that be? My clothes are already too tight and I've felt the baby flutter."

Dr. Oberman nodded in understanding. "You're new at this. It's your first time. A lot of first time moms experience those things early on. It's because your body hasn't been through it before, so the changes come earlier than for more experienced moms."

That made sense and Lyric felt at ease.

Leaning over the machine, the doctor flipped a switch. The sounds of a quick, whooshing heartbeat filled the air.

Lyric's own heart seemed to be caught in her throat. Time momentarily stood still as she listened to her baby's heartbeat for the first time. Then the tears came and she squeezed Marcus' hand even harder. "That's my baby," she whispered in awe.

Marcus was quite in awe himself. He knew this would be cool, but hearing that little heartbeat was downright miraculous! His eyes got a little moist.

He bent over to kiss Lyric's forehead and their eyes locked for a split second. And then the moment was over.

Marcus broke the spell. "It's amazing!"

Later, Lyric would look back and try to figure out all of the things she had felt at that moment. And, more interestingly, how Marcus' sweet and brotherly kiss had made her feel.

＼＼

On the way to the Coulters' Labor Day barbecue, Lyric tried calling Austin, only to get voicemail. Lyric left a message. "I saw our baby today." She worked on keeping her voice even. "The baby was just miraculous." Here, her voice broke. "I heard the heartbeat, saw the little developing arms and legs." Fighting for control, Lyric took a few deep breaths and continued. "You don't know what you're missing, Austin. I was scared and nervous, but Marcus graciously offered to accompany me since you were apparently too busy. Perhaps you'll go next time." And then she hung up.

Driving, Marcus eyed her. "You okay?"

Breathing deeply, Lyric answered, "Fine, I suppose. Austin didn't answer. He really did miss out today."

"Well, that was his choice," Marcus ventured.

"I know." Turning to look at him, Lyric said, "Thank you for coming today. I was really nervous and scared, but mostly – I would've really hated hearing the baby's heartbeat and seeing the baby for the first time all alone. I'm glad you could share in the excitement and experience the same joy I did."

Marcus smiled and glanced at her. "It really was my pleasure. Now I know why Rachel and Levi were always so jazzed after their baby appointments. Seeing it in person, rather than just the little pictures they showed
afterward, was quite amazing."

"Miraculous!" Lyric enthused.

"Exactly!"

They pulled up in front of Marcus' parents' house. Levi and Rachel were already there, judging by their 4Runner parked by the sidewalk.

As soon as Marcus and Lyric entered, Rachel and Lynne descended on them, almost as if they'd been lying in wait.

"So, how'd it go?" Lynne asked, obviously anxious to hear all.

"It was amazing!" Lyric gushed as they all migrated toward the living room.

"Did you get to see the baby? Did you hear the heartbeat?" Rachel wanted to know.

Lyric nodded, then dramatically produced the pictures the doctor had given her. There were girly shrieks and exclamations as Lyric told the other two women all about her appointment.

Marcus looked at the scene of women and was grateful. '*Thank you, Jesus, for giving Lyric women who can share in her joy during this special time of her life.*'

He then decided he needed to seek out some testosterone.

He found his dad and brother in the backyard with Hailey and Zachary running around and playing.

"Hey, dude!" Levi greeted his brother. "Just got back from the baby appointment, I take it?"

"Yep," Marcus grinned.

"Pretty cool, huh? Glad you could finally experience that."

"It was awesome!"

Kurt turned from the grill where he was barbecuing to join the conversation. "We didn't have all that fancy stuff when you boys were babies. Glad you could see that baby. From the sounds of it, it's quite marvelous."

"It is, Dad," Marcus agreed. Then he went on to tell them about what the doctor had said and how the baby looked and hearing the heartbeat for the first time. "She's showing mom and Rachel the pictures now. I know she'd be thrilled to show you guys, too."

Kurt grinned at his youngest son. "I'm very proud of you, Marcus. You've done a great deal for Lyric. It seems as though she's really needed a friend and someone to watch out for her and you've unquestionably stepped in to be there for her in whatever she needs. You've become sort of her protector and now you're being there for her in this pregnancy when most guys wouldn't give her a second thought. Especially because she has a baby on the way. It takes a real man to help someone out the way you have with Lyric. You should be proud of yourself. I know God is."

"Thanks, Dad." Marcus felt a bit uncomfortable. "I'm just trying to do the right thing, like you taught me."

There were sounds of women then.

"Kurt, Levi, come see Lyric's baby!" Lynne encouraged. "The baby looks just like you, Lyric."

Lyric laughed with Lynne. It was hard to tell any distinguishing features from the grainy black-and-grey photo.

Lyric wasn't used to so much attention and flushed as they all gathered around, even Zachary and Hailey, to see her baby.

` ` ` `

Lyric started noticing definite changes. Mood changes. Weight gain. Cravings. And her emotional state was a mess.

At first, she thought the emotions were due to her still being mad at Austin for not going to the doctor. She clued in, however, when the Home Shopping Network made her cry.

They had been selling slow cookers and one of the spokeswomen mentioned that a person could start a batch of soup before leaving in the morning and come home to a "home cooked meal like grandma used to make."

Since both of her grandmas had died before she was born, Lyric had no recollection of a grandmother. And yet, the Home Shopping Network's sentiment wasn't lost on Lyric as tears dripped off her chin and she flipped past the channel.

"Well played, Home Shopping Network, well played," she mumbled.

The start of the following week brought with it a phone call.

Lyric had been napping on the couch when the ring startled her awake. Groggily, she answered. "Hello?"

"Lyric?"

"Yeah?" Her brain kicked in then and she registered the caller. "Austin?"

"I wanna go. I wanna meet our baby, too."

It took a few moments for Lyric to process that and for her mouth to properly engage. "What? What are you talking about?"

"When do you go to the doc again? For the kid? I wanna go, too."

"Oh, ummm…" she had to think. Marcus had made sure she stopped at the receptionist desk on the way out to make another appointment. She had tried resisting, reminding him she could only afford that appointment because of the money Austin had given her. Finally, she was forced to give in when Marcus walked up to the desk himself and made the appointment. In the car, he had told her he'd pay for it himself if it came to that.

He'd looked at her with his piercing green eyes and the look she'd come to recognize when he was being stubborn and told her, "You and your baby need to stay healthy. You need to take care of yourself. You matter, too."

He'd added the last part to himself, but she'd heard it.

Ever since she'd come to the City, she'd never had anyone tell her they cared about her and about what happened to her or that she mattered. Until Marcus. Weirdly, it made her think of her parents. Deep down, she knew they'd love to know about their grandchild. Pride kept her from going back home, though, so she tried not to think about it too much.

"Lyric? Lyric?" sounded in her ear, bringing her back to reality.

"Uh, sorry. Um, it's next month. My appointments are only once a month, for now. As it gets closer, probably around the holidays, it'll be every two weeks."

"Alright. Let me know and I'll be there." Pause. "Unless you want to move back in before then."

Suddenly very weary, Lyric answered, "I don't think so, Austin. I'm pregnant and way too tired to even think about moving anywhere."

"Is it because of *him*?" Austin spat. "He treats you better than me, huh? He better keep his hands off of you! You're mine!"

Lyric wasn't prepared for the onslaught and could feel herself cowering, even on the phone, reverting to the only defense she knew, and started to whimper.

"Well? Does he?"

Making herself calm down and realize there was no way Austin could physically attack her on the phone, Lyric's breathing slowed and became even again. Patiently, she explained. "It has nothing to do with *Marcus.*" She purposefully emphasized his name. "And, honestly, Austin, yes, he *does* treat me better than you ever did! And do you know why?" she boldly asked. Then added, "It's precisely because he *doesn't* touch me!" The last words were delivered in a courageous blow, full of the anger and rage she'd harbored toward Austin over the past year-and-a-half.

Calmly now, she told him, "Goodbye, Austin." She was shaking as she set the phone down.

'*You know Marcus would be proud of you,*' a little voice told her.

And then Lyric was stunned to discover that she didn't really want Austin going to the doctor with her, after all. If she was being honest with herself, she had, somewhere along the way, begun to think of that small exam room as hers – and Marcus', if she were being *completely* honest.

'Stupid, stupid girl!' she chided. *'Austin has a right. Marcus doesn't. Austin should be there if he wants to be. It's his right, his baby.'*

Marcus walked in then, to Lyric's pacing and heard her give voice to her inner thoughts. "His right! His baby!"

The door shut, making Lyric jump and turn, cheeks scarlet. "Marcus! You scared me!"

Smiling and showing his dimples to full advantage, Marcus replied, "What are you yelling about?"

Waving her hand in dismissal, she answered huffily, "Austin!"

Willing himself to show no emotion at the name, Marcus simply questioned, "Oh?"

"Yeah. He called. He's decided he wants to go to the next appointment with me."

"That's good," Marcus ventured hesitantly. "Sounds as if he's having a possible change of heart." It made Marcus cringe to give Austin any credit.

Lyric puffed her cheeks up and then blew them out again. "Yeah. He still wants me to 'move home'," she air quoted. "I think that's why he's even making an effort. I think he misses me – well, beating on me, anyway."

Marcus was surprised at the admission. Lyric usually got prickly when talking about Austin.

Walking over and sinking into the sofa, Lyric joining him, Marcus casually draped an arm around her shoulder and squeezed. "You don't have to let him, you know."

Resigned, Lyric sighed. "Yes, I do. It's his baby, too. He has the right. Besides, if you tell Austin no, he just tries that much harder to get his way. And he usually ends up succeeding. It's easier just to give in."

"You don't give yourself enough credit, Lyric," Marcus chuckled. "You're much more understanding and gracious than I'd be. You do have a good point."

"Aren't you people supposed to be the gracious and understanding ones?" Lyric asked, teasing.

"You people?" Marcus asked, bemused.

"You know, Christians."

That brought him up short. He was being a lousy witness to Lyric where Austin was concerned.

Leveling a look at Lyric, Marcus tried to find the words to explain. Smirking, he began, "You make it sound as though Christians are some type of alien. We're human, too, and make mistakes, just like everyone else." Carefully, he chose his next words. "I don't have to…love the action, but you're right – I'm supposed to love the person. Hate the sin, love the sinner, if you will." Stopping, he tried to introduce the topic of Austin. "Where Austin is concerned, I have a hard time remembering that and that God is the ultimate judge. Especially when I see innocent people being hurt."

Unconsciously, his eyes flicked over Lyric, then back to her face.

"I *do* have to remember that, as much as *I* hate to see it, God hates it more and it hurts Him to see it, too. He made those people, and He loves them. More than I *ever* could and He even loves the ones doing the hurting. They're probably hurting, too; but it's not up to me to fix it."

Marcus turned fully toward Lyric so he could look her directly in the eye as he said, "I'm sorry for having the hate in my heart that I've had toward Austin. If I get the chance, I will apologize to him, as well. I will honestly try harder to be more accepting of him."

It was clearly not the direction Lyric would have expected the conversation to go. She'd never had anyone apologize like that to her before. "It's alright, Marcus. I was only teasing."

"I needed to hear it. I want to help you and be here for you. And it wouldn't help for you to have more ammunition to dislike Austin nor would it help to excuse my behavior toward him."

They sat in companionable silence for awhile, side by side.

Marcus broke it by laying a hand over Lyric's and quietly telling her, "You make God proud, Lyric. I hope you know that. You're willing to give Austin another chance, at least for the baby's sake, despite your history with him."

Touched, and full of hormones, Lyric's eyes filled with tears. Clearing her throat, she managed, "Thank you, Marcus."

"Can I ask you something?"

"Sure."

"Have you contacted your parents and told them the good news?"

Horrified, Lyric spluttered, "No! I couldn't do that!"

"Why not?"

"They're probably ashamed enough of me already. Why add fuel to the fire?"

"Do you know for certain that they are?"

"How could they *not* be?"

"I'll take that as a no, then."

"You don't understand, Marcus. You're such a goody-two-shoes! *You* never left home at eighteen! I basically threw everything they gave me and did for me, back in their face. I was a rebellious teenager, trying to find myself, I suppose. It doesn't excuse what I did, though. I can never go home. *I'm a disgrace!*" Sobbing now, Lyric added, "They're good, kind and wonderful people, who deserve a better daughter than I've been."

Lyric hunched over, weeping, face in her hands.

Marcus slid forward and folded her into his side, letting her cry. When he heard her sobs turn into sniffles, he ventured, "Seems to me you're sorry for what you've done. I bet they'd forgive you – maybe they already have."

Lyric stared at Marcus, baffled. "You know, they're like you. They love God, too. They did try teaching me about Him." She hung her head. "It didn't stick. I fell into the wrong crowd and it only got worse. Then I left for New York and haven't looked back."

"It seems to me that you've been doing some changing since then. I'd bet they'd like to hear about it."

"I just can't, Marcus. It's too late."

Knowing better than to push any more than he already had, Marcus asked only one more question. "Will you do something?"

Puffing up her cheeks and then expelling her breath, she cautiously agreed. "Alright. As long as it doesn't involve me contacting my parents."

"Nope. Do you have a Bible?"

How did he *know*? She still carried the one her parents gave her in the third grade.

"Read Luke 15:11-32."

Giving him a wary look, Lyric acquiesced, "Alright."

Chapter 12
Help one person at a time, and always start with the person nearest you
Mother Teresa

Lyric sat staring at her Bible. She was floored! It had taken her a whole week to finally read the passage Marcus had suggested. Now, as it stared back up at her, she felt the beginning prick of tears. She certainly saw herself in the story of the prodigal son. Remembering back to her Sunday school classes, she could vaguely recall the story, but had never applied it personally. Had never needed to – until now.

The son in the story had a home much like hers. Loving parents…at least, the dad from the story had been. There had been no real rhyme or reason for them, her or the prodigal, to leave their homes. They simply had. She'd told herself that it was to get away from the stuffiness of her life, but it all added up to the same thing. She had wanted to rebel and find "fun" and "adventure". Instead, here she was. Pregnant. Unmarried. In the Bible times, she would have been cast out and then stoned. Although…that brought to mind another story she remembered from her church days. Jesus had treated an adulterous woman, who was going to be stoned, kindly and gently. He'd forgiven her and literally saved her life! *Maybe* Jesus could forgive *her*, too?

'No! I've made too many mistakes. Jesus is for people like Marcus – who deserve Him.'

And yet, she couldn't explain why she had a hollow, empty feeling whenever she thought about God or Jesus – as if she were missing something.

She pushed the feeling away this time and stood up. Suddenly, she doubled over. There had been a definite tightening, like a cramp, in her abdomen.

"No, baby," she panted, "you aren't supposed to come yet. You're way too early! You'll die if you come out now."

She was only thirteen weeks along. Is this what a miscarriage felt like? Wasn't she supposed to be past the risky first trimester by now?

Slowly, she sat back down. She was supposed to leave for work in an hour, but feared she'd make things worse by going.

Sweat beaded on her forehead and upper lip as she tried to concentrate and decide what to do.

Slowly in…slowly out…she breathed for some minutes, despite the late summer heat trying to distract her.

There. No more pain. She waited a few more minutes to be sure. She should be fine. Carefully, she stood to get ready for work, and felt another pang low in her back.

Sitting down heavily, she broke into tears. It was her fault. She was having a miscarriage, she knew it. God knew she didn't deserve a baby and He was taking the baby back. Her crying turned to panicked pleadings. "Oh, no! Don't take my baby! Please! Please, let me keep my baby! I love my baby! Please!" She wasn't sure who, exactly, she was pleading with. She supposed it'd have to be God.

Until that moment, she hadn't realized how true that was. She loved her baby, yes, but it still felt abstract. She'd equated the baby with needing to have a piece of Austin. Her relationship with him was so rocky, she didn't know if he'd really stay with her. Some messed up part of her wanted a piece of him to hold onto forever. At that moment, however, crying out to Whoever would hear her, she realized she *did* love her baby, pure and simple. No strings attached, and not even because the baby was also from Austin. Lately, a part of her yearned for Austin not to be involved at all. It'd be much easier, in a way, with just her and the baby.

Calming down, Lyric realized she needed to call off from work. Summoning her courage, she gave standing another try and carefully walked to the phone, trying to dispel her panic at the pain now low in her abdomen as well as her back.

On the first ring, Mr. Butterman answered, "Hello, Butterman's Health Food."

"Uh, hello, Mr. Butterman, it's Lyric."

"Lyric! My favorite employee…but don't tell Camilla I said so," he teased.

"Um, Mr. Butterman, I'm going to have to call off from work. I'm, um–" she burst into tears. "I don't know what's going on with my baby, but I might have to see a doctor."

Lyric gripped the phone tight as she stood there, quelling panic at the pain she kept feeling.

Alarm filled Mr. Butterman's voice as he told her, "I'm taking you off the books for the week. You only had one more day this week, anyway." Concern replaced the alarm as he told her, "Take care, dear, and let me know if I can be of any help at all."

'*No!*' her mind screamed, '*I need the money!*' But practicality won out. She didn't know *what* was going on. Her baby was probably dead. She couldn't afford an extra doctor's appointment, much less a trip to the hospital.

Instead, she answered, "Um, yeah, that may be best. Thank you, Mr. Butterman."

"I hope everything works out alright, dearie."

They said their goodbyes and hung up.

Lyric suddenly felt the need to use the bathroom. In case she needed it, she took the cordless phone with her.

She let out a scream as she was confronted with blood. It seemed like it was everywhere! She cleaned herself up as best as she could and simply sat there, numb. She was going to die, as well, she just knew it. And she could do nothing. She couldn't possibly get down to get a cab by herself in this state, she was barely able to make it to her bed. Marcus wasn't there to drive her, either. Besides, she'd have no money to pay the hospital bill. She still wasn't sure how she'd scrape enough together to pay for the birth. Not that she'd need it *now*.

'*Call Austin!* Popped in her head. But, even as she wearily crawled into bed, she couldn't bring herself to. She knew it was a bad idea. She didn't even want him near her. Especially if he found out she lost their baby. He'd probably hit her.

Despairing, Lyric cried herself into oblivion.

`````````````````````````````````````````````````````````````````````````

When Marcus walked into the apartment, he wasn't alarmed. Nothing seemed out of place or amiss. Many times when he'd get home, Lyric would already be in bed, poor thing. Pregnancy made her exhausted.

However, one detail caught his eye. As he went to listen to his messages on the answering machine, he realized the phone was missing. He stared at the empty cradle, confused. He pushed the page button to locate the phone. Distantly, he heard it. Following the beep-beep-beep of the signal, he was led to Lyric's room.

He found Lyric curled up on her side, facing away from the door, buried in covers. Silently, he tip-toed over to the other side of the bed, to her bedside table that she was borrowing from him, to retrieve the phone and silence its paging. As he bent over and grabbed it, Lyric's eyes flew open. He could just make out her panicked expression from the light spilling in from the living room coupled with the faint light coming in from the window.

The sun was going down but hadn't quite set yet since it was summer and it got darker later.

Her expression stopped him cold.

"I'm sorry for waking you," he quickly and quietly apologized. "I couldn't find the phone," he lamely explained.

"So - so–" she stopped, confused, " – I'm still alive?"

Even more alarmed, Marcus flipped on the small lamp atop the table – another one of his hand-me-downs. "Watch your eyes," he warned as he did so.

Suddenly, Lyric was crying and struggling to sit up. Her head felt woozy. "I brought it in here 'cause I thought I might need it. But then, I figured I'd die instead."

Marcus sat down, hard, on the edge of the bed and looked closely at Lyric. She looked very pale. "What's going on?" he asked severely.

"I think I miscarried…or am about to. I'm bleeding – well, I *was,* I don't know if I've stopped yet. I thought about calling Austin," she rambled on, "but then I found I didn't want to. Then I fell asleep."
`````````````````````````````````````````````````````````````````````````

Marcus quickly punched the phone on and hit a speed dial number.

"Dr. Oberman? Hi. This is Lyric Bell's roommate. She needs to talk to you."

Shaky and nauseated, Lyric took the phone Marcus handed her.

"You tell him everything!" Marcus demanded. He was frightened, worried and angry that Lyric wouldn't have called him – someone – *anyone,* yes, even Austin, to help her!

"Hello?" she answered nervously. She didn't know if she could handle hearing about her miscarriage already.

"Yes," Marcus heard Lyric answer the doctor's question. Pause. "Yes, I felt some abdominal and back pain earlier." Pause. "No, I fell asleep." Pause. Then tears. "No, I didn't know!" Pause. "I can't! I don't have the money –"

Marcus snatched the phone from Lyric. "Dr. Oberman? What does she need to do? I'll cover the expense."

As he talked to the doctor, Marcus carefully moved to sit next to Lyric and grabbed her hand, squeezing it lightly.

Tears coursed down Lyric's cheeks now.

Marcus finally ended his conversation with Dr. Oberman and turned to Lyric. "Get up – carefully – we're going to the hospital. He thinks you might have something called placenta abruption. Lyric – you could've died if I hadn't found you! He thinks you're probably still bleeding. We need to go to the hospital *now.* Why didn't you call me?"

"It wouldn't have helped," she weakly protested. Her brain felt fuzzy. "I have no money for an extra hospital visit."

"Lyric," Marcus scolded, worry making his tone harsh, "I've *told* you I'll help!"

Grabbing her hand, Marcus tried to carefully help Lyric to her feet. She stumbled, but he caught her by the elbow.

Embarrassed, Lyric indicated the sheets. "I owe you new bedding." Looking down at herself, she faintly asked, "Could you maybe get me a towel to sit on for the car?" And then she fell back onto the bed, eyes closed.

Marcus noticed her blood-soaked pants then. He ran to the bathroom cupboard, grabbed a towel and then came back and swiftly scooped Lyric up.

"Lyric! Can you hear me?" he asked, even as he hurried through the apartment, grabbing his keys and wallet off of the counter on his way out.

She only mumbled gibberish in response.

Doing double time, he hoofed it to the parking garage. After settling a limp Lyric into the passenger seat, he grabbed his cell and dialed 911. He didn't know the hospital's number, but he was hoping 911 could transfer him…or something.

"911, what's your emergency?" the dispatcher answered.

Marcus sped out of the parking garage. He gave his location and said,

"My friend is mostly passed out from blood loss…I think. Possible miscarriage. I'm enroute to the hospital. Could you – transfer me – or tell them I'm coming – or something?" Marcus had never been so freaked out in his life!

"I'm sorry, sir, we don't usually – "

"Please!" he interrupted abruptly. "I don't know what to do!"

Gentling her tone, the dispatcher replied, "Calm down, sir. I will let them know you're on your way. You're going to Grace Hospital?"

"Yes, ma'am."

Soothingly, she told Marcus, "I'll let them know."

He snapped his phone shut and stomped on the accelerator.

'Please, Lord, save her!' he begged God. *'Don't let her die!'*

"Lyric, please talk to me!"

"Austin," she mumbled.

Of course she *would* want that loser.

"He's not here," he told her. Trying to remind himself of the new leaf he was trying to turn over in regard to Austin, Marcus muttered to himself in resignation. "Maybe we *should* call him."

That got a definitive reaction from Lyric. "No!" Her voice was so weak and quiet, it didn't carry her intended vehemence.

They presently pulled into the ER parking lot.

"Stay here," Marcus ordered as he ran to get somebody to help Lyric.

Soon, he returned with two medics who were wheeling a stretcher. They carefully lifted a barely lucid Lyric.

Marcus followed them in.

"Are you family?" the receptionist asked as Marcus grabbed the paperwork thrust at him.

"No," he automatically replied, distracted by the forms and walking behind Lyric's stretcher.

"I'm sorry, sir. You can't go back there."

Marcus halted abruptly. "I need to. She's my – my sister – sort of."

Lyric faintly called out, "Where's Marcus? Marcus?!" panic lacing her voice.

Giving the receptionist a tight smile, he said, "Excuse me, I'm needed." And he walked off to follow Lyric.

Finally, Lyric was settled into a room. It was determined she had lost a lot of blood and needed a blood transfusion. The baby's condition was unknown.

\`\`

"How are you feeling this morning?" Marcus had opened his eyes to Lyric looking at him.

He had spent the night in the vinyl-cushioned chair by Lyric's bed.

Lyric yawned. "Fine, I guess."

She caught sight of the clock. "Hey, aren't you supposed to be at work?"

"Nope, not today. I'm playing hookey."

Glancing back at Marcus, she told him, "Thank you. You saved my life – and the baby's too."

He merely shrugged, but told her seriously, "You scared me." Leaning on the rail of an arm rest on her bed, Marcus told her, "Don't ever do that again. If you ever need me, call my cell phone."

Lyric simply nodded. "I know. I scared myself, too."

Breaking the tension, Marcus stood and stretched. "I'm going to get breakfast. You'll probably get yours soon, but do you want anything? Having any cravings?" he smiled.

"Nope, I'm fine. Really. Go on."

"Suit yourself," he grinned and was gone.

Alone, Lyric felt the fear of what might have been grip her. '*I'm okay. Baby's fine.*' She mentally scolded herself.

She warily checked the sheets and her gown. All seemed unblemished.

Tentatively, she spoke. "If you're there, God, I just want to say thank you for sparing my baby."

She felt kind of stupid…until a sudden feeling of peace stole over her.

The doctor had told her she'd need lots of rest, so she promptly closed her eyes to revel in the momentary peace.

'''

The next day, Lyric was released from the hospital. When she found out Marcus had taken the rest of the week off of work, she tried to protest.

"You don't have to do this. Really. I'm fine."

"I know, but I want to. Friends help each other out."

Lyric had always found it hard to ask for, and accept, help – even if she needed to. She knew this about herself and tried to be gracious, instead of annoyed, which was being ridiculous, she knew. *Why* did she feel annoyed? It *annoyed* her to feel that way! Instead, she teased, "Well…I suppose after all we went through with the hospital, you'll pass for a friend."

"I didn't want you to be lonely, since it sounds like you can't do much else but watch T.V. Besides, *someone* needs to nurse you back to health." He jokingly winked.

It touched her that Marcus seemed to care so much. She felt herself getting choked up. '*Oh, great, here come the hormones!*' she scolded.

"Thank you, Marcus," she was finally able to voice. "It really means a lot."

Marcus merely waved it off. "It was nothing."

Chapter 13

There is no friendship, no love, like that of a mother for her child--
Henry Ward Beecher

Lyric tried to get comfortable in the backless gown on the papered exam table. She checked the clock on the mint green wall again. *'Where is he?'* she wondered for what seemed like the twentieth time.

She'd called to remind Austin of the doctor appointment set for 1:00 that day. Last night when she'd talked to him, he'd said he'd be there! The hands on the clock now read 1:32 and Austin still hadn't shown.

It was good he'd missed the exam twenty minutes ago, though. It was part of her follow-up from her hospital visit and she hadn't told Austin about it. Part of her feared he'd be angry – and she knew what happened when he got angry.

She suddenly found herself wishing she had asked Marcus to come today instead. She should've known Austin wouldn't have. That would have been selfish, though, asking Marcus, after all he had done for her already. She'd completely turned his whole world upside-down, she was sure. He'd have never allowed her to be his roommate, had he known – probably. Probably he wished he could kick her out. Probably he regrets ever meeting her.

Horrified, Lyric felt hot tears streaming from her eyes. "Stupid hormones!" she spat.

What did it matter? She figured eventually she'd have to go back to live with Austin anyway. Marcus just needed an excuse. Something along the lines of, "It'd be best for all concerned if you returned home with Austin, where you belong." He'd probably kindly wait until the day she left the hospital after the baby was born. She could hear Marcus now.

"I'll show him," Lyric muttered.

Except, how? He'd be right. Where else could Lyric go, but back to Austin? She didn't have the money to get her own place.

A quick knock and Dr. Oberman entered. Baffled, he took in Lyric's face. "Are you in pain?" His wide, gray eyes were full of concern.

"Just self-pity," Lyric informed him. "And stupid hormones," she added, then hiccupped.

Dr. Oberman perched on his rolling stool and faced Lyric. "Do you want to talk about it?

And the water works began. Lyric spilled out her whole story – she started with meeting Marcus, but didn't share why she had left Austin. She simply said that Austin wasn't a very good boyfriend. Ending, she lamented the fact that Austin hadn't bothered to show up for her appointment that day, even though he said he would. "And now you probably have some horrible news to tell me about my lab work I had done and no one will be here with me when I hear it!"

Dr. Oberman smiled sympathetically and shook his head. "Actually, it's not horrible. I do want to do an ultrasound for a final check. You did have a placenta abruption, but it seems as though your rest has helped immensely. How's that going? Still lying low?"

"Yes. It's going very well. I took the rest of the week off from work and laid around the apartment all weekend. And my…roommate…had taken the time off while I was in the hospital as well as the day I was released and the following day. He was very helpful and barely let me off the couch or out of bed to even use the bathroom!" She was still skeptical Marcus could care so much for her in such a short amount of time. What was his angle? Men usually wanted *something.*

"That was nice of him."

Lyric sniffed, ridiculously feeling tears again. "I know," she sniffled, "and he doesn't deserve to be caught up in this mess. He's a good person!"

Dr. Oberman understandingly patted her knee. "It sounds like it."

Getting up, Dr. Oberman grabbed a pair of gloves and snapped them on. "You should be able to *slowly* add a *little* more activity, but don't overdo it. If you see any more spotting of *any kind,* call me immediately and *go to the hospital,* okay?"

"Okay," Lyric nodded her consent.

Lying back as Dr. Oberman indicated, she asked, "What are you checking?"

"Just the baby. Making sure all is well. We'll check the growth, too. When you were in the hospital, there were some indicators that you're farther along than I originally thought."

Lyric tried to relax as Dr. Oberman wheeled the portable ultrasound machine closer. Soon the *whoosh –whoosh* of the baby's heart filled the room. Once again, Lyric found herself blinking back tears as the blurry image of her baby came on the screen.

'*Stupid Austin is missing seeing his baby–*again*!'* His loss, Lyric resigned.

After taking a few measurements, Dr. Oberman cleaned the gel off of Lyric's belly. "Yep, you're a week farther than I'd originally thought. Your new due date is January thirtieth. That also means that at your next appointment, you could find out the baby's sex – if you want."

Lyric's heart swelled. "Yes," she heard herself say. "I'd like that very much."

As Lyric was changing and preparing to leave, she was determined she would not be alone next time. Even if it meant she personally went to Austin's first and dragged him there physically.

She still couldn't quite believe he'd missed the appointment. Okay… maybe it wasn't so shocking. It still hurt, though. And *why* did she continually let herself get hurt by him all of the time?

Angrily walking toward the subway, Lyric whipped out her cell phone Marcus got her to carry around. She left a curt message for Austin. "You. Are. An. Idiot. And I hate you. Why weren't you at the doctor appointment today? I was really anxious about it. The next appointment is in a few weeks and we can find out if the baby is a boy or girl so you better be there or– " she thought fast for a threat, " – or I'll just get Marcus to go."

There. That'll get to him! With a satisfied smirk, Lyric put her phone back in her purse and walked onto the subway.

When she emerged, her phone beeped, alerting her to a missed call and voicemail. The readout said: AUSTIN.

Quickly, Lyric punched in her voicemail code, only to hear Austin say, "Hey, babe, sorry I missed your call. I just woke up."

Rolling her eyes, Lyric glanced at her watch. 3:01 in the afternoon! Still, she couldn't muster surprise. It only meant he had spent the night and early morning hours shooting up. Heroin was his drug of choice.

The message continued. "Anyway, I forgot about the appointment. Sorry. I can't go to the next one, either. I'm busy all that week – I'm sure of it. Sorry." And that was it. Not even a good-bye.

Hot, angry tears beaded on Lyric's eyelashes as she rapidly tried blinking them away. *'He's so uncaring!'*

She turned down her street and hurried up to the apartment and let herself in. Her tears were uncontrollable now that she was no longer on the street for all to see.

Why couldn't Austin care? About his baby, at the very least! Why couldn't he be excited? The irony wasn't lost on her that her roommate, someone she had met by chance, was more excited about her baby than the baby's own father! And not just Marcus, but his *entire* family! Last time she'd talked to Lynne and Rachel, the idea of a baby shower in the future was even thrown around.

Lately, Lyric felt exhausted anytime she thought of Austin. It felt as though he didn't care about her anymore. And that made her feel alone. She didn't know *who* to turn to for advice. Usually girls turned to their mothers for pregnancy advice, but she simply couldn't. Her mother wasn't there. Lyric took full responsibility for that one, though.

She sat curled up on the couch until Marcus got home. It was dark in the apartment by then because she hadn't bothered to turn on a light.

As Marcus came in, he flipped the switch, which startled Lyric from her dozing.

Sitting up, she fixed Marcus with an accusing glare. "Where were you?"

Flabbergasted at her forceful accusation, Marcus took a few steps back. "Um?" not sure what to say.

"Um? Um! That's all? I really needed you today!"

"Uh...I'm...sorry?" Where was the script for life when you needed it? Although, he hadn't felt the need for one until he had a pregnant woman living with him.

'*Remember, Marcus, she's pregnant,*' he coolly reminded himself.

"I went to my appointment today and Austin didn't show." And then her accusation of Marcus hit her and she began to cry in remorse and shame. She was horrified at herself! "I'm s-sorry," she managed, gasping through sobs. "You d-don't deserve me t-tearing your head off l-like that. You have n-nothing to do with it."

Marcus knelt down by Lyric and tried comforting her until she calmed down.

After a few moments of composure and Lyric's sobs had turned into hiccups, Marcus bit back a smile as he asked, straight-faced, "So, how are those hormonal mood swings treating you?"

Blowing out a breath, Lyric didn't miss a beat. "Oh, they're not too bad."

She saw Marcus duck his head as he shook with laughter. Slugging him in the arm, she joined in.

Later, after dinner, Marcus and Lyric hung out on the couch watching T.V.

During a commercial, Marcus momentarily muted the television. "So...I've been thinking...if you really need someone to go to the doctor with you, I'd be happy to be the one to go."

Lyric started trying to protest, "Oh, no, Marcus, it's okay – "

"No, really, I mean it! You were really upset earlier. And you don't need any more stress, especially after being in the hospital. And I know my mom and Rachel would both be thrilled to go with you if, you know," he teasingly ducked his head, "I don't suffice."

Lyric could still hardly believe she had only known Marcus about three months. She bit her lip, considering.

The truth was, she would prefer any of the three – Marcus, Lynne or Rachel – to Austin accompanying her. In fact, she probably knew Marcus better than Austin, in some ways. Marcus had always been open and honest. Instinctively, she had trusted him, even from the day she walked into this apartment for an interview. She had *never* trusted Austin like that.

Turning to him, Lyric smiled and declared, "Oh...I suppose you'll do."

"If you let me know when your appointments are, I'll do my best to ar-range my schedule. If I can't make it, make sure to call my mom or Rachel, or both, 'cause I know they'd love to go."

Lyric felt a bit embarrassed and awkward. She wasn't used to anybody accommodating their schedule for her. The fact that Marcus was so ready and willing touched her more than she'd realized it would.

"Thank you, Marcus," she told him sincerely. Then, beaming, she informed him, "I get to find out if the baby's a boy or girl next time!"

Marcus matched her enthusiasm. "I'm definitely there for that!"

`'''''''''''''''''''''''''''''''''''''''''''''''''''''''''''''''''''''''''''''''`

Lyric squeezed Marcus' hand as the technician squirted gel onto her belly.

Marcus was seated in a chair that had been placed discreetly up by Lyric's head.

The ultra sound tech started right in. "Body measures good. Head looks great, too." He moved the Doppler over Lyric's abdomen. "All of the organs are where they should be." The technician took his time and explained everything he was doing as he measured and checked Lyric's baby.

Finally, he declared, "Okay, kids, are you ready to find out the gender of your baby?"

Lyric concentrated on not looking at Marcus as she became flummoxed and blushed. "He's not mine...er, with me...he's not with me. We're just friends."

The tech winked knowingly. "Ah, I see."

Lyric knew he most certainly did not. However, she was too excited to press the point. Instead, she insisted, "Please! Tell us the sex of the baby!"

The Doppler was put back in place. After moving it around a bit, the ultra sound guy asked, "Do you see it?"

Lyric squinted as Marcus leaned forward and wondered aloud, "Is that his--"

"Yep," the tech answered. "You're having a boy!"

"A boy!" Lyric gasped, teary-eyed.

"A boy!" Marcus whooped.

Lyric couldn't take her eyes off of the image of her son.

Marcus was awed by the picture of the tiny baby. He leaned over and kissed Lyric's forehead in a brotherly gesture and murmured, "Congratulations, mama."

`'''''''''''''''''''''''''''''''''''''''''''''''''''''''''''''''''''''''''''''''`

Lyric didn't hear from Austin, but she didn't dwell on it – much. There were moments when she'd panic, thinking she would be alone in raising their son. But then Marcus would be there, chasing her fears away. He was unaware, however, of how much Lyric began counting on him merely for her own peace of mind.

One night, she got up for a cup of tea. She had been getting uncomfortable lately, causing her to not sleep well. She was nearing twenty weeks of pregnancy, and it was the end of September, to boot.

This time, she awoke because of movement inside of her, rather than her usual aches and pains. Groggy with sleep, she hadn't realized what it was, at first. After a few minutes, nothing more happened, but she was awake, so decided on a cup of tea.

Finally, she settled herself at the table with her tea, growing belly and all. She had been getting awkward in her movements lately, having to hoist her stomach around everywhere she went. At least, that's what it felt like.

She took another sip of tea and suddenly felt a movement, much like the one that had awoken her. Only this time, she was wide awake! It had been a definite kick! She immediately dropped her hands to either side of her belly and whispered with a smile, "Well, hello, baby boy."

Oh, how she yearned to share this moment with someone! Her eyes drifted toward Marcus' closed bedroom door. Did she dare? He would share in her excitement, she just knew it! Just then, her baby boy jabbed her again, almost as if urging her. She gave in, getting to her feet and heading for Marcus' door.

Standing directly in front of the door, she hesitated, not sure how to proceed. Should she knock? Feeling bold, she pushed his door open, hearing soft snoring. She realized this was the first time ever seeing Marcus asleep. Tiptoeing in, she soon stood by his side in another conundrum. How to wake him?

She decided on the gentle-as-possible approach. Bending down, she gently shook his exposed, muscular shoulder. Even sleeping, he looked strong and she felt an overwhelming sense of security.

Softly she called, "Marcus, Marcus."

Marcus stirred and slit his eyes open, "Huh?"

Lyric couldn't contain her excitement anymore. Forgetting to whisper, she exulted, "The baby...I think he kicked me!"

Still sleepy, Marcus blinked his eyes and tried to wake more fully. "Is everything okay?"

"Yes!" Lyric squealed, "The baby kicked!"

Marcus immediately sat up and turned his bedside lamp on. "What?! No way!" His excitement matched hers.

Impulsively, Lyric plunked herself down on the edge of his bed and grabbed his hand to hold it to her stomach. "Here! Feel!"

They sat for a few minutes in silence. Then the baby kicked her hard. Marcus looked at Lyric in awe. "I felt that!"

Without thinking, Marcus leaned down and addressed Lyric's stomach, "Are you going to play for the Cowboys, buddy? That was *some* kick!"

Awkwardly, he straightened up, missing the tender look on Lyric's face as he had spoken to her son.

"Sorry," he mumbled, "that was probably too personal. Got carried away in the moment." He was actually blushing! Lyric noted.

"When Rachel was pregnant, she encouraged all of us to talk to their babies so they would recognize our voices." He looked chagrined. "Of course, we didn't hunch over her belly like I just did."

Slightly shaken at her reaction to Marcus' obvious excitement, Lyric barely whispered, "Don't worry about it." She stood up. As normally as possible, she stated, "I think I'll go back to bed now. I'm pretty tired."

Snuggled in her bed, Lyric pondered her reaction. To her, it had felt almost intimate, yet he hadn't touched her, except to feel her baby boy kick. And she had prompted that. Somehow, Marcus talking to her unborn son had felt more personal than his hand on her stomach. And she presently felt herself wondering if Marcus had felt it, too. He *had* seemed unsettled, but she didn't know if it was *only* because he'd feared he'd been too personal, as he'd stated, and apologized for.

Had Lyric given any thought to Austin, she might have found it peculiar that she didn't mind at all that he hadn't been there to share in this milestone. As it happened, Austin wasn't even considered as an afterthought.

\\\

Marcus lay awake for quite a while after Lyric went to bed, thinking of her and the baby. Mostly the baby. He was sorely embarrassed that he'd had such audacity as to talk to her son like that, hunkered next to her stomach. As if he had any right to do such an intimate thing! He'd have to apologize – again – and profusely. He had no claim on either of them, other than being Lyric's friend. But he wasn't the father nor Lyric's husband or even boyfriend. He had been so excited, he hadn't given his actions any proper thought. Weirdly, at the time, it had felt natural. He'd acted the same way he'd seen Levi act with Rachel when she was pregnant – although, he *was* the husband *and* father. Despite his debacle, he was honored Lyric had chosen to wake him up to share the experience. Still…it had given him no license to behave so intimately and he aimed to remedy the situation as soon as possible.

The next morning, Marcus mustered up his courage. "Lyric, I really am sorry about my actions last night. I believe they were way too personal and I was out of line. I had no right. Please forgive me."

Lyric's heart dropped. Was he sorry she woke him up, too?

'Stop it!' she told herself.

No, she'd seen his excitement. It had mirrored her own. He truly was only sorry for what he perceived as inappropriate behavior. Sighing, she swallowed her mouthful of Cheerios. Really, she shouldn't have been surprised that he'd do something of this nature.

"Quite frankly, Marcus, I'm too tired and worn out to try and appease you with a lame line like, 'That's okay,' 'Don't worry about it,' or 'Don't let it happen again.' Truthfully, I liked it. It made me feel less alone, like there really *is* someone else out there who cares about my son, too. It made me feel…special, if I'm being honest. You didn't bite my head off when I woke you, either. You genuinely shared in my excitement. It was…nice. You've been here for me this whole time, even when I was too stupid to realize it and appreciate what I have. And you had every right to kick me out. The fact is, I *want* my son to know who's important in his little life – and, yes, I *want* him to recognize their voice. And, if you don't mind, I would be very grateful if you continued doing what you're doing. You're really all I have."

Lyric stopped and blushed, embarrassed by her somewhat bold confession.

Marcus smiled, happier to hear her words than he knew he should be. "That's not true. You have my family, too."

Lyric smiled. "I was wondering…" she hesitated, trying to figure out her wording. "I'd really like to go to the family dinners on Sundays, if I still can. And I do realize it would mean I'd have to go to church, even though I'm not quite sure God's ready for me yet."

Marcus only grinned and said, "Oh, He's ready!"

True to his word, Marcus took care of Lyric. And though not much of a cook, he managed to run to the corner deli for sandwiches or ordered in pizza or Chinese.

On one such deli run, Lyric found herself, once again, thanking God! Twice in one week *must* be a new record.

Glancing toward the ceiling, just in case God needed positive visual I.D., Lyric spoke aloud, "I think, maybe, You had a hand in me finding Marcus. If so, thank you. You should be really proud of him."

Chapter 14
*A little child born yesterday, a thing on mother's milk
and kisses fed*
Homer

"I got them!" Marcus announced as he came through the door. "Chips, ice cream and *green* grapes." He emphasized because Lyric had been very specific.

"Sorry it took so long. The line was atrocious!"

Lyric jumped up and made a mad grab for the Original Lay's Potato Chips with Ridges.

"You remembered the dip, right?" she asked anxiously.

Marcus grinned and pulled out Reser's French Onion Dip. "Of course! You can't have potato chips without onion dip!"

"Thank you *so much,* Marcus!" Then Lyric dug in still standing at the kitchen counter.

Marcus sat at the table. He was secretly amused at the amount of food she was able to pack away at one sitting – er, standing – lately. Her figure was filling out as the baby grew, making up for the lack of it when she had first come to him. It pleased Marcus to see Lyric looking so healthy. She really did have the legendary pregnancy glow. He thought it made her already delicately pretty features even more beautiful.

Marcus remembered how well Rachel had looked in pregnancy. It seemed to have transformed her as well. He marveled at the wonder of pregnant women. Before Lyric, he had never experienced a full pregnancy. Sure, he'd been around Rachel when she was pregnant at all of the Sunday dinners, holidays, and anytime in between they chanced to get together, but he hadn't been privy to the day-to-day experiences. He found he had actually been enjoying watching Lyric bloom and blossom in pregnancy.

After devouring half the bag of chips and most of the dip, Lyric finally sat down, hands folded over her belly, satisfied.

"Apparently you needed salt," Marcus noted, giving her a quirky smile. Lyric laughed. "Or I just needed potato chips."

So far, Marcus had made it to one out of only two doctor appointments. That's how he knew cravings were literally the body craving certain nutrients or vitamins it was missing.

For some reason, Marcus had felt irrationally guilty about missing the appointment, despite the fact that there would be plenty more and Rachel had been able to go. Along with the guilt was immense disappointment. He had to keep reminding himself he had no claim on Lyric or the baby other than friendship. Despite that, he'd made Lyric and Rachel fill him in, with great detail, about the appointment. He smiled at the memory that Lyric had, thankfully, launched right in with very little prompting, eager to share about her son's growth.

` ` ` `

"Hey, Lyric," sounded down the line.

"Oh, hey, Rachel," Lyric returned.

"So Mom and I were thinking. We could have your baby shower the Saturday after Thanksgiving. What do you think?"

Lyric thought it was endearing that Rachel referred to her mother-in-law, Lynne, as Mom.

Lyric chuckled. "Um, Rachel, this is only September."

Rachel giggled. "Oh, I know, but we're *so* excited!"

Lyric smiled. It felt wonderful being able to share her joy with others. She hadn't heard from Austin in a couple of months and she only felt relief for it.

"That sounds fine, Rachel. Thank you. And tell Mrs. Coulter thank you, too. I mean, I'll tell her in person when I next see her, but you'll probably see her first. I really appreciate you two being willing to do this for me."

"Oh, pshaw, Lyric. It'll be fun! We love you, you know. And you'll hurt Mom's feelings if you continue calling her Mrs. Coulter. At least call her Lynne," Rachel suggested.

She had said it all very matter-of-factly and Lyric knew she meant it nicely and not as an insult.

"I'll try, Rachel. It's very different having a family again. I have to get used to it."

There was a moment's pause of hesitation. Then Rachel broke it softly. "We could invite your mom to the shower, you know."

Lyric cringed. Between her and Marcus, the Coulters were apprised of her relationship with her parents. Over the last several weeks, as she and Rachel bonded, Lyric had opportunity to share more details with her. She appreciated Rachel's nonjudgmental attitude and understanding about it all.

Quietly, Lyric answered, "I don't think so, Rachel."

Brightly, Rachel continued on as if nothing had been said. "Okay, well, you get a list together of who you want to invite and we'll invite the ladies from church. Are you opposed to having it in the church bulletin?"

"Rachel, you and your family are really the only people I know. Besides Camilla from work. I suppose you could make an invitation for her, but I can always tell her at work, too. And, no, I'm not opposed to the bulletin, but I don't really know any ladies from church."

"Alright. I'm sure some will come. They are very supportive. And why don't you try to get Camilla's address all the same? We'd still like to send her a formal invitation."

"Alright, I'll try to remember."

"Hey, when's your next appointment? Is Marcus able to go?"

"Next week. I think so, but I'll let you know if he can't. His classes don't start again for a couple of weeks, so he would only need to check with his work."

"Well, let me know if you need me or Mom to go."

"Will do. And thanks."

Lyric hung up feeling excited anticipation for what the next few months would bring.

vvvvvvvvvvvvvvvvvvvvvvvvvvvvvvvvvvvvvvvvvvvvvvvvvvvvvvvvvvvvvvvvvvvvvvvvvvvvvvvvvv

"Oh, and Rachel called. Apparently she and your mom want to throw me a shower the Saturday after Thanksgiving." Lyric then filled Marcus in on their conversation.

Lyric and Marcus were having their usual evening chat. They didn't consciously plan them. They just happened.

"That sounds fun!" Marcus enthused.

"Yeah. I'm looking forward to it."

"And what name have you chosen to have put on all of those presents?" Marcus teased.

Lyric still hadn't settled on a name for her baby boy and Marcus liked teasing her about it.

Lyric pretended to sulk and then threw a pillow from the couch at Marcus, sitting in one of the chairs. "Quiet, you!"

"You know, Marcus is a *great* name," Marcus continued, relentless. "And James."

"James?"

"Yeah! That's my middle name."

Feeling ornery, Lyric retorted, "Well, thanks for taking two names out of the running. Now I only have to narrow it down by about two hundred more."

Marcus grinned. "You're welcome."

vvvvvvvvvvvvvvvvvvvvvvvvvvvvvvvvvvvvvvvvvvvvvvvvvvvvvvvvvvvvvvvvvvvvvvvvvvvvvvvvvv

A couple of months passed in Lyric's pregnancy. They were blessedly uneventful, except for celebrating Marcus' twenty-fifth birthday at the beginning of October and celebrating Zachary's fifth just that past week-end.

An added bonus, Marcus had been able to make it to the doctor appointments. Lynne had even accompanied them to one appointment. It felt to Lyric like she had her mother there. Lynne even got misty-eyed when she heard the heartbeat.

Now the holidays were upon them. And just a month after Christmas, Lyric would be holding her baby boy.

"I am really looking forward to Thanksgiving tomorrow with your family," Lyric told Marcus.

Teasing, Marcus smirked, "Yeah, there'll be some good eats there."

Lyric good-naturedly rolled her eyes. "I don't *always* think about food nowadays – just *most* of the time. Besides, I wasn't talking about the food. I meant your family." She paused thoughtfully. "Although, turkey sounds really good right now…" her voice trailed off at the thought.

"That's probably just the protein talking."

Lyric laughed outright. "No, seriously. I love holding your adorable twin niece and nephew. I can't believe they're nine months old already! I've literally known them for over half their life." She pondered that for half a second. "Weird!"

Marcus chuckled. "They are all looking forward to you being there. And I think Sydney and Logan recognize you. Did you see how Sydney had lifted her chubby little arms out to you last Sunday?"

Lyric beamed. "Yeah, I did. It felt pretty good. She's such a sweetie."

They relapsed into silence for awhile.

Hesitating for a moment, Marcus finally broke the silence. "Ummmm…so…your parents won't want to see you tomorrow?"

Lyric, flustered, ducked her head to hide the ashamed tears that surfaced. "Maybe, but this will mark the fourth Thanksgiving without them." Quietly, she added, "I wouldn't want to ruin their holiday. I'm just a disappointment to them now."

"From what you've told me of them, they've probably forgiven you."

Lyric merely shrugged. "Maybe."

Marcus cleared his throat nervously, trying to broach the difficult subject his mom had asked him about. "You know…it's not too late to invite your mom to the shower. It's still three days away."

Lyric could only shake her head as tears tracked down her cheeks.

Lynne had been so concerned about Lyric's relationship with her mother, she'd asked Marcus if he would give it one last valiant effort to convince Lyric to invite her mother to the baby shower for her grandson. His only grandmother. It was very clear Austin was not involved and, besides, no one knew anything about his parents.

Softly, Marcus put words to his thoughts. "Your parents are the only grandparents your son will have."

Unexpected pleasure filled Lyric when Marcus phrased it like that, 'your son.'

Deciding to try to lighten the mood, Marcus asked, "Are you excited about the shower?"

Lyric felt apprehension. Not because she was afraid of being accepted. She already knew she was. She had been attending church regularly with Marcus and his family throughout the past few months and each Sunday, several people always came up to introduce themselves or, for the ones she had already gotten to know, ask how she was feeling. And she could tell they genuinely cared. These were the people who made up most of the guests to the baby shower.

No, her apprehension was because she didn't belong. As welcoming as they had been, she was still a sinner. She wasn't a member of the church nor did she really have any claim there, other than the Coulters. She was afraid she'd feel awkward at her own shower!

Hesitantly, she answered, "I don't know. I suppose it'll help having it at your parents' house. It's just strange, having most of my guests be people I hardly know."

"I happen to know there are some expert quilt and baby blanket-making grandma-types in our church who love blessing new mommies with their creations. And one older gentleman always gifts every new baby with a wooden rattle he makes especially for them. My mom still has mine and Levi's. And Levi and Rachel's kids each have one, too. In fact, I have it on good authority that he's had one done for your baby for quite awhile and his wife will be bringing it for you to the shower."

Lyric felt her eyes grow wide with astonishment. "Really?"

"Really."

"He doesn't even know me!"

"So?" was Marcus' challenge.

Lyric was quiet for a few moments. Finally, "Okay, I guess I feel a little better. He's coming in about eight weeks, so I suppose I should do what I can to get ready."

"Rachel only had one of hers on time. One came about a week early and the twins were four weeks early. Babies are unpredictable, so I'm told."

`''''''''''''''''''''''''''''''''''''''''''''''''''''''''''''''''''''''''''''''''''''''''''''''''`

Lyric sat there, looking around, feeling loved by these virtual strangers.

Lynne and Rachel had done a beautiful job with the baby shower. Baby blue and white streamers draped from the vaulted ceiling, it flooded the gift and cake tables. It seemed like everywhere she looked, Lyric saw blue-and-white celebrating her son. It was a bit overwhelming, but in a good way. She was still in awe that all of these people came just for her, despite them not really knowing her.

Camilla sat, poised to take notes, beside Lyric. It was time to open the gifts.

The gifts were not only useful, but sweet and thoughtful. At least half were handmade, lending to the air of love that was prevalent.

There were many oohs and ahs with each new gift that was unwrapped. There was a new, handmade baby blanket...and here was a baby quilt... and, oh, there was the wooden rattle!

"Thank you, everyone!" Lyric sincerely expressed after she had unwrapped the last gift.

There were many well-wishes as the party wound down and guests began to file out. After the door had been closed after the last guest, Lyric went to seek out Rachel and Lynne.

Uncharacteristic of her nature, Lyric threw her arms first around Rachel, then around Lynne. A bit weepy with gratitude, Lyric wiped her eyes and told them, "Thank you *so* much for the shower!"

As women do, there were sudden tears all around as they embraced again. That was how Kurt, Levi and Marcus found them upon entering the house.

They had taken Zachary, Hailey and the twins to the park and then out for ice cream afterward. Luckily, it had been a clear autumn day. Despite the chill in the air, the children had played hard and were now tuckered out.

Lynne spotted the men coming in, first. "Hi, guys, how was the park?"

The trio of women broke up as a favorable report was given.

Marcus came up to Lyric then. "Can I see all the presents you got?"

Caught off guard, Lyric stuttered, "Um, um, sure, uh, if you *really* want to."

Marcus smiled, eyes sparkling. "I *really* want to."

He followed her over to the couch, which was full of, and surrounded by, gifts. For the next hour, Marcus enthusiastically perused the gifts with Lyric...and she wondered at the ridiculous giddiness she felt upon being able to share the wonderful things she had received, with Marcus.

Afterward, as planned, they stayed for dinner with the rest of the family.

Lyric felt so special. She couldn't remember the last time she'd felt that way.

Shortly following dinner, Marcus loaded up his car with Lyric's presents. Good-byes were said all around. Then Hailey rushed up to Marcus and threw her arms around his legs. "Bye-bye, Unca Mawcus."

He picked her up in a hug. "Bye, Hailey."

Hailey reached toward Lyric then. "Lywic, need a hug!"

Relinquishing his hold on Hailey to Lyric, Marcus handed her over.

Lyric held Hailey's light weight in her arms and buried her face in the small girl's dark curls, deeply breathing in her sweet scent. With a final kiss on the cheek, Lyric set Hailey down. "Bye, Hailey."

Quiet Zachary merely waved his farewell from the floor, surrounded by Hot Wheels.

And Marcus and Lyric walked into the night.

,,,

December ninth dawned dreary and rainy.

'Perfect', Lyric told herself. *'Happy birthday to me!'*

It was a Sunday.

"Happy birthday, Lyric," Marcus told her, subdued, sliding her a cup of decaf across the counter. He knew she wasn't a morning person and wished it could be regular coffee, but all the pregnancy books said caffeine was a 'no-no' for pregnant women.

Flabbergasted, Lyric asked, "How did you know?"

Marcus chuckled. "I, uh, still have your application you filled out to live here. Remember?"

Lyric felt a thrill that reached her toes. Instead of trying to decipher the sensation, she simply took her cup of coffee and turned to go get ready for church calling, "Thank you" over her shoulder.

After church, as usual, they headed for Kurt and Lynne's.

As Lyric walked into their house, she gasped. There was pink and silver everywhere! In the living room, pink tulle was artfully swooped across the mantel and any other place that stood still, it seemed. Silver streamers fluttered down from the ceiling and silver vases of pink flowers and roses were scattered among side tables. Dazedly wandering through to the dining room, she was greeted with the same pink and silver theme on the table. A pretty pink tablecloth with matching pink candles in silver holders graced the table. A large silver vase held another enormous bouquet of the flowers she had seen in the living room.

"What on earth…" Lyric whispered aloud.

Following behind, the adult Coulters had watched her carefully.

"Happy birthday, Lyric!" Lynne exulted then, unable to keep her excitement in.

Lyric spun around, surprised to find she had an audience. "How did you know?!"

Rachel, looking very much like she had a secret, blurted out, "Marcus told us!"

Lyric was too bewildered to speak. Why would they do this?

Had she been coherent, she would've known the answer. They loved her. Plain and simple. They considered her family.

Lynne spoke up then. "We didn't know your favorite food, but Marcus said you liked pasta, so I made chicken alfredo for dinner."

Stricken again with surprise, Lyric's mouth dropped open. How did Marcus know she liked pasta?

Realizing she was being rude, Lyric managed through a thick throat, "Thank you, Lynne! Actually, my favorite food is anything Italian and I do like my pasta – any kind, really."

Zachary and Hailey found the grownups then.

Zachary tugged on his dad's pant leg. "Did you show her?" he whispered loudly, shyly indicating Lyric.

"Yes, we did. And she liked it a lot."

Zachary grinned.

"We he'ped," Hailey informed Lyric. "Gwammy put fwowes in da bases. I he'ped. And Zachy, too."

Lyric smiled and fondled Hailey's curls. "You both did a great job! The flowers are very pretty. Grammy did a good job picking them out, too." Lyric smiled at Lynne.

Soon they were all seated for Lynne's delicious alfredo.

As she looked around, Lyric knew this was her most memorable birthday to date.

⹊⹊⹊

It was a white Christmas! Lyric had her nose pressed against the living room window, just like a little kid.

"I still can't believe it, Marcus! It's *snowing* on *Christmas!*"

Ridiculously, Lyric felt the familiar tears gathering. She was *so* over the hormones pregnancy caused. She wasn't usually such a *girl!*

Marcus had to admit, Lyric's excitement was catching. He came to stand beside Lyric at the window. "Cool!"

Reaching out, Marcus slid his arm around Lyric's shoulders and gave her a side squeeze. "Merry Christmas, Lyric."

"Merry Christmas, Marcus."

Feeling suddenly self-conscious with Marcus' arm around her, Lyric tactfully stepped away. "I better go get ready to go to your parents'. It's gonna take us awhile."

She stood in front of her closet trying to decide what to wear, which wasn't like her. Usually she grabbed the first thing she saw that was presentable. She'd never felt this way before! Sort of queasy, but in a good way…and it most definitely had nothing to do with the pregnancy. And it made no sense!

Frustrated with herself, she reached out to pluck a red sweater from its hanger. *Why* did she suddenly care *what* she wore? It wouldn't make much of a difference! With only four weeks of pregnancy left, she looked and felt like a fat cow in anything she put on her ever-expanding body.

However, when she stepped out of her room, Marcus complimented, "You look really pretty, Lyric."

Blushing, she answered, "Thank you."

The drive was slow going. With each mile they got closer, though, Lyric felt apprehensive.

"Do – are – I mean, Christmas is such a big holiday. Is it, I just, well – I'm not family. Usually Christmas is so – *intimate*, meant just for family. I'm not –"

"You're family, Lyric," Marcus curtly cut her off. He hadn't intended to speak so harshly.

"Sorry," he apologized. "I really wish you understood how special you are to my family. You *are* one of us."

'Just not special to you, huh, Marcus?' she wanted to ask. Immediately followed by a disconcerting question, why did she suddenly care so much what Marcus thought of her?

Soon, they were turning down Kurt and Lynne's street and pulling up in front of their house.

Apprehension filled her. She had gotten Kurt and Lynne and Levi and Rachel small gifts. What if they hated them? What if they laughed at her?

'Stop it!' she commanded herself. '*You* know *they are not like that!'*

Lynne and Rachel had told her they loved decorating for Christmas. It was evident as soon as she stepped through the door. The house was elegantly decorated in festive red and green.

The Christmas dinner was lovely. And all too soon, they commenced with coffee and pie around the Christmas tree – a Coulter tradition.

Lyric felt awkward handing out her gifts but she found herself ready to be done and over with that part. She had gotten each of the children a toy appropriate for their age. She had never been any good at getting gifts, especially on a budget. Just getting what little gifts she had, had nearly drained her checking account. The Coulters had all been so kind to her that she *wanted* to get them all *something*.

She had given Kurt a new grilling set, only because she knew he liked to barbecue, not because she thought he particularly needed a new set.

To Lynne, she gave a pair of turquoise earrings, both of their birthstone. At her party, she had discovered Lynne's birthday was also in December, on the twenty-seventh.

For Levi, all she knew was, he loved his wife, his children – and golfing. So she gave him a set of tees engraved with his name.

To Rachel she gave an organizer. Lyric had found out she'd done most of the planning and prep work for both the baby's shower and her birthday.

Although she hadn't known what their reactions to her gifts would be, she was still shocked.

Both Kurt and Levi had gotten up and came over to engulf her in a hug.

One thing Lyric had discovered about the Coulters over the last several months, they were a huggy family.

Lynne and Rachel were both moved by what they perceived were thoughtful gifts and tears accompanied their hugs.

Lyric still thought her offerings were pretty insignificant, but the recipients certainly hadn't made her feel that way.

Turning to Marcus, she presented her last gift. Her heart thudded. His had taken the most thought. And it had taken her forever to come up with an idea.

Marcus ripped the wrapping paper off eagerly, the epitome of a kid on Christmas. In his lap lay a black Bible engraved in gold lettering with:

Marcus James Coulter

Lyric had seen, on occasion, when Marcus would be reading his Bible, it seemed worn out and falling apart. Still, she knew some people cherished that about their Bibles. She had no idea if Marcus was one of those people. Still, the idea of getting him a new Bible had stuck in her mind. She had even gone into one of those Christian bookstores to buy it. She waited on pins and needles for his reaction.

His face lit up when he smiled at her. "Thank you, Lyric! I've needed a new Bible. How did you know?"

All eyes on her, Lyric flushed. "Oh, just observation." And then she giggled, everyone joining in.

Levi played Santa then, clambering under the tree.

One by one, presents were given out and opened. Lyric was shocked by how many had her name on them. Clothes and bath salts, bath oils and bubble bath, books and stationery and even a few toys for her baby were among the gifts she received from Kurt and Lynne, and Levi and Rachel.

Amidst the festivities, Hailey bounced up to Lyric and perched herself on Lyric's lap and handed her a stack of papers. After careful examination, Lyric saw that they were all stapled together like a little booklet of coloring pages Hailey had made just for her.

"Mewy Cwis'mas, Lywic." Hailey then gave her a sloppy kiss on the cheek.

"Thank you, Hailey," Lyric returned, "and Merry Christmas to you, too."

Seeming bolstered by his younger sister's friendliness, Zachary shyly approached and silently handed a folded piece of paper to Lyric.

On it was a drawing with a blue sky and a smiling sun. Two figures were drawn among flowers and they were holding hands. One was of a tall girl with curly blond hair and the other was a black-haired little boy with green eyes, just like Zachary had. In childish printing and with adult help, Lyric guessed, it read: Merry Christmas.

Lyric grew misty-eyed. "Aw, Zachary, it's you and me!"

Zachary smiled and nodded.

Lyric leaned down and gave him a hug. Surprising her, he hugged back.

The other adults were starting to clean up and Lyric pitched in to help.

Marcus came over then. "I have something for you." He handed her a small box.

She opened it. Inside, on black velvet, lay a silver chain with a dark red baby bootie pendant.

"The bootie is a real garnet, which will be the baby's birthstone."

Leftover emotions from Zachary's picture formed into real tears that fell down Lyric's cheeks now. She'd never been given *real* jewelry before. And certainly nothing so pretty or with such precious meaning.

Impulsively, she threw her arms around Marcus and kissed him full on the lips, then almost immediately jumped back, terribly embarrassed. "Oops! Sorry!"

Frustrated at her own forward behavior, Lyric didn't know quite what to do, so simply spun on her heel and walked away.

∿∿∿

Nothing was said about the kiss. Lyric was too embarrassed and Marcus wisely kept quiet on the subject. They both thought of it from time to time, however.

Time passed and it suddenly seemed as though Lyric's due date was looming.

She could admit she was scared. How would she know what to do as a mother? She could care for her son much easier in the womb. And the pain made her nervous, too. She'd researched extensively about drugs versus a natural birth without drugs. She'd talked to Rachel a lot, too. It was, at least, a once-a-week occurrence, if not more, now, and always baby-related. Sometimes Rachel would call to check on her, usually while Marcus was at work, to make sure Lyric wasn't in labor and alone. Sometimes Lyric would call with a baby question. Their conversations were never less than an hour and they generally moved through a wide range of topics, growing more personal as the two became closer.

During one such conversation, Rachel confided that with Zachary, she'd had the drugs and secretly wished now that she hadn't. He was her first-born and she could barely remember her response or emotions when she first saw him. With Hailey, she hadn't had the drugs and, although there was pain, it had seemed to disappear once she initially laid eyes on her little miracle. With Sydney and Logan, she had to have a C-section, since Logan had been trying to push Sydney out of the way.

Lyric had finally decided no on the drugs and had her birth plan ready. Now all she had to do was wait. And every time she thought about the birth, she felt very alone without a daddy for her baby.

Marcus and his family had been very supportive, but part of her felt as though there was an expiration date – as if it was too good to last. She knew she'd probably do something to inadvertently disappoint them and that would be that. How did she get so lucky to have the Coulters in her life, anyway? She most certainly didn't deserve them. Marcus himself had volunteered to be her birth partner when she went into labor. It had been discussed at a doctor appointment and Lyric had frozen when the doctor had asked her who her person was. Obviously the logical choice would be the baby's father. Lyric only cringed now when she thought of Austin. He seemed to have taken himself out of the picture. Marcus had later, at home, offered himself, if she wanted. She had readily agreed.

However, she had never discussed with Marcus what she'd do if she went into labor while he was at work or school. She hadn't given any thought to how she'd get to the hospital if he wasn't there to take her. She'd sort of just assumed he'd be there and hadn't wanted to think of the what ifs.

Lately, she'd found herself tentatively praying to God. *'If You care, could You please hold off on the birth of my baby for when Marcus is home.'*

That was all she allowed herself to pray, not wanting to press her luck. Of course, God might not answer her prayer, but she needed all of the help she could get.

\\\

The inevitable happened. It was Friday afternoon, January 25, 2003, when Lyric felt a few tugs and twinges in her abdomen.

She'd been curled up with a book; since she was on maternity leave, she got to read to her heart's content. It was one of her favorite pastimes.

In the middle of a sentence, she stiffened and froze.

After a few minutes, nothing more happened and she continued reading. Right at the end of the chapter, she felt another stab of mild pain.

'Okay, breathe,' she instructed herself. She remembered the doctor telling her the beginnings of labor could be slow.

'Don't panic,' she lectured.

"I'm okay," she reassured herself aloud as she struggled to sit up. Another stab of pain pierced her then and she found it difficult to breathe. Or was that just panic because she was alone?

Pulling herself together, she waited a few minutes more. When no pain followed, she reassured again aloud, "I'm okay."

Marcus was due home in only a few more hours. If the doctor was right, this was a slow process and she should be able to make it until then. The jolt of pain that followed that thought had her doubting.

Time it, she remembered. She was supposed to time the contractions. Good. That gave her something to do while she waited for Marcus.

She got up, suddenly needing to pace, and then she was leaning over an end table, trying to breathe through the pain. Her eyes swiftly went to the clock on the wall: 4:28.

Wasn't this labor coming on a little fast?

"No. Stop panicking, Lyric. You're okay. It just feels that way because you're alone. Marcus will be home with enough time to take you to the hospital."

The out-loud reasoning seemed to calm her a little bit – until the next contraction had her bracing the back of the couch. Her pacing through the apartment had led her back through the living room. The DVD player's clock read 4:41.

Was that too close or was thirteen minutes between contractions okay? Should she head to the hospital? She could feel herself beginning to panic.

"It's only thirteen minutes, Lyric, calm down!"

Trying to relax, she sat down, only to feel the uncomfortable pressure. She leaned forward, hand on either side of her belly, trying not to cry.

Was this much pain normal? Or was she just being a wimp? Should she call Marcus? Rachel? Maybe Lynne?

Her eye jumped to the clock. 4:54.

Still thirteen minutes apart. That was good. Consistency was key. Or was she confusing that with childrearing? She'd been reading a lot of those types of books, too.

"Ow!" she moaned as tears of worry sprang to her eyes.

5:05.

Uh, oh. Eleven minutes. They were coming closer!

Fighting panic, Lyric acted on instinct. She gingerly got up and grabbed her overnight bag by the door. She had carefully packed it two weeks ago per doctor's orders.

Slowly, she made her way to the elevator of the apartment building, stopping once to ride out a contraction. She checked her watch she'd remembered to strap on. The hands pointed to 5:16.

Finally, she made it out of the apartment building, then stopped. Now what? She couldn't walk all the way to the subway! Nor did she think she'd have time to call Lynne or Rachel and wait for them to drive all the way into the City to take her to the hospital. But cabs were expensive.

She began to cry, and in the midst of crying, she had to lean over a nearby stair railing to combat another contraction. She was scared and confused and didn't know what to do. She glanced at her watch. 5:26. Ten minutes! It'd been nearly an hour since her contractions had really begun. Now they were even closer! Not good, she knew that much, since she wasn't at the hospital yet.

Gritting her teeth, she hailed a cab.

During her ride, Lyric silently pleaded that the baby stay in until she made it to the hospital. She had felt definite pressure that had her worrying.

As soon as she rushed into the ER, she was quickly checked in and admitted. It probably helped that she told them she had timed her contractions on her nearly hour-long cab ride over and her contractions had accelerated to five minutes apart.

It wasn't until after Lyric had changed into a gown and was in bed, hooked up to all of the monitors and able to relax and catch her breath that she realized she hadn't told anybody where she was.

'Lyric', she scolded, 'Stupid girl. Now you most certainly will be alone for the birth of your son!'

She knew exactly where her phone was...in her pants pocket...her pants that were on the floor of her bedroom.

Alone in her hospital room, she bowed forward then and groaned in pain as another contraction hit and drove all thoughts of phones from her mind.

Silent tears slid down her cheeks.

vvvvvvvvvvvvvvvvvvvvvvvvvvvvvvvvvvvvvvvvvvvvvvvvvvvvvvvvvvvvvvvvvvvvvvvvvvvvvvvv

Marcus walked into a dark and silent apartment. He flicked on a switch, surprised Lyric hadn't fallen asleep on the couch with the table lamp on while reading, like usual.

'*She must've just gone to bed*,' he tried to reassure himself, despite the nagging feeling that something was off.

Just checking, he walked through the living room to her slightly open bedroom door. He cautiously opened it and peeked in. He didn't want the light from the living room waking her if she was sleeping. Yet, he couldn't make out any form on her bed. Flicking on her light, he confirmed his suspicion. She wasn't there!

He turned around, uselessly calling out her name. "Lyric!"

Quickening his step, he hurried to the bathroom to check. All was dark.

'*Oh, Lord, what happened?*' Marcus prayed.

Circling back to the living room, he glanced at the door. It was then he realized, with a jolt, that her overnight bag was gone.

Giving it no more thought, Marcus grabbed his keys and cell phone and bolted out the door.

He drove like a mad man, worried. Why hadn't she called? Did something happen to prevent her calling? Was she taken by ambulance?

Marcus screeched to a halt in a parking space outside the hospital and sprinted through the automatic doors, barely taking the time to read the map to find the birthing center in the hospital.

Once there, he was stopped at a set of locked doors. He silently railed in frustration as he picked up the phone on the wall, as a sign above it instructed.

A pleasant voice answered, "How may I help you?"

"Yes, um, my name's Marcus Coulter." He bent slightly forward, trying to catch his breath. "I'm here for Lyric Bell."

A moment's pause.

"Hm. I'll have to verify. She has no list of accepted visitors."

"Please! I'm not merely visiting. I'm supposed to be her, er, person."

What had Dr. Oberman called it? Oh, yeah. Birthing partner!

"I'm her birthing partner."

Even as he answered confidently, there was a seed of doubt. Did Lyric want him there after all? He *was* in her plan as her birthing partner…but, then, *why* did she not call him before going to the hospital?

He heard in his ear a curt, "Well, why didn't you come in with her, then?"

Chagrined that her question so closely matched his own, Marcus bit back a retort.

The voice continued on, "Hold, please, I'll check."

Marcus wanted to hit something, even as he felt tears sting his eyes.

His reaction startled him, as he wasn't prone to violence – at least, pre-Lyric. She brought out a protective instinct he'd had no idea he possessed.

And he honestly couldn't remember the last time he'd cried. These tears were of fear. Fear that he was too late.

ˏˏ

Lyric was trying not to panic. The contractions seemed to be staying at five minutes, meaning she was no longer making progress. Still, she valiantly fought to keep the tears at bay. Not from the physical pain, but from the knowledge that she would end up bringing her son into the world all alone.

A nurse walked in then. "There's a gentleman out there, saying he's supposed to be here with you. A Marcus Coulter?"

Marcus? He'd found her?!

She suddenly felt herself laughing, giddy with relief. Crazy, she knew, but she felt lighter already. "Yes! Please let him in!" she practically shouted, causing the nurse to scurry backwards out the door.

ˏˏ

"Come on back, Mr. Coulter," suddenly greeted him through the phone he held, white-knuckled, against his ear.

And then he heard the click of the lock on the door being released.

Frantically, he shoved through the door.

"Which room?" he called, even as he passed the nurses' station.

"Behind you, Mr. Coulter!" one of the nurses replied. "You just passed it. Room 208."

"Thank you," he replied as he bolted through the open door.

"Lyric?" he called out as he parted the privacy curtain. He was relieved to finally see her.

"Marcus!" she wailed.

Alarmed, Marcus quickly went to her side. "What's the matter? Are you okay?"

"I'm so scared!" she spluttered, trying to get all of her explaining out of the way. "I'm sorry I forgot to call. I just thought…it all happened so fast…or so it seemed, being all alone. And then I get here, and things slowed down. And I – "

"It's okay, Lyric," Marcus stopped her flood of words.

"How did you know I was here?"

"I finally noticed your bag was gone. I'd searched the entire apartment, looking for you and finally noticed it missing."

"I'm so glad you're here! You'll stay, won't you?"

Marcus grabbed her hand and squeezed. "Of course."

Although, he felt suddenly apprehensive. He couldn't imagine the doctor exposing anything, knowing their situation, and he planned to stay by Lyric's head, but still...

And, suddenly, everything seemed to happen at once.

Lyric's grip tightened in Marcus', making him question her fragile appearance.

A nurse paged the doctor.

Lyric let out a loud groan. Even as Dr. Oberman went under the sheet to check her, Lyric broke out in a sweat and her pain increased. She grunted and moaned.

Why had nobody warned her about the intensity of the pain?

"Good news, kids!" Dr. Oberman announced, "Lyric, you're dilated to ten. You'll likely be ready to push soon."

Lyric's eyes flashed to Marcus'. "I think he was waiting for you." She indicated her belly.

The next hour was filled with grunts and groans and other unearthly sounds Marcus had never heard Lyric emit before. He had a hard time hearing Lyric in such agony. Was that normal? Surely something was wrong! Yet, Dr. Oberman seemed reassuring enough.

"You're doing great, Lyric. That contraction's almost over," Dr. Oberman told her as he watched the monitor. "Try to rest until the next one. Then I want you to push, okay?"

And Lyric did, crying out in pain as she did so. It seemed to do no good.

Marcus absently rubbed his thumb across Lyric's hand as he held it and she squeezed. But when she was in pain, he thought his hand might fall off! Wisely, he kept that little tidbit to himself.

Marcus stayed by her side, nearest her head. Occasionally, he reached across with his other hand to brush her long locks of hair out of her eyes. Hair fell in her face from the ponytail that she had haphazardly thrown up.

Lyric struggled to right herself, trying to get purchase on the bed to better brace herself for contractions.

Trying to aid her, Marcus let go of her hand momentarily.

Mistaking the gesture, Lyric panicked. "No! Marcus, please stay! I need you!"

Instantly, he grabbed her hand again and leaned close to her ear. "I will stay as long as you want me," he promised.

Lyric had time to reward him with a weak smile before the end began.

"Lyric," the doctor called, "are you ready for your first *big* push? A good contraction's coming."

"Wait!" she feebly cried, "I'm not ready! I can't do this. I need – I need – " and her free hand grasped the railing on the bed, as she prepared to bear down.

"Push, Lyric," the doctor instructed. "Now!"

Lyric tried pushing, leaning forward squeezing Marcus' hand until her knuckles were white, but she could find no purchase. Nothing to anchor her so she felt like she would slip right off the bed.

"I can't!" she wailed.

"I see a head, Lyric. Come, now, let's try again. A couple more good pushes and you'll be done."

Marcus, forced to clothe in scrubs before entering the room, made sure he could murmur encouragement in her ear. "You hear that? You did well, Lyric. The doctor said he can see the little head now. Two more like that and – " his throat caught " – and you'll be able to meet your son."

Lyric turned her wild, half-crazed eyes on him. "Are you sure? I just don't think I can."

"Yes. You can."

Lyric leaned forward again, trying to brace herself. "I can't do this!" And suddenly, she sat up. "I need – something – behind me. I need–" she broke off with a contraction, trying to bear down, but could only give a weak push.

"Lyric, you have to try," the doctor insisted.

"You!" he snapped at Marcus. "Get on the bed behind her and grab under her arms. She needs the support."

Marcus hesitated. Is that what Lyric would want? It seemed – his thoughts were interrupted.

"Now! Her contraction is peaking!"

Marcus didn't know what that meant, but the doctor's orders were insistent enough that he obeyed without another thought. He carefully positioned himself behind Lyric, arms under hers, elbows used to brace, and his hands were still free for Lyric's gripping. He could no longer see Lyric's face, but he kept talking to her in low, soothing tones as she tried pushing again.

"It's okay. You're doing great." And, finally, getting excited, "One more push, Lyric! That's all. You can do it, I'm right here with you."

And, seemingly, as abruptly as it had started, it was over.

Lyric sank back against Marcus, exhausted, as she watched the doctor and nurses wipe off her baby and swaddle him. The bath would come later.

Marcus wasn't sure what to do. Lyric was still slumped against him, but she'd be handed her baby soon. Surely she'd want a few minutes of privacy.

Before Marcus could contemplate further, Lyric had her baby in her arms.

"Do you see him, Marcus?"

He peered over her shoulder.

"Isn't he perfect?" Her voice broke.

"Yes, he is," he quietly agreed, feeling like an intruder on her perfect moment. He couldn't possibly move.

She leaned her head back against Marcus' chest, snuggling her baby close, and shut her eyes to revel in the sweetness of her baby son.

"Thank you for being here," she murmured.

"You're welcome," he whispered.

The doctor and nurses had left the room promising to be back shortly.

Marcus gazed at the perfect, tiny form of Lyric's son.

"He really is beautiful, Lyric." And he bent forward and kissed her forehead.

He'd done it out of sheer instinct. He had kissed Rachel's forehead in the same brotherly way after she'd had her babies. Each time. Of course, he hadn't been in such an intimate position, sitting behind her. Yet, this kiss had felt oddly, and unsettlingly, different – and it had nothing to do with the fact that Lyric still leaned back against him. And the thing was, he didn't know if it was a good odd or not.

Lyric opened her eyes then and looked up at Marcus and smiled contently.

She struggled to sit up then, nuzzling her son.

A nurse came bustling in then with paperwork. Another followed with supplies for a bath and other instruments to do the necessary checks on a newborn.

As the nurses bathed the baby, Lyric leaned forward, releasing Marcus from his prison, while she perused the paperwork.

Marcus took the chair next to her bed.

"Name of child," she muttered. Then answered herself, "Lucas James."

Marcus perked up. "James?"

Lyric eyed him speculatively. "Um, yeah," she answered, unsure.

He cracked a smile. "I thought that was out of the running."

Lyric bit her lip, "I know." She then confessed, "I named him after you." Suddenly worried, she asked, "Is that okay?"

Marcus grinned, his eyes softening as he looked toward Lucas. "I am honored."

Lyric's worried eyes met Marcus' then. "I don't know if I should give Lucas my last name or Austin's."

'Remain calm!' Marcus commanded as his anger flared. He breathed deep to keep his composure. Why would she give Austin any claim to that precious baby, after all he'd put her through? Austin didn't deserve it! He tried calming down. She hadn't exactly asked his opinion. It was none of his business, anyway.

Then she did ask. "What do you think? I mean, he hasn't been around lately nor taken an interest in Lucas, but Lucas is his baby, too." Lyric suddenly smiled. "It feels strange using Lucas' name. I like it!"

Marcus smiled, too, despite the subject of his former thoughts.

He worked to keep his voice even and his answer kind. "I think you deserve to have Lucas carry your name. You *are* his mommy, after all." He winked then, hoping to convince her of his nonchalance.

Lyric grinned. "You're right. Austin *chose* not to be involved. *I* get to choose his name. It's Lucas James Bell."

A nurse came over then and handed Lucas to his mother.

"Would you like to hold your namesake, Marcus?" Lyric offered.

Gently, Marcus took the tiny infant into his big arms. Lucas was so small and fragile. Marcus marveled, just as he had done when he first held his nieces and nephews.

Lyric leaned over and loosened the blanket a little so she could grab a tiny hand. Instantly, Lucas gripped her finger. With tears in her eyes at the wonderment of this miracle, she softly introduced her son. "Lucas, meet your very special friend, Marcus."

Chapter 15

Reflect on your present blessings, of which every man has many,
not on your past misfortunes, of which all men have some
Charles Dickens

Lynne and Rachel came to the hospital every day Lyric was there, clucking and fussing and bringing gifts for little Lucas.

Lyric wasn't used to so much attention, but reveled in the adoration they shared for her miraculously perfect son.

Secretly, she had worried that God would punish her by causing something to go wrong or for Lucas to have some deformity that would make caring for him that much more difficult. The love for her son knew no bounds.

Marcus was surprised at how quickly little Lucas' hold on him took effect. Suddenly, it was hard for Marcus to remember what life had been like before Lucas was born. That had been as recent as three days ago. He jumped at any chance he was given to hold Lucas. Imagine that! Sure, he'd held his nieces and nephews, but once they leaked goo, he passed them off. With Lucas, for some reason – maybe because he was Lyric's baby – he didn't care what form or color said goo came in, he'd hold Lucas all day if he could. He'd even changed a few diapers already – and of his own volition!

"How are you today, dear?" Lynne came bustling in. She went over to Lyric and plumped her pillow and tucked the covers in more securely around her frame. And she did it all without being intrusive, somehow.

Lyric turned an amused gaze on Marcus. They had shared a secret joke a time or two about Lynne's mother hen. Lyric didn't mind, though. She adored Lynne.

Marcus grinned back, clutching little Lucas to his big, broad chest.

"I'm ready to be out of here," Lyric confessed, answering Lynne's question. "I've had enough of the hospital and its food."

Lynne chuckled. "It's only been three days, dear. Let them pamper you here more."

Without thinking, Lyric blurted out, "But Marcus does such a better job of taking care of me at home, than they do here!" Then she turned bright red.

Marcus' laugh shook Lucas and he began to stir and whimper.

Lyric held out her arms, trying to hide her embarrassment. "He's probably hungry."

Lynne shot her son a fond look. "Of course he does," she responded to Lyric's earlier statement. "I taught him well," she shamelessly, and teasingly, boasted.

Marcus carefully transferred Lucas to his mother's arms.

Lyric promptly, and discreetly, began nursing Lucas.

"Knock, knock!" Rachel cheerfully announced her presence. She carried in an enormous bouquet of red roses.

"These are for you," she told Lyric as she set them on the portable bedside table. "I figured the new mama needed presents, too." She produced a gift bag that had been dangling from the crook of her arm and handed it to Lyric.

"Thank you!" Lyric enthused. She dug into the bag, pulling out bubble bath, hand lotion, body spray, and other bath products scented in lavender vanilla. She inhaled.

"Mm! I love this scent, Rachel. Thank you!"

Rachel waved it off. "It's just a little pampering kit for when you get home."

"*If* I *ever* get to go home. I'm hoping it'll be today."

"So soon?"

"Well...they *did* say if I was up and moving around. I took a shower this morning. It felt *so* good!"

"Oh, how I remember those days!" Rachel laughed.

Lucas finished eating and Lyric peered down at him, marveling again at his tiny perfection.

Lynne noticed and asked hopefully, "Can I hold him?"

Lyric nuzzled her son's tiny head and answered, "Of course."

After that, it was a tie of who held him the most, Rachel or Lynne, until they left.

Lyric used the time to try to get some rest.

Marcus ended up dozing in his chair, as well, as he had been at the hospital nearly as long as Lyric. A couple of hours later, a nurse came bustling in. "Time to check stats again," she cheerfully told Lyric.

Lyric groaned. "Can't I go home *yet?*"

The nurse's eyes twinkled. "Maybe. You have to be able to walk the hall. If you're able to accomplish that, the doctor will probably release you."

Relief flooded Lyric. "Let's go, then!"

"Hold your horses, dearie," the nurse chuckled. "Let me make the checks on you and your handsome son first."

The nurse performed her duties efficiently and in record time. Lucas decided he was hungry again.

After feeding Lucas – *again*, and yet another nurse came in to check vitals – *again*, Lyric was allowed to walk the hall. A couple of hours later, *another* nurse came in with forms and happily announced, "You are free to go home!"

`````````````````````````````````````````````````````````````````````````````

The first few days home were all about adjustment. Lyric felt a bit like
`````````````````````````````````````````````````````````````````````````````

her life had taken on a surreal quality. But she jumped in with both feet and soon had a routine, of sorts, in place; as much as she could have with a newborn, in any case.

One evening, she awaited Marcus' coming home. She was exhausted because Lucas had been up off-and-on most of the night. She could feel tears of frustration gathering. Lucas had been fussy all day and she had barely been able to put him down without him immediately crying, even if he was asleep. She had scarcely been able to grab a small snack here and there and so hadn't eaten much all day. And she desperately craved a shower. The last one she'd had was just before leaving the hospital two days ago.

When Marcus finally walked in, he assessed the disheveled Lyric and asked the wrong question, judging by the reaction that followed. "What happened?"

Lyric immediately dissolved into tears. "I n-need a sh-shower!"

Although that barely touched the tip of the iceberg, she couldn't seem to articulate anything else.

Marcus put his stuff away, noting the dirty diapers piled in the trash can and the dishes in the sink.

Lyric was standing in the middle of the living room, gently jostling a fussing Lucas.

Looking at Lucas, Marcus asked, "Have you fed him?"

"Of course I have!" she snapped. "I'm not a *neglectful* mother. I just don't know what he wants! I'm a *terrible* mother."

Marcus thought back on his words and cringed. "Sorry. I only asked because I was going to offer to take him so you could shower."

Lyric's tears immediately stopped and she brightened. "Okay."

Gently, she transferred the still-squalling newborn from her arms to Marcus'. And then she shot off to the bathroom.

Marcus puzzled. He thought mood swings were only reserved for *pregnant* women.

Lyric was elated. She wondered at her sanity that a simple shower could elicit so much pleasure. She took her time, enjoying the steaming stream, knowing that her son was safe.

It was a strange conundrum – she didn't know if she could have taken even one more second of Lucas' crying, yet she knew that if something happened to him, she'd be crushed and feel at a loss without him.

Marcus had fixed a simple snack of cheese, crackers, and grapes, one-handedly. He was preparing to settle down with the now-quiet Lucas when there was a knock on the door.

Who would be coming at nearly eight o'clock at night? His mom and Rachel hated coming into the City. Besides, they would've called first. And Sunday was only a few days away. Surely they could hold out until then to get their Lucas fix.

Marcus peeked through the peephole and groaned. What was he going to do now? There was no way to avoid it. His only problem was Lucas.

He eyed the bathroom, still hearing the water running. Lyric hadn't finished her shower yet.

Should he put Lucas down? He was awake, though, and would surely fuss.

Marcus finally wrenched the door open with an unwelcome expression.

"Well, if it isn't my son!" Austin Wood sneered at Marcus.

"What do you want, Austin?"

"My son, of course!"

"And what gives you the right to him?" Marcus hotly countered.

"He's mine!" Austin turned on a nasty smile. "And you can't keep him from me."

"That would be Lyric's decision."

"Where is the little wench? She needs to come home and be a family."

"Austin!" Lyric had come in behind Marcus. She could scarcely breathe. This couldn't be happening! "What are you doing here?"

"I came to get my son and take you two home, where you belong."

Lyric knew better. Austin could care less about family. With him, it was a matter of simply wanting what he couldn't have.

"No. I don't want to go with you. You are not my home anymore."

Austin started to come in then, but Marcus put a hand up to stop him.

"Lyric, why don't you come get Lucas?" Marcus suggested.

"Lucas?" Austin sputtered. "You named him without me?!" Austin was livid. It was *his* kid, too! He had rights, as the father. "That's a dumb name."

Lyric willed herself to stay quiet as she gathered Lucas to her, protectively.

"Why don't you take him into your room?" Marcus directed.

Lyric immediately wheeled around, not meeting Austin's gaze.

"Hey, where are you taking him? Where are you going?" Austin whined. "I want to see my son!" Austin took another step forward.

Again stopping him with a raised hand, Marcus told him in a deadly quiet voice, "You need to leave. You have no claim to him. You were not around during Lyric's pregnancy and you care nothing for either of them. Leave her alone! I'm going to call the police – I'm sure they'd be interested in looking up your record. My suggestion? Don't. Come. Back. Forget about Lucas. Forget about Lyric."

Austin leered at Marcus and asked with thick meaning, "Yeah? What's *she* to *you?* Maybe he's not my kid at all. Maybe he's yours." He gave Marcus a knowing wink and made a few more lewd suggestions.

Incensed that Austin would disgustingly objectify Lyric in that way, Marcus punched Austin in the face.

"Don't *ever* talk like that about her again!"

Austin was too stunned to react, giving Marcus ample time to push him further into the hall and away from the door.

"Ow!" Austin howled. "You can't do this! You'll be sorry!"

Marcus quickly closed and locked the door, panting from the physical exertion.

He leaned, stunned, against the door. Why? Why did he always succumb to violence when he had to deal with Austin? And yet, a tiny, miniscule part of him had really gotten a certain satisfaction from punching Austin Wood.

Idly, Marcus wondered if Austin would, indeed, come back. Resigned, he realized the answer. Probably.

Lyric poked her head out of the bedroom. "What's going on? Where's Austin?"

Marcus eyed her, deciding what to tell Lyric. Simplicity was always best. "Gone."

Lyric came all of the way out then. "Oh. How did you get him to leave?"

Chagrined, Marcus admitted, "I punched him."

"Again?" Lyric grinned, then giggled.

Marcus frowned.

"You'd think he'd have learned from the first time," Lyric snickered, trying to bite back her mirth, seeing Marcus was not amused.

"It isn't funny, Lyric," Marcus groused. "The Bible doesn't condone violence to solve problems. I was brought up better than that. It's like – it's as if – I don't know…he's my vice, or something."

Finally sobering, Lyric told Marcus, "He deserved it, you know. I almost gave in and let him see Lucas."

Seeing Marcus' horrified expression, Lyric quickly reassured, "I won't! It was only a fleeting thought."

Marcus and Lyric had drifted toward the living room and each took a seat.

"He *is* Lucas' father, after all," Lyric explained.

"He doesn't deserve you. Either of you," Marcus spat.

In a small voice, Lyric agreed. "I know."

"He wasn't here through any of the doctors' appointments or even the birth! He's despicable!" Marcus continued, vehemently.

Lyric cut in. "I know, Marcus!"

"If he comes back, we're *not* opening the door; we're calling the police."

"Okay," Lyric acquiesced.

"Where's Lucas?" Marcus had an inexplicable need to see him. To physically check him over and make sure he was alright. It didn't make sense, but he couldn't shake the feeling.

"He's on my bed, asleep."

The whimper and cry belied Lyric's words and she smiled.

Remembering from earlier, Marcus altered his words. "Is he fed?"

"Yep. And changed." Lyric grinned. "You wanna go get him, don't you?"

Eagerly, Marcus asked, "Can I?"

"Of course!"
Marcus quickly jumped up and loped off.

Lyric couldn't help but notice how Marcus was with Lucas. He was so sweet and caring, treating Lucas like another little nephew…only, Lyric sensed something more, hidden underneath.

As she snuggled Lucas one night, she mused into his tiny ear, "Marcus is the kind of man you *deserve* to have as your daddy."

Pausing, Lyric breathed in the baby scent of his sweet, little head. Tears pricked her eyes.

"I'm sorry," she murmured. "I've made so many mistakes that affect you. I'll do better, I promise."

Marcus could no more explain his feelings toward Lucas, than he could of his feelings he'd initially had toward Lyric that first day she came to his apartment for an interview. He couldn't deny it, though. He felt extremely protective of Lyric's innocent son. He delighted in holding him, caring for him. Every time Lucas' little hand wrapped around his finger, Marcus could feel him wrapping around his heart. He simply couldn't contemplate the future because he was afraid to look too closely. One day, Lyric would move on, taking Lucas with her. Eventually, she was bound to find someone – a good guy to be Lucas' dad. Since Marcus couldn't bear the thought of Lucas leaving, he simply closed it off. For now, they were here. Lucas was here. And that's all he would think about. And yet…what if he could convince Lyric to stay, to never leave? Would she be willing to do what it took?

Chapter 16
*He felt now that he was not simply close to her, but that
he did not know where he ended and she began*
Leo Tolstoy

Marcus, once again, felt his course of action change without his consent. As he watched and listened and witnessed Lyric with her son, Marcus had to finally admit his feelings. To himself, at least.

He found himself on the phone with his best friend, Andrew, his brother, Levi, and his mom. A lot. What should he do? How should he proceed?

All Marcus was certain of was that the more he thought of Lyric leaving one day, the more scared he was of losing her.

Lucas and Lyric weren't attached to him in any way. He had no claim to them, but he yearned for it.

For now, he tried being satisfied with the little bit of involvement he could safely have. He could take Lucas so Lyric could get a shower. He could check Lucas' diapers. Mundane, everyday things had never held so much appeal to Marcus before.

And Marcus never had feelings so much greater than himself before. There was nothing he wouldn't do for Lyric or Lucas. They were quickly becoming his world. And yet, he had to pause to think and reflect. In so doing, he realized he knew next to nothing about Lyric's feelings for him.

He knew she was passionate about her son. He knew she adored his family and they adored her. And he also knew that she would leave him someday. Maybe even to go back to Austin. The thought made him sick. Because he also happened to know that she did not feel worthy of love.

If she would only believe him, he would show her. How he would tell her, if he thought she would understand. He *could* make her understand! Only, he was afraid, that to Lyric, he would always simply be Marcus.

'''

"Can you believe Lucas is a month old already?" Lyric asked as she bathed him in the kitchen sink.

She delighted in her little boy and looked forward to the evening bath, before snuggles and his first few hours of the night that he slept through. Usually, it was from 8:00 p.m. to anywhere from 10:30 p.m. to midnight, before he woke up again. After that, however, it had been hit and miss as to when he'd sleep again. Right now, Lyric didn't mind much, but knew she would, once she went back to work. She tried not to think about it or worry too much.

Marcus was seated at the table doing homework, as usual.

Marcus looked up, smiling in response to her query. "Now that's hard to believe."

Lyric turned to Lucas and grinned at him as she finished gently washing him with Johnson's baby shampoo.

Toweling him dry, Lucas began to fuss. Soon enough, Lyric had him dressed in fleecy pajamas and swaddled in a blanket. She walked to the chair in the living room, facing away from Marcus, to nurse.

Marcus had free reign then to watch Lyric without being detected.

He admired her tenacity at being a good mother. He knew she struggled at times, frustrated when Lucas cried and she didn't know why. Or when she'd tell Marcus how Lucas wouldn't go back to sleep after eating at two in the morning and was still awake for his next feeding. She would wearily smile even as he secretly worried about the dark circles under her eyes. He had offered to hold baby Lucas while she slept, even if it was the wee hours of the morning. So far, however, she hadn't taken him up on it.

As he watched her then, from behind, he longed to go to her and ask her if he could take care of them. For always. If they could be his. For always.

Instead, Marcus simply continued to watch. And wait.

`````````````````````````````````````````````````````````````````````````````````

The day finally came when Lyric had to return to work.

She had had quite a lengthy interview process, with Marcus' help, to choose someone to care for Lucas while she was working. He was only six weeks old.

"You've had experience with interviews. Anyone stand out to you? You know, like I did with you for the apartment?" Lyric teased Marcus.

He grinned. "I'm sure we'll find the perfect person. God will send her...or him."

Lyric wasn't so sure, but Marcus proved to be right. They found a grandmotherly type who checked out and had excellent references. And she was willing to watch Lucas at their apartment, a very important condition for Lyric.

Her name was Mary Roberts, but both Marcus and Lyric were so awed by her, they could only call her Mrs. Roberts, despite her insistence of, "Please, call me Mary." As a compromise, they called her Miss Mary.

Miss Mary was a widow. Ever since losing her husband, she had worked as a nanny. Both Marcus and Lyric agreed that she was perfect for the job and gladly hired her.

`````````````````````````````````````````````````````````````````````````````````

Lyric going back to work went well for a few weeks. Until one night, Lucas woke up fussing, as usual. Only this time, he wouldn't stop and absolutely could not be consoled. Usually, he was pretty easy to get back to sleep now. Lyric was stumped by Lucas' cries. Surely Marcus would be woken up and irritated with the crying baby. Any minute now, he'd come to investigate. And he'd probably be angry.

'Don't confuse Marcus with Austin,' Lyric chastised herself. *'He's not like that!'*

In fact, she reflected that he had told her to wake him up if she felt she needed to. It *had* been half an hour of crying already.

She chewed her lower lip as she held Lucas tight against her body and gently jostled him, contemplating.

After another hour of trying various holding positions, a few diaper checks and even another attempted feeding, to no avail, Lyric decided to chance it. She knew her hesitancy to wake Marcus was based on her fears of what *Austin's* reaction would've been, rather than Marcus himself. Taking a deep breath, she headed for Marcus' door.

He had warned her he was a sound sleeper, but she had laid Lucas in his bassinette in her room, still crying. She had read in one of her books it was okay to do that if you needed a break from a crying baby. And she desperately needed one now. She felt on the verge of tears herself, so great was her frustration in not being able to calm down her own baby. And fatigue, along with worry, were factors…and were her two constant companions lately. Especially with going back to work.

Hesitantly, she entered Marcus' room. Standing by his bed, she could make out his form from the glow of the digital numbers on his alarm clock.

He looked so peaceful and boyish lying on his back, one arm flung across his forehead, the other dangling by his side, his mouth slightly open.

Lyric was amused to find that he didn't snore. He only breathed soft and deep and even.

Lyric bent over and quietly called his name, "Marcus," as she touched his shoulder.

Marcus mumbled something as he turned on his side toward her, still asleep.

Again, she tried, "Marcus."

His eyes fluttered as she said his name once again, finally opening them all the way, though unfocused.

Suddenly alert, seeing Lyric there, Marcus rubbed his eyes to clear them, sitting up. "Is something wrong?"

Uncertainly, Lyric answered honestly. "I don't know!" And then she burst into tears. Finally, through garbled speech and tears, she got out, "Lucas won't stop crying and I don't know what to do! It's been nearly two hours now and nothing I do seems to help. Maybe I should call Miss Mary. Maybe I should call the doctor!"

Marcus threw back the covers and got up.

Lyric was promptly convinced she was delirious from lack of sleep. As she watched Marcus pad into her bedroom in his white t-shirt and blue plaid flannel pants, hair mussed, she felt a spark of – something. What, she didn't know. Only that it wasn't altogether unpleasant – just confusing.

"Hey, little man," Marcus greeted as he lifted Lucas into his arms. "What seems to be the trouble?"

Lucas' gusty sobs were the only reply.

Lyric, still in tears, panicked. "See? What's wrong? He's never cried so long before."

Lyric slumped onto her bed, exhaustion taking over.

"Why don't you stay in here and try to sleep and I'll take Lucas into the living room?"

Lyric simply nodded and curled up, knees to chest, giving in. However, she knew she wouldn't be able to sleep with Lucas away from her in the other room.

Marcus left, shutting the door.

Tossing and turning for nearly an hour, Lyric heard the change immediately. She sat up when she realized she really was hearing silence!

Holding her breath, she tip-toed to her door and peeked out. She saw Marcus sitting in a chair and heard him murmuring to Lucas. Lyric came out then and Marcus looked up.

"Is he asleep?"

"Nope, just looking around. Did you get any sleep?"

"No. I couldn't with him out here."

Lyric sat down on the couch, opposite Marcus' chair.

"Do you want me to take him now?" Lyric offered.

"You should try to sleep. Especially now that he's stopped crying."

Lyric leaned forward to look into her son's face. He looked quite content.

"What do you think was wrong with him?" she wanted to know.

"Who knows," Marcus answered. "There are a lot of things it could be when an infant's involved."

Lyric was unsure, but Lucas seemed fine now.

Almost as in reassurance to her unspoken fear, Lucas flashed a big grin.

Stunned, Marcus and Lyric both looked at each other in surprise.

"Did he just...?" Marcus began.

"He just smiled!" Lyric exulted, feeling her tears form again.

After a few moments of silently gazing at Lucas, Marcus noticed that Lyric was starting to nod off.

"Lyric, I really am good here if you want to go to bed. I can bring Lucas in when he gets hungry or falls asleep."

Yawning, Lyric stretched and made herself stand up, conceding defeat, but feeling doubtful. What if Marcus was only *pretending* he didn't mind?

She immediately shook the thought away. This was *Marcus!* She knew better.

However, she cast a furtive worried glance in Marcus' direction and then a thought stopped her. *Why* was he so nice to her? No, he was *more* than merely nice. He was *good* to her. Too good. Better than she deserved. Why did he care so much for her baby? And, as she got the feeling lately, why did he *seem* to care at all about her? She was nothing special. She wasn't dumb enough to believe she actually deserved it. He was too good for her and she was nothing. And the fact that he'd been acting quite the opposite unnerved her.

Reluctantly, Lyric made her way to bed.

Although she didn't fall into a deep sleep, she dozed.

Marcus reveled in the quiet time with Lucas and could understand why some mothers cherished the early morning hours when their newborns awoke to eat.

Marcus couldn't tear his eyes away from Lucas. He spent time taking in Lucas' tiny hands and fingers, the top of his wee head to his baby toes. And Lucas blessed Marcus with another quick grin.

After another hour or so, Lucas' little eyes drifted closed. Marcus sat still, holding Lucas' warm body upright against his chest now, momentarily pressed his face against the top of Lucas' precious head and inhaled deeply. For another half hour, Marcus dozed, ensuring Lucas was sound asleep.

Sighing, Marcus murmured, "I wish I could take care of you always, little buddy."

Marcus finally stood up and quietly took Lucas to Lyric's room to lay him in his bassinette.

The room was in shadows, but lit by the pearl gray dawn breaking outside the window.

Turning, Marcus simply stood, mesmerized by Lyric's sleeping form. She was so beautiful…and she didn't even know it.

He finally willed his feet to move, but as he passed by Lyric to walk out of the room, he paused by her side. Hesitating only a fraction of a second, he bent and kissed her forehead and whispered, "I love you." Then he walked out of the room.

Little did he know that Lyric hadn't been completely asleep.

Lyric had been slightly roused from her light slumber when Marcus came in to lay Lucas down, but she figured she'd fall right back to sleep as soon as Marcus left. However, she'd heard Marcus when he stopped by her side and she had sensed his closeness. She had not dared open her eyes then for fear of breaking the spell. Somehow, she'd sensed something in that stillness, just before Marcus bent to kiss her forehead.

What she hadn't counted on were his sweet, wonderful words that both thrilled her and filled her with dread.

That was why, as soon as she heard her door's soft click, her eyes flew open and filled with tears. She tried convincing herself she was only overly tired. That was why she cried. But, deep down, she knew. It was because she and Marcus could never be. He was too good for her.

''

Several nights in a row produced the same pattern. Lyric couldn't get Lucas to stop crying and go back to sleep so she would, eventually, wake Marcus.

But she never spoke of the kiss that first night. Until one night, overwrought, she could no longer stand keeping the secret.

Marcus had gotten Lucas to quiet down, but Lucas was still awake.

"Go ahead, Lyric, go on to bed. I'll bring Lucas in when he's asleep. I bet you're really tired."

Lyric knew Marcus was only concerned, but she'd had enough and wanted to hear everything from his own lips. So, instead of simply complying, she remarked, "Fine, as long as you don't kiss me this time."

"Wha–"

"I know what you did that first night last week. I wasn't totally asleep."

Lyric cringed, knowing she was being unnecessarily harsh, but she couldn't let her guard down, only to eventually be hurt.

Marcus turned a satisfying, to Lyric, shade of red.

"I'm sorry. I didn't know–"

"That's right; because if you had, you wouldn't have said you loved me, would you?"

Marcus was silenced, knowing she spoke the truth, but it wasn't for the reason she probably thought: that he was ashamed to admit it aloud so he whispered it to her sleeping form. It was because he didn't want to lead her on. He was a Christian and couldn't pursue someone who wasn't. It would let God down. There was no way to explain that without making her more upset. Sighing, he realized he was defeated. "Probably not."

Lyric was shocked to find the sting hurt more than she had thought it would. He may as well have slapped her in the face. That was the language she understood, anyway. At least she knew how he really felt, she tried convincing herself. No illusions.

She was horrified to find tears which choked her and made her squeak, "Well, at least that's cleared up."

At first, Marcus was subdued. "That didn't come out right. I mean, it – it's just that – " he paused, stumped.

Suddenly, he blurted out, "I'm sitting here, holding your son, wishing he were mine. So I might as well say it. I do love you, Lyric. I wish I could have a real claim on you and Lucas. *I* want to be the one to take care of you. Always. I can't marry you now, but I have high hopes that someday I can. So, yes, I love you and that will never change."

Through his little speech, Lyric eyed him skeptically. She couldn't believe what she was hearing! This wasn't right. He shouldn't settle for her!

At first, Marcus thought that maybe Lyric was softening. She looked ready to cry – happy? – tears.

And then, in the next moment, she was spitting out venom. "Don't you *ever* lie like that to me again, Marcus Coulter!" And she slammed her door.

Chapter 17

I climbed up the door and opened the stairs, said my pajamas and put on my prayers, then I turned off the bed and crawled into the light. All because you kissed me goodnight!
Author unknown

The following days and weeks were awkward. Lyric didn't feel ready to apologize just yet for her outburst, however. She was able to confess to herself that she knew Marcus had been serious. Marcus wouldn't lie to her. She *knew* that. Which begged the question – why the outburst? Deep down, she knew. Fear. The only man she had really opened up to had been Austin.

No, she realized, he hadn't been the only one. She had told things to Marcus she had never told Austin. Austin knew nothing of her estrangement from her parents. And he had never asked. She should have known then that Austin didn't really care for her.

'*You are a stupid girl! Accept Marcus! He loves you, you know he does. And you know you've been falling for him, too.*'

Her argument was halted when she remembered the biggest barrier wasn't her. It was God. She remembered well Marcus' words. He had even told her awhile ago – before she felt anything stronger than friendship for him – that he wouldn't date a non-Christian. That counted her out.

"Besides, I don't deserve him!" she resolutely convinced herself aloud.

"What, dear?" Miss Mary asked, as Lyric walked from her room out into the living room.

Lyric had forgotten Miss Mary was there. She had been so preoccupied lately with thoughts of Marcus, she could scarcely remember what she was doing in the moment.

"Uh…nothing…" Lyric dismissed. Then a thought struck.

Lyric had been getting close to Miss Mary for the past few months, as she had cared for Lucas. Especially now that Lyric had recently acquired full-time status. Which meant double the amount on her paychecks! It had felt good to start being able to set aside a little in savings each month. It had felt equally good, and liberating, to tell Marcus she would be paying for Miss Mary from now on.

Marcus had insisted, at first, to pay Miss Mary. And her bank account had forced her to agree.

Plopping down on the couch, Lyric asked now, "Miss Mary, what do you think of Marcus?"

Miss Mary's brown eyes sparkled knowingly. "I think he's a fine young man."

Lyric felt she could confide in Miss Mary and she jumped in with both feet. "A few weeks ago, he told me he loves me."

Carefully keeping her voice neutral, Miss Mary asked, "And what did you say?"

Shame-faced, Lyric admitted, "I stormed out and yelled at him on the way."

Biting back an understanding smile, Miss Mary questioned, "And why did you do that?"

"I–I'm scared. I've never known anyone like him. He's so good. *Too* good! For me, at least."

"Nonsense, Lyric, dear."

Lyric wouldn't be convinced. "Plus, I know he really shouldn't seriously consider me, being that he's a Christian and I'm not."

"But you go to church every Sunday with him."

"Ye-e-es," Lyric agreed, uncertain where Miss Mary was going with her statement.

"So, why aren't you?" Miss Mary asked, frankly.

"Aren't what?"

"A Christian! It's not hard to become one. Acting like one proves challenging, but that's where God's love, help and grace come in."

"I don't know." Lyric wished the conversation was over. It was becoming uncomfortable, but she'd started it. She didn't know it would lead down this path.

"I used to be – sort of." Lyric paused on a thought. "Well, no, not really. I tried using my parents' faith to get me by."

"But that's not how it works, is it?" Miss Mary gently questioned.

Quietly, Lyric answered, "No."

After a few silent moments, Lyric wanted to know, "Miss Mary, are you?"

"For about forty years," the cheerful woman grinned.

Lyric should have known! The plump, older woman, who looked a lot like Granny from Looney Tunes, exuded grace and God.

"I'm surrounded by Christians!" Lyric moaned.

"And that's a bad thing?"

Lyric cringed at how ungrateful she probably sounded. She thought back to Austin and knew there were worse things she could be surrounded by.

"Well, I suppose not. It's just…I…I feel so…I'm not a good person. When I was with Austin and surrounded by that lifestyle, at least I fit in. I was as bad as they were. Now, all I'm surrounded with is Marcus and his family – and you – and you're all – you're just *good.* And I don't belong!"

"Why ever not, dear? We've *all* made mistakes and done things we aren't proud of. Even Marcus and his family. Have they judged you? Treated you harshly, unfairly?"

"No, of course not! I adore all of them. Rachel is so sweet. She's Marcus' sister-in-law. And his mom – wow! And even his brother and dad have made me feel welcomed and accepted – "

"Lyric!" Miss Mary excitedly interrupted. "Did you hear what you said? You said *they made you feel accepted!* My bet is, they would be thrilled to have you join their family. The only thing holding you back is *you*."

Standing, Lyric suddenly felt that she had had as much as she could stand. She leaned down to smother Lucas' face in kisses, as Miss Mary held him in her arms.

"Bye, bye little man!"

Looking at Miss Mary, she stiffly informed her, "I need to leave for work now. Thank you for the – advice."

As Lyric closed the door, she was sure she heard Miss Mary call after her, "Think about what I said."

And, much to Lyric's chagrin, she did.

\\\

That evening, Lyric let herself in when she got home. She wasn't sure if Marcus had beat her home or not. If Miss Mary was still there, Lyric wasn't sure she could stand it.

"Hey, Lyric," Marcus softly called. He was in the chair holding a sleeping Lucas.

Lyric made up her mind then. She had something to tell him that had been a long time coming.

"Marcus," she began, sitting across from him on the couch. "I know I should have said something earlier. I need to apologize for a few weeks ago. I really don't think you were lying. I was – caught off guard, is all. It was…unfathomable, to me, that'd you'd love me. So – I'm sorry."

Marcus merely smiled. "You've already been forgiven, Lyric."

Groaning, Lyric bemoaned, "Not you, too! Yeah, yeah. God loves me and all that, and He's already forgiven me."

Marcus surprised Lyric by laughing outright. Giving her a bemusedly puzzled expression, he explained, "While you're right, actually, that's not what I meant. I meant me! I already forgave you for that."

"Oh," was all she could think to say.

"Miss Mary left food. It's in the fridge. I already ate."

More so for something to do than because she was actually hungry, because she really wasn't, Lyric headed for the kitchen. Marcus made her uncomfortable. No, lately, he downright unnerved her with whatever it was that was going on between them.

Just as she finished eating, Lucas woke up hungry. He was getting so big! He was six months old today.

Lyric planted herself on the couch and she and Marcus settled into their comfortable routine for the evening. He watched a game while she read. Like clockwork, around 10 p.m., Lyric snapped her book shut, intent on bed. As usual, Marcus looked up and offered, "I'll take the first shift."

He already had Lucas in the crook of his arm, having taken him earlier in the evening, shortly after Lyric had been done feeding him. Marcus glanced down at Lucas and was rewarded with a one-toothed grin. Lucas had cut his first tooth on the bottom just last month.

Lucas slept much better now. Yet, his own personal agenda dictated he stay awake for a couple more hours. Then he'd be hungry. Lyric would feed him and Marcus would finally go to bed. After that, Lucas would sleep the rest of the night, until at least six o'clock.

Smiling, Lyric made her usual reply. "Thank you." Then she smothered Lucas' face in kisses and bid Marcus goodnight.

```````````````````````````````````````````````````````````````````````

Lyric had a hard time getting comfortable. She refused to admit it was less physical and more because Miss Mary's words kept running through her head.

Finally, the clock showed Lucas would be wanting her soon, if he didn't already.

Resigned, she got up and padded into the living room. She found Marcus snoring softly, mouth slightly open, and Lucas held close against his chest, also sleeping.

Leaning forward, Lyric meant to simply awaken Marcus. Instead, she was overcome with emotion at seeing the man who meant more to her than anyone else, save Lucas, sleeping so peacefully, yet protectively, with her son, that she softly kissed his forehead.

Never did she imagine it would lead to what happened next…the moment that changed everything.

Leaning down as she was, left hand supporting her on the arm of the sofa, she was at eye level with Marcus. In the next moment, when he opened his eyes, he looked directly into hers.

Slightly off-balance at Marcus' close proximity and frank gaze, Lyric began to straighten. Everything happened so fast then, Lyric was left teetering.

Marcus gently shifted Lucas to his left side, grabbed Lyric's wrist that was supporting her, firmly keeping her in place, and simply met her lips with his.

Caught off-guard, Lyric felt herself leaning in, melting, with the kiss.

Alarm bells sounded in her head, alerting her to the danger this presented. This was all wrong! She had no right to be kissing him! Or did he kiss her? No, she'd started it. She'd kissed his forehead, awakening him.

She immediately jumped up then. Swiftly and calmly, she took Lucas and, without a word or backward glance, she hurried to her room.

```````````````````````````````````````````````````````````````````````

The next morning, both were wary. They only exchanged pleasantries. Until Marcus was about to leave. He cornered her in the kitchen.

"Lyric," he began seriously, "we need to discuss our situation here."

Lyric's heart sank. The kiss! She knew it'd ruin everything. Bucking up, she decided to hear Marcus out.

"I won't – " he seemed stumped.

Incredulously, Lyric noticed he was…blushing!

"After last night, well…I don't trust myself. Around you, that is. That kiss – wow! I'll try to leave you alone, but – I love you. And that kiss – "

"Was inappropriate," Lyric finished. "And I am sorry."

Marcus was gobsmacked. "*You're* sorry?" Shamefaced, he admitted, "*I* did it! I'm the one who started it."

Lyric turned red. Did he not know? If Marcus could 'fess up, so could she. Hesitantly, she told him, "Ye-e-e-es…I woke you up with my, er–"

"I know. You kissed my forehead. Big deal. I took it too far."

"No, Marcus, you didn't. I should have resisted."

Marcus smirked. "Let's call it a draw, then."

Almost immediately, he turned extremely grave. "We need to discuss what to do. I don't want to kick you out of your home, but I think we're in dangerous territory. At least, I am. So…I'll start looking for another place to live."

"But, Marcus, I can't afford this place on my own! I make more, sure, but I don't think I could afford to stay here on my own!"

Lyric panicked. What had she done? All because of a stupid kiss! Except…it *hadn't* been a stupid kiss. It had been wonderful.

"We'll work something out. *I* will work something out. In the meantime, I promise not to touch you. It'd be…inappropriate."

"Inappropriate?"

"Yes. My feelings for you – they change things. I'm beyond merely trying to save you now. And I can't lie to myself anymore, using that as an excuse. I want you to be mine. It sounds selfish, I know, but…I – I desire you for myself. I would marry you – but I realize you aren't in the same place as I am."

"Don't leave, Marcus!" Lyric cringed, hearing the pleading in her voice. "It's *my* fault. *I'm* the one causing the problem. *I'll* leave."

Although, they both knew the only place she could go to on her own was back to Austin. Neither wanted that.

"Don't be silly. You have Lucas now. I'll start apartment hunting tomorrow." He tried sounding reasonable, even as his heart was breaking.

It wasn't as if they wouldn't see each other. There would still be Sunday dinners…he hoped. And then it hit him…this could very well change everything about their relationship. It was more than a mere change of address.

At the door, Marcus turned and offered a sad little smile. And with that, he was gone.

Unexplainable panic assailed Lyric. Why did it bother her so much that Marcus was leaving?

Okay…she knew why. She loved him, too. And she knew they didn't belong together. He was too good for her.

Lucas wiggled and fussed in her arms, clearly ready for his own breakfast.

Sitting down to nurse, Lyric grabbed the phone and, fighting tears of sudden helplessness, she dialed Rachel.

As soon as she heard Rachel's greeting, Lyric dove in. "Hey, Rachel, it's Lyric."

"Hey, Lyric! How are you?"

Biting her lip, Lyric willed the tears away, but they came anyway. "Not too good, I'm afraid," she choked out.

"What's going on, hon? Do I need to come over?"

"No, no, it's – Marcus."

"What did he do?" Rachel's indignant demand would have been comical under any other circumstances.

Instead, Lyric started crying in earnest. "He's – he's – leaving!"

"What? What do you mean?"

Struggling to gain composure, Lyric confessed, "Well, we kissed last night and – "

"Hang on," Rachel interrupted, "you *kissed?!*" She squealed.

"Yes, but – "

"It's about time!"

"Rachel!"

"Sorry, go on."

"He's leaving because of it!"

Rachel sighed. She deduced that Lyric felt it was her own fault. And she guessed Marcus' reasoning – she knew him better than Lyric did. The Coulter men were honorable.

Softly she explained, "Honey, it's because he loves you."

"How do you know?"

"Please – " she lightly laughed, "his mom and I know these things. Anyway, when you first came to live with him, he was rescuing you. Saving you from your situation. From Austin. Now, his feelings have developed and he doesn't want to be tempted by you. To risk compromising you."

"Tempted by me?" Lyric snorted, incredulous. "As if!"

"He is," Rachel insisted. "And it has reached a dangerous point where he would be putting his faith and morals in jeopardy if he continues to live with you."

Lyric grew silent and thoughtful. She was developing a plan. The only way she knew out of the situation was growing in her mind.

"Lyric?" Rachel finally asked, "are you still there?"

"Yes. Only thinking. So…this has nothing to do with me being a bad person?"

"Lyric!" Rachel hissed, aghast, "You're not a bad person." Laughing lightly, she finished, "Just his siren, is all."

Lyric rolled her eyes. Sobering, she quietly asked, "Rachel…do you think – do you think he's too good for me?"

"Pssh!" Rachel answered. "*You're* too good for *him.* Seriously."

"Yeah, right," Lyric breathed, more to herself. Aloud, she decided, "I'll *try* not to take his leaving too personally."

"Well, I'd say it's not about you, but…it sorta is," Rachel chuckled. "Although, not in the way you might think. It's because you love him, too, you know."

Lyric meant to try to deny it, but instead, found herself grousing, "How does everyone know this already?"

Rachel answered simply. "Easy. You two are perfect for each other."

Chapter 18
You know you're in love when you don't want to fall asleep because reality is finally better than your dreams
Dr. Seuss

Lyric wouldn't admit she was pacing as she walked to and fro, bouncing Lucas. She had convinced herself it was because Lucas was fussy and she was trying to lull him to sleep. Except, Lucas was asleep and had been for the last twenty minutes.

Deep down, Lyric knew the truth. Marcus was due home soon and she needed to talk to him. Now!

Glancing at the clock, Lyric resigned herself to finally laying Lucas down. Deciding to be productive in the time she had left before Marcus came home, she went to start some dinner.

She needed something that was time-consuming. So she decided on lasagna. All those layers needed extra time and prep work to prepare so she set to the task.

As she worked, she thought. If she and Marcus couldn't live together, she should be the one to leave. It was only fair. Marcus didn't need to leave his home for her sake!

Where to go, though? That was the question – the one she'd started pondering during her conversation with Rachel.

Although staying in New York seemed ideal, Lyric wasn't sure she could, knowing Marcus would be there – somewhere – forgetting about her; for there had been no indication they would even see each other again. To Lyric, this was more than living in separate places. It was the end.

She would always remember Marcus as having done her an extremely good deed by taking her in and not kicking her out when he found out about Lucas. And she was sure his God was proud of him. But, like so many things, all good things must come to an end.

Tears pooled in her eyes as she popped the lasagna in the oven. It wasn't fair! She loved Marcus, but she couldn't have him.

"You reap what you sow," she bitterly chided herself aloud.

She succumbed to a pathetic pity party. If she deserved Marcus, if she was good enough for him, he would be willing to make it work. Wouldn't he? He simply must not love her back – at least, not as much as she loved him. She was unlovable.

'What about the kiss?' a niggling voice asked.

If Marcus didn't have any sort of feelings for her, why did he kiss her? He wasn't the sort to give out his affection lightly.

He'd said he loved her, but was it only a product of the moment? Again, she knew Marcus wouldn't lie about something like that.

Yet, it made no sense! She was only fit for men like Austin. Surely she wasn't attractive to Marcus – her strawberry-blond hair always managed to look stringy – at least, to her. Her blue eyes were too light to be pretty.

And putting appearances aside, her past alone must be a turn-off. It was too sordid. It was messy. It would almost be regrettable, if it weren't for Lucas.

Lucas...Marcus' love for her son was unexplainable. And *why* was she allowed such a perfect gift? She could barely remember her life six months ago, before Lucas was born.

Lyric turned toward the door at the sound of Marcus arriving home.

Marcus stepped through the door, saw Lyric and flashed her a smile.

They both felt awkward still and Lyric turned to retreat to the safety of her bedroom.

"Lyric," Marcus' voice stopped her.

She didn't turn, but stood still.

"Are you okay? Have you been crying?"

Curse her swollen, red eyes and the tearstains on her cheeks!

Mumbling, she answered, "It's nothing to concern yourself with."

"Is it Lucas? Is he fussing again?" A mixture of worry and sympathy colored his words.

Finally turning, Lyric felt all of her pent up frustrations and misgivings come tumbling out as she spat, "It is none of your concern! I'm not...Lucas isn't...nothing is!"

Marcus now knew the kiss had been a bad idea. However, he had been under the impression Lyric felt the same, otherwise he wouldn't have risked it. He'd hoped she would open up to him. He hadn't expected this – this horrible, cutting, furious reaction.

"I – I – wish it was," he faltered, yet determined to go on. He had something to say and he *would* make her listen this time. "I desperately *want* you to be my concern. *And* Lucas. I *want* you two in my life. Very much."

Lyric's look was stony, but Marcus could see an internal struggle underneath.

"I don't see why," she retorted. "I have nothing to offer you. And I know you can't marry me because I'm not a Christian." Gathering steam now, Lyric seemed unable to stop. "And I'll never be one. I don't want to be!" Defiance had crept into her voice.

Marcus sensed a deeper issue and asked quietly, "You don't want to, or you think you can't?"

Lyric felt heat flush her cheeks. How could he see through her so easily? Her guard was already up, so instead of admitting her fears, she remained silent, resolute.

"You're a smart girl. You'll make the right decision, with or without me. I know you feel rejected by me moving out, but it has nothing to do with that. I'm saving us both from temptation and preserving your innocence."

It had been a long time since anyone had called her smart…and even longer since anyone concerned themselves with her innocence, since it was long gone, anyway. Feeling the tears come, Lyric quickly turned and walked away.

ˏˏ

The day of reckoning came. Marcus found an apartment.

"I can move in September first," he told Lyric.

"That's great!" Lyric mustered fake enthusiasm.

It was the end she had dreaded. After September first, she would never see Marcus again.

Marcus wasn't fooled. "We'll still be friends, Lyric. Right? We'll still see each other. And you'll keep coming to church…? Won't you?"

Lyric swallowed, her throat suddenly tight. She couldn't lie to him. "Um…I don't know." Evasive was good. "It seems friends always mean well when saying these things at good-byes, but neither attempts to stay in touch. It's inevitable – it's called life." She gave a self-deprecating shrug.

Not to be dissuaded, Marcus emphatically countered, "Well, we still have two weeks."

Two weeks for her to finish getting her plans in place.

"I *will* stay in touch," Marcus vowed.

If only he knew he wouldn't be able to keep his promise, Lyric reflected.

Marcus suddenly felt desperate, as if he truly was losing her. It was unsettling. They *would* still see each other. Just in case, he appealed to her sensitive side. "My family would miss you. Think about that. What about my mom and Rachel – and the kids?"

Lyric faltered at that, but quickly regained her composure.

Marcus longed to touch her, to fold her into his arms. His voice took on quiet urgency. "Please, Lyric, don't give up on us! I know you don't understand, but I truly believe God brought us together and He has *some* plan to keep us together, somehow. He knew I'd love you and Lucas and desire to make you my family, permanently. Please…just, *please* don't give up on us!"

Lyric longed to embrace Marcus' words. She longed to believe they could be true. Her guard got in the way.

"Stop it," Lyric begged, frantic. "Please, Marcus, stop! I don't belong with you, I never will! There is no way your God would let you settle for someone like me."

It was too much, all this hoping. Of course she wanted Marcus, but she didn't deserve him. She loved him too much to allow him to stoop down to her level. It had to be good-bye.

Marcus risked a couple of steps toward Lyric; anything that would put him closer to her. He longed to reach out, but he refrained.

"Lyric, *why*? Why do you reject me? I thought I had proved myself to you. You have simply bloomed since moving in here almost a year-and-a-half ago. You aren't the same girl you were then. You've grown, you've evolved. I truly wish you could see your own worth the way I do – the way God does."

Lyric began shaking, overwrought at all that was and all that would be. The emotions made her exhausted. Yet, she could feel a chink in her closely guarded armor fall away – and she couldn't allow that to happen.

The first part of her plan was done.

'*No turning back now,*' she firmly told herself.

Her plan was as good as set in stone. Really, what else could she do? She had no choice but the course of action she had set in place.

Being rejected or, rather, *feeling* rejected makes one act in ways that don't make a whole lot of sense.

Now came the waiting game. The waiting would drive Lyric nuts, she knew. She had always been impatient. Patience wasn't her forte.

She sat silently, contemplating the enormous change that was about to occur in her and Lucas' lives. She could admit to herself she was a little more than scared. And suddenly, she found herself praying aloud!

"G-God?" she began tentatively. "If You're there – and can hear me – I was wondering..." she paused, unsure where to go from there. How did one beseech the heavens, anyway? Especially from one insignificant human. Her troubles seemed pretty small, in the grand scheme of things. Would He even care about her worries? There were more important people He could be listening to in that moment. There were billions of people on earth – who was she to Him? Would He even be listening?

Lyric gathered her courage and finished in a hesitant rush. "Could You, possibly, give me a sign? Something to show I should stay...for Marcus...for Lucas. Maybe stopping this thing I've already started?"

Lyric fretted. Second thoughts and doubts assailed her. What had she done? Had she completely ruined her life? Had she completely ruined Lucas' future?

Trying to remain calm through her overwhelming fears, she finished. "I don't fully know what I've done, God, but I fear I may have made a terrible mistake and don't know how to fix it."

Part of Lyric's hesitancy was because she hadn't fully completed her plan. She had only worked out the first part. The next part was, as yet, unplanned, unknown. And that was scarier than the first part. But, it was done. No way to go back now.

The next two weeks until Marcus left moved painfully slow, and yet, unbearably fast. Lyric wasn't sure she was quite ready to employ her plan yet. It seemed too soon. She had agonized over every detail. She saw no way out of it. God hadn't provided an alternative option. No surprise there, she supposed. Still, she was a little disappointed. She'd hoped He'd intervene and she could have a happily ever after – but this was real life, not some fictitious romance novel.

'Stop the pity party, Lyric. You know you brought this all on yourself. Why would you even think *God would give the likes of* you *a second glance? Besides, you* know *Marcus deserves someone better than you. You're doing him a favor by following through.'*

Secretly, she'd been finishing up last minute preparations. Still, she kept hoping fate, or God, whichever, would intervene.

Two days before Marcus left dawned bright and sunny. Hot, actually. It was Lyric's day of reckoning. The day she had been planning for, dreading and anticipating all at once. She had taken the day off from work – and all the days afterward. In essence, she had quit. Her plan hinged on it. It was all unbeknownst to Marcus, however.

He greeted her with a chipper, "Good morning," as he waited for his toast to pop up. It was just another day to him. He had taken the summer semester off, but still had his job at the bank.

Lyric tried to act as normal as possible as she returned his morning greeting.

"When is Miss Mary going to be here?" Marcus asked.

Sometimes, when it worked, Marcus and Lyric would leave together and travel together to work until they had to part ways.

"Later," came Lyric's breezy lie. And she felt terrible for it.

Another final detail had been letting Miss Mary go. Of course, she had deduced what Lyric was doing and tried talking her out of it, but to no avail.

Marcus' face fell a little. "I thought we would be able to go to work together one last time."

Lyric's heart dropped. She hadn't thought about that. "Oh. No. Sorry," she muttered, suddenly rethinking everything.

Too soon, Marcus was getting ready to leave for work. Hesitating at the door, he looked back. "Hey, maybe we could get a movie and pizza tomorrow night. Sort of as a farewell since tomorrow night will be my last night here with you."

Lyric forced herself to smile cheerily, even as she willed the tears away.

"Ok...so...see ya tonight?"

Lyric gave a small wave and bile rose in her throat as she lied to Marcus for the last time. "Yeah...see ya."

As soon as the door shut, Lyric forced herself to carry out her plan.

She called a taxi then went to gather her things. Two bags each, for her and Lucas. That was it. That was all she could manage to take with her since she'd be alone.

After securing Lucas in his carrier and trundling everything together by the door, she went back to her room for one final item.

Returning to the living room, she placed the letter she had spent hours trying to write, on Marcus' chair, propped up so he wouldn't miss it.

Then, without a backward glance, she hoisted two bags over each arm, picked up Lucas, and left Marcus and his apartment behind.

Chapter 19
'Tis better to have loved and lost than never to have loved at all
Alfred, Lord Tennyson

Marcus noticed the eerie silence first and knew, instinctively, that something was wrong.

Rushing through the living room to Lyric's bedroom, he broke a cardinal rule: violating her privacy.

He yanked out her dresser drawers and found them empty. The same result was produced when he threw open the door to her miniscule closet.

Despair enveloped him when the realization hit. Lyric had left. She took her beautiful, enchanting, smart, funny, exquisite, engaging self off – Lucas with her.

Slowly he trudged back into the living room, fully intending to slump into his chair and ponder his next course of action. The letter stopped him.

He grabbed it and frantically tore it open, reading:

Dear Marcus,

Writing this, and following through on what I have determined I must do, are the two hardest things I've ever faced.

When I left Austin—

Marcus stopped, heart in his throat. His first thought was, *'Oh, no! She's gone back to him!'*

Forcing himself to focus, Marcus read on:

When I left Austin, it was hard to take that step, but it led me to you. Your support and encouragement, even though you didn't know me at the time, gave me the strength and resolve I needed to follow through on the decision to leave that part of my life behind. To you I will be eternally grateful. I hate to think what would have happened, not only to me, but to Lucas, too, had I stayed. It makes me shudder.

'Thank you, God, she isn't going back to him. But, where is she, then?'

Marcus' heart was thudding hard now. He tried concentrating so he could finish the letter and, hopefully, have the mystery solved.

And now to the kiss...I suppose you could say that's why I left. When you told me you had to leave, the morning after the kiss, I felt rejected. I realize now, and should have then, that you weren't rejecting me. I know you told me that, but I'm just now realizing that you were really trying to act in the best interest of both of us. You, to keep your purity intact and me because, somehow, you really do value me. Enough to leave me so you wouldn't compromise either of us. We both know you would have regretted it if anything untoward had happened. And now I realize you would have regretted it more for my sake, than for your own.

Heart in throat, and swallowing the lump there, Marcus continued on.

Marcus, you will never know how truly sorry I am for leaving, but it seemed the only way. It was unfair for you to have to give up your home for me. Your willingness to do that finally made it real—you do love me, just as you said you did!
    And...I love you, too.

Tears pricked Marcus' eyes as he read the beautiful words that were too late.

I am so sorry I didn't have the courage to tell you that in person. I was afraid you wouldn't let me leave and that I'd allow you to talk me into staying.
    In loving you, I had to leave. You deserve someone much better than me. Someone who shares your faith and trust in God — and without my history, without my baggage.
    And, yes, I know you love Lucas, too. More than you know, I regret that he'll never know you. I think I regret

that most of all. He's innocent in all of this and deserves to know one good man. I promise to tell him all about you. And I'll do my best to find someone, someday, that he can look up to. Whoever he might be will never measure up to you, but I'll try for Lucas' sake. I'll tell Lucas about you and call you my hero.

Finally, I regret that the last words I spoke to you were lies. I hate it, in fact. If you can forgive me, please let these be my last words to you:

I will always love you. I will never forget you. You will always be my hero.

Love,

Lyric

For a long while, Marcus lost track of time as he unashamedly spent his tears.

'*Why?'* his whole soul seemed to cry out. He yearned to have Lyric back. And Lucas, too. What could he have done differently to keep her from leaving? To show her he *only* wanted *her* and no one else. That she did deserve to have him because *she* was the best thing to have happened to *him*.

Marcus felt at a loss and didn't know what to do. Where could he start looking? There were endless possibilities! Did she take a train? A plane? A bus? Was she still in the City? Did she leave the City?

The tone of her letter gave him a hunch that she had. Again, where? Did she finally go home to reconcile?

For some reason, he thought not. So, where? Where could she have gone?

Marcus found himself on the phone, calling around, searching for the last person who may have talked to her.

Mr. Butterman only said she had put in her two week's notice and her last day had been two days before. Lyric had never told him where she was going, only that she needed a new life for Lucas and herself. Mr. Butterman had thought that sounded reasonable.

Camilla, Lyric's co-worker friend, intimated that all Lyric had told her was similar to what she'd told Mr. Butterman.

"And that she was thinking of heading north," Camilla added.

"North? As in Canada?"

"I don't know. I suppose."

Marcus could almost hear the shrug of her shoulders. He thanked her and rang off.

'Who else?' he wondered.

Miss Mary! Surely Lyric would have told Miss Mary she was no longer needed, at the very least. Obviously, Miss Mary hadn't been over earlier, as Lyric had said. One of the things she regretted, lying to him.

"Hello?" Miss Mary's cheery voice answered.

"Hello, Miss Mary. It's Marcus Coulter."

"Marcus! Good to hear from you. You're calling about Lyric, I presume."

"How'd you know?"

Miss Mary sighed and clucked her tongue. "She told me she was leaving and I had a feeling she wasn't going to tell you." Softening her voice, she added, "I'm sorry, hon. I tried talking her out of it, but that girl is stubborn. Anything I can do to help?"

"Do you know where she went?"

"Sorry, I don't, but she did mention taking a train."

"A train?"

"Yes, sir. And taking it as far as it would go."

Marcus groaned. It could be *any* train going *anywhere*!

"As far as it would go," Marcus repeated slowly, his mind working. Suddenly, "North!"

"North?" Miss Mary queried.

"Yes! Camilla told me Lyric mentioned she was going north!" Marcus practically shouted. "And the trains all only go as far north as Canada."

It would take time, but it would be doable. He *would* track her down! He was determined.

"Go get her, honey," Miss Mary enthused.

"I will – as soon as I figure out which part of Canada she's gone to."

An unknown knowledge settled in then, convincing him he was on the right track – literally and figuratively.

"Good luck! And keep me posted."

"Will do, Miss Mary."

"And, Marcus?"

"Yes, ma'am?"

"Invite me to the wedding."

＼＼＼

Despite heavy fees, Marcus let his new lease go. Staying where he was would help Lyric find him, should she decide to come back.

Over the next few weeks, when he wasn't working, he would alternately try calling Lyric's cell phone and investigate trains. Their departure times and where they had been headed the day of Saturday, August 30, 2003.

Marcus hadn't realized how many trains went to Canada just from Grand Central Station! And what part of Canada had she headed? And *did* she leave from GCS, or somewhere else?

If only she'd answer her phone!

It had only taken a couple of days for Marcus to tell his family. Mainly because he had waited until Sunday dinner. Of course they wondered where she was when he showed up at church without her. The only explanation he offered was that he would explain later.

As soon as Lynne set down the last dish of food on the table, she promptly sat down and demanded, "Alright, spill it."

Uncomfortably clearing his throat, Marcus told his family all he knew and what he had found out up to that point. Which hadn't been much.

"Oh, Marcus!" Rachel groaned when he was done.

"What?" he asked, bewildered by her slightly scolding tone.

His mother answered, already in tune with Rachel's thoughts. "You scared her off, that's what! Making her feel all rejected like that." She sighed in mock exasperation. "Mind you, I completely agree with you needing to move out...but, love has to be handled delicately."

Mother- and daughter–in–law exchanged pitying glances.

"I'll help you look for her," Levi offered.

"Me, too," Kurt, Marcus' dad, put in.

Marcus had shared his thoughts about the train Lyric had taken and its possible destination.

"I just don't know where to start. So many trains, so little time," he lightly quipped. "Mostly, I've been trying to call her. Of course, it goes right to voicemail."

"Well don't leave one!" his alarmed mother advised.

"I won't!" he defended, then sheepishly added, "Anymore."

Rachel rolled her eyes. "Let her be, for now," she warned. "Or you'll drive her away even further."

Marcus had taken that to heart. After that day, any time he called Lyric, he'd merely hang up, hard as it was. Chagrined, he thought of the messages he'd left already. Four in all, just in the first two days she'd been gone – two each day. All had been begging her to reconsider, pleading that she'd come home, and gushing out his love for her. He cringed. Alright, he conceded, his mom and Rachel had a point. Lyric probably found him pathetic...if she'd even listened to the messages.

Now, nearly a month later, Marcus was starting to feel desperate. Would he *ever* find Lyric? And even if he did figure out what train she took and where she was headed, it didn't answer where she *was*, now.

It took nearly another month before Marcus thought of a possible solution. Andrew! Of course! Surely he'd have an ingenious way of searching and finding things out. He was a computer whiz, after all.

Marcus felt a little dense not to have thought of it sooner. It seemed a call to his best friend was in order.

Saturday, August 30, 2003

Lyric stared out the train's window, anticipation knotting her stomach. Or was it the fear of the unknown? She wasn't sure. All she knew was, she had arrived! She grabbed Lucas' seat and swung the bags over her shoulders. The twelve hour train ride had been brutal, giving her too much time to think. Too much time to doubt whether or not she had made a mistake by leaving.

Several times, she had determined that at the next stop she'd turn right back around and go home to Marcus. *Home.* No. He wasn't her home any longer. She would get a new home for her and Lucas.

Now that she had arrived, she resolved to stay. She had to. Surely, by now, Marcus would have seen her letter. She hoped he could understand and forgive her one day.

As the train began unloading, she murmured to Lucas, "Okay, baby boy, here we go. Time to start our new life."

Terrified, she tried to keep her immediate focus on the very next goal. Finding her hotel. Then, in a couple of days, after she was sort of settled, she'd start her new job.

After that, things were hazy. As were her plans for Lucas. What would she do with him? There were no Miss Marys here. And no Marcuses, either.

She tried swallowing the panic and, once again, refocused her thoughts. *'Let the day's trouble be enough for the day,'* she immediately recited.

Huh. It would seem that even thousands of miles away, Marcus was still rubbing off on her.

Taking a deep breath, she slowly exited the train with her fellow passengers, finally stepping into Toronto, Canada.

Chapter 20
Nothing compares with the finding of true love;
because once you do your heart is complete
Author unknown

"Hello?" The jovial voice did not match Marcus' mood.

"Hey, man, it's Marcus."

"Oh, hey, Marcus! Good to hear from ya! How's it goin'?"

Marcus swallowed hard. He hadn't cried so much since he was a little kid, but felt as if he would start at any minute.

"Um, well…not so good."

"Aw, man, I'm sorry. Anything I can do to help?"

Marcus cleared his throat. "As a matter of fact…" he trailed off. The constriction in his throat tightened.

"What's going on? Marcus, are you okay?" Alarm now colored Andrew's words.

"It's Lyric."

"Okay…?" Andrew's question was left hanging.

"She left. I can't find her. I was hoping you'd be able to help."

"Maybe you'd better start at the beginning, buddy."

Marcus took a deep breath and began again, ending with, "So I was hoping you could use your computer expertise to try to find her. I'm almost certain she took a train to Canada."

"Dude!" Andrew exclaimed. He let out a long, deep breath. "Okay, it's possible, but it's gonna take a while. There are a *lot* of trains. And Canada's huge!"

"Couldn't you just put her name in a data system, or something?" Marcus asked, hopefully.

Andrew laughed outright. "In a perfect world. This isn't some movie, Marcus. Real life doesn't work like that. Besides, that's called hacking. It's illegal."

Turning serious again, Andrew stated, "You've gotta give me at least a month to see how far I can get. And even then, I can't guarantee I'll know where she is. Maybe what train she took and where it went. Okay? I promise, I'll have *something.*"

Resigned, Marcus puffed then blew out his cheeks. "Okay."

He gave a grudging, "Thanks, Andrew," before hanging up.

\\

September 2003

Lyric was proud of herself. She'd had enough forethought to get a temporary visa so she could procure a job. She'd done a phone interview while still in New York for the waitressing job that would now pay her bills. Admittedly, the manager was taken aback that Lyric had wanted a phone interview for a measly waitressing position. Lyric, emotionally raw at the time, had spilled all – probably more than she should have, but the kind manager lady hadn't seemed put off and called back, giving her the job. Lyric wondered if the lady had just felt sorry for her, but was grateful she would have a job when she got there. She'd only needed a temporary work visa, which she promptly got.

Now, she could concentrate on getting Canadian citizenship.

She vaguely wondered if she'd need her passport for that. They hadn't looked at it when she boarded the train in New York nor when she had got off in Toronto. She thought she heard somewhere they were really only concerned about it when re-entering the States.

No matter, she had to be there a few years before she'd be eligible to apply for citizenship but, starting early could only help, she reasoned. Besides, it made her decision to stay feel that much more permanent. She had been in Toronto for only about a month.

The hardest part had been finding a childcare facility for Lucas. It had caused her great anxiety and made her feel Marcus' absence keenly.

She hadn't understood the feeling, at first, because it made more sense for her to miss Miss Mary rather than Marcus. At least, that's how she *thought* she should feel. Despite her best efforts not to, she'd analyzed her feelings and found she missed the completeness she felt with Marcus. Weirdly enough, Marcus had felt like family. When it had been her, Lucas and Marcus, she felt like she had a little place in the big world. It had felt right. It had felt like – *home.*

In the end, Lyric had hired a babysitter through a nanny agency. While they specialized in nanny placement, they also helped with finding more short-term childcare, as well.

There were times Lyric allowed herself, briefly, to reminisce about Miss Mary and the Coulters. After that first time, however, while worrying about childcare, Lyric had not permitted herself to think about Marcus. It was still too painful and much too sad.

\ \

"Alright, Andrew, it's been at least a month. Do you have anything to tell me? Do you have a report?"

Marcus had taken the weekend to visit Andrew in Boston. He had needed to feel as if he were *doing* something to find Lyric, not merely sitting at home, twiddling his thumbs, waiting for Andrew's call.

Right then, he was sitting across from Andrew in a diner in Boston.

"I'm getting closer. I've narrowed it down to two trains." He paused for suspense, leaning closer. "Judging she's in Canada."

"I'm fairly certain. It's just something in my gut telling me and I've learned to trust that instinct."

"Well, then, *if* she is in Canada, she's – "

Marcus instinctively leaned forward, interrupting Andrew and scarcely breathed, "Where?"

"Either in Toronto or Montreal."

Curious, Andrew leaned forward himself. "Is she worth it? I only met her the one time. She seemed sweet." He hesitated. "Before I go any further in trying to locate her, I only want to be sure all my labor won't be in vain."

"She is *absolutely* worth it, man. I'm worried sick about her and Lucas. I can't eat. I can't sleep. I'm devastated she left. In short, I love her! If only I had found out sooner, I could have stopped her from leaving."

Andrew contemplated Marcus for a bit, then agreed. "I'll do everything I can, but the holidays are coming. That will hinder progress."

Marcus felt a lump in his throat, thick with despair. Would he never find her?

Thursday was Thanksgiving. This year, he'd rather skip the holidays, thinking back to the previous Christmas – and Lyric's kiss.

Quietly, Marcus answered, "Thank you."

,,,

The whole month of November, Marcus had been on the phone daily with either Andrew, his dad, Levi, his mom or Rachel, seeking advice, words of comfort or even encouragement. He could admit that he was a broken man.

And, from the men, he was also trying to determine what course of action he should take, what he could *do* next.

From the women, he gleaned insight into how the female mind worked and what Lyric might have been thinking, where she might have decided to settle.

Shortly after returning from Boston, Marcus was talking to Rachel. During the conversation, she had a suggestion he had not yet thought of – and probably never would have on his own.

"Have you tried finding her parents? Maybe they would have some insight into where she may be. Besides, you know, or knew, where their daughter was. A daughter they haven't seen or heard from in five years, or so. I can't imagine either Hailey or Sydney leaving home and not knowing where they were. Well…you know, I'm sure, a taste of that – with Lucas.

"Anyway, I'm sure her parents would appreciate a call, in any case. Even if they have nothing to add."

Marcus was stunned. Why hadn't he considered this?

"Thanks, Rachel. I think I will."

Hanging up, Marcus contemplated what he could do to find Lyric's parents.

He had to go off the assumption their last name was Bell, too. Had Lyric ever mentioned their names? He couldn't remember.

Something niggled at the back of his mind.

Vaguely, he also wondered if he still had Lyric's rental agreement.

Still mulling over what his brain was trying to conjure, he padded to his bedroom and fished the lockbox out from underneath his bed. Pawing through his keys, he found the key to the box and opened it. He rifled through the papers until he found it. Lyric's rental agreement.

Staring at it, he tried to remember what was working his mind.

Turning to the last page, he looked at Lyric's signature. She had signed it, *Lyric J. Bell.* The "J", what did it mean?

The worrying in his brain grew stronger. Quickly flipping to the first page and her personal information, Marcus read Lyric's full name. *Lyric Jacqueline Bell.*

"I'm named for my mom. At least, my middle name is," came flashing back.

That was it! That's what he'd been trying to remember! He now had Lyric's mom's name! Jacqueline Bell.

He knew they lived in upstate New York. Hopefully a Google search of upstate New York would turn up a Jacqueline Bell and the place Lyric had grown up. Wherever that was....

The next day, he was sharing the results of his find over the phone with his mom.

"There are over thirty Jacqueline Bells in upstate New York, mom! Not as bad as I expected...but, that's all judging that *one* of them is *the* one. Nevertheless, I'll have to wait until next week, with Thanksgiving being tomorrow and all, before I can start calling."

"I'm so glad you found *something*, though, honey."

"I really hope Andrew can find Lyric soon. I want her home before Christmas."

There was a moment of silence. Enough that it made Marcus nervous. "What? What is it, mom?"

"Well..." Lynne trailed off. Taking a breath, she tried again. "Well, it's very obvious to everyone you love Lyric and we all have suspected for a while that she is in love with you, too." She paused again, seeming to pick her words carefully.

"I think all that has already been established. So...what?"

"You need to proceed with caution, Marcus. Lyric left because she was scared of her feelings and because she doesn't feel worthy of you."

"I know, mom, but when I go after her, she'll see how much she means to me. She'll know how much I love her."

"And that will be yet *another* thing you have done for her."

Marcus was clueless. "Yeah? And?"

"What has she given you, Marcus?" Lynne asked gently. "No doubt she'll still feel unworthy because she feels inadequate. She'll feel she has nothing to offer you in return."

"That's enough, that's all I need of her!" Marcus protested. "All I want is her. I'll take her and nothing else, if she'll have me."

"Yes, *I* know that, Marcus." Lynne sounded sad. "Son...she needs to feel she has something to offer *you*, if you want her to come home. If you go after her, saving her yet again...well, there's a very real chance she'll resent you."

Frustrated and desperate tears mingled in Marcus' eyes. Taking a shaky breath, his voice caught as he insisted, "But, Mom, *I love her.* I want her to come home." His voice broke on the last part.

Lynne was quiet. Then, "I know you do, Son. But you may need to wait for her to come to you. If she loves you as much as you love her, she's probably just as miserable as you are."

Absurd as it seemed, Marcus felt a tiny spark of hope at that. "You really think so?" he asked almost eagerly.

Chuckling, Lynne answered, "It's a very real possibility. I would say she is probably feeling much the same way. And, Marcus?"

"Yeah, Mom?"

"I've seen the way that girl has looked at you, especially in the last few months. She loves you and, I bet, right about now, ready to come home."

Marcus thought on his mom's words a lot, hoping they were true. Hoping that she was right.

\`\`

Present

Lyric looked out her apartment window again. In the distance, she could see Lake Erie. She had always found the ocean calm and peaceful. Even now, as she looked at the open water, she felt a bit more serene than she had a few moments ago.

Lucas was teething and hadn't been sleeping well. He had been up several times the night before and now he had started in on his fussing again. Lucas seemed inconsolable and Lyric tried the best she could to calm him down and make him feel better, but nothing worked. She had frozen washcloths and teething rings. She had even tried small bits of ice, but none of it worked. She had rubbed Orajel on his tender gums and had given him baby Tylenol, but still he fussed.

While rubbing the Orajel, Lyric had discovered the rubbing seemed to feel good because he had stopped fussing while she did that. As soon as she had stopped rubbing, he had begun his crying again. So, now, she was rubbing his gums and standing, staring out the window, absentmindedly gazing at the ocean and thinking of where she had been this time last year.

This time last year, Lynne and Rachel had thrown her a beautiful baby shower.

Lucas. Her eyes flickered to him. He had changed everything. If it wasn't for him, she would probably still be with Austin. The thought made her shudder.

Lucas had saved her life. Lucas and Marcus.

Marcus had given her the resolve to stick to her decision and not go back to Austin.

Lucas had given her the courage to leave in the first place.

Both of them had saved her life, no question. Reality was, she could be dead. Austin's beatings had left her unable to move on more than one occasion. Just after she had found out she was pregnant, she had elicited Austin's wrath because she had forgotten to pick up some beer on her way home from work. She had been tired and hadn't felt well, thanks to her all-day morning sickness. Thankfully, he hadn't kicked her in the stomach that time. It had been a favorite place to concentrate his rage. Instead, he had focused on her face. And that was the last time he had been able to lay a hand on her. Less than a week later, she saw Marcus' ad. In the meantime, she had done everything exactly as Austin wanted, careful to steer clear of his wrath. If he hadn't been drunk or stoned most of the time, he probably would have suspected something. As it was, he didn't and, mercifully, Lyric was able to make her escape.

"Thank you, God," she mused aloud, then stopped. Had she said that aloud? Was she *actually* thanking God? When had she ever done that before?

'*Marcus,*' she seethed inwardly, gritting her teeth.

Sure, she'd been going to church with him, but she hadn't made it personal, or anything. It had been a means of seeing his family.

But now…perhaps it was because she was utterly alone for the first time in her life and *had* to rely on God, to some degree. She knew it had to be more than just chance that she had gotten her job—and over the phone in another country, nonetheless! Nor was it mere chance that her temporary visa had been processed without one little hitch.

Glancing one last time toward the water, Lyric felt tears gather as she now thought of whom she had left across the expanse of water. She turned away from the window. It only reminded her of how very far away she was from those who loved her and cared about her.

Not for the first time, Lyric felt the regret wash over her and the sorrow at how she had left. Recently, she had finally begun to open her heart to the memories of Marcus, as painful as they were. She dearly missed him.

Looking down at the sleeping face of Lucas, she kissed him and nuzzled his neck. A pain shot through her as she realized Marcus wouldn't be there for Lucas' first Christmas or birthday. And she *knew* Marcus would give anything to be. Even if it meant he would be walking up and down the short hallway, rubbing Lucas' gums. And he would do it gladly.

She sighed, resigned. Just another way she had successfully disappointed him, she was sure.

For the seeming thousandth time, she wondered, *'What have I done?'* More importantly, could it be undone?

Chapter 21

Look not mournfully into the past, it comes not back again.
Wisely improve the present, it is thine. Go forth to meet the
shadowy future without fear and with a manly heart
Henry Wadsworth Longfellow

Marcus spent the weeks after Thanksgiving searching for Lyric's parents. He suddenly found himself obsessed with the only two people in the world who knew Lyric better than he did. When he finally located their phone number, however, what would he say? How could he explain what he needed to know? Would they welcome his call or view him as an intrusion?

He picked up the phone to call yet another Jacqueline Bell. He only had three phone numbers left to try.

It started out the way all of the other calls had.

"Hello," a friendly voice answered.

"Mrs. Bell? Mrs. Jacqueline Bell?"

"This is she."

He still got nervous at this part not knowing if they'd hang up on a stranger. So far, no one had. They had all been surprisingly polite.

"Er, um, you don't know me. My name is Marcus Coulter."

"Hello, Mr. Coulter. How may I help you?" Her answer was cooly polite.

After twenty-seven calls, he would have thought it would get easier to say the next words. It wasn't. He still stuttered.

"Is your daughter – I mean, do you have a daughter? Named Lyric?"

Unexpectedly, Marcus heard a sharp intake of breath and then a soft, "Lyric?"

Marcus was tongue-tied. He realized at that moment that he hadn't really expected to find the right Jacqueline Bell.

"Um, yes," he tried to explain. "Well…I don't know where she is now…" he trailed off, realizing he was going to start babbling.

"I'm sorry, Mrs. Bell. Let me start again. Up until about three-and-a-half months ago, she was living with me. Since May of last year, in fact."

His face suddenly turned red as he realized what it might have sounded like to her, Lyric's mother. "Completely innocent, I assure you."

Marcus heard a rustling on the other end.

"Hold on, Mr. Coulter, would you?"

"Sure."

He heard her muffled, excited voice. "Will! I have news! Of Lyric!"

More scuffling and then she was back. Excitedly, she asked, "You know Lyric? She's been living with you? I – I'm just so…dazed!"

A click sounded in Marcus' ear, as if another phone had been picked up.

"My husband's on the phone in the other room. Will you please tell us all you know?"

"Hello, Mr. Bell," Marcus greeted. "My name is Marcus Coulter. As I was telling your wife, I know Lyric. She had been living with me since a year ago May – completely innocently, as a roommate. She left at the end of August."

Marcus cringed. It was still too painful to relive the memory.

"Anyway, I think it may be prudent if we could meet in person so I can explain everything," Marcus suggested. "I think it only fair that I tell you what I know, but it's a long story."

"Mr. Coulter, please, when can you meet?" Jacqueline asked eagerly, clutching the phone tightly. She could scarcely believe they had news of Lyric! And they would have more!

"When and where would you like to meet?" William Bell asked.

"I live in the City," Marcus informed them, not knowing if he should offer to meet them in their home. They knew nothing about him, however, and may not want him in their home. Yet, they may not feel comfortable coming to his apartment, either.

Tentatively, he told them, "We could meet at my apartment, for privacy, but I understand if you would rather meet somewhere more public. I am only thinking of discretion."

'A young man calling his former roommate's parents purely to let them know of her whereabouts is a decent thing to do,' William mused to himself.

Aloud, "Your apartment is fine, Marcus. Thank you for the call. Is tomorrow too soon to meet?"

Marcus didn't give himself a moment for hesitation. Having Lyric's parents know all that he knew about her was very important to him. They deserved this.

"Tomorrow sounds perfect, Mr. Bell."

\\

Marcus was nervous as he waited for the knock on his door, announcing the arrival of the Bells. He prayed the meeting would go well.

'Please, God.'

He glanced at the clock. 4:45. He only had fifteen more minutes until the appointed time. He had already set out cheese and crackers, some fruit and bottles of water for a light snack. Simply, there was nothing left to do, but wait.

And time dragged on.

Finally, he heard the sound he'd been anticipating.

Opening the door, he ushered the couple inside with a polite, "Hello, Mr. Bell, Mrs. Bell. Won't you please come in?"

Quickly, Marcus noticed that William Bell was formidable. No wonder he hadn't seemed to mind coming to a stranger's apartment. Even in New York City. He had a commanding presence and Marcus bet no one would dare cross him – and if they did, he could take care of himself.

If Marcus hadn't talked to him first over the phone, he would be too scared now to even open his mouth! Since he had, he had heard the soft tenor of Mr. Bell's voice and his overwhelming concern for his daughter. So Marcus knew he wasn't *all* intimidating.

Still, William Bell had the bearing and demeanor of someone who had been in the military, which was very likely. Lyric hadn't said much about her parents, not to mention the smaller details of whether or not her dad could kill a person with his pinky finger!

Marcus suddenly wished they had had *that* conversation.

Mr. Bell's sandy-colored hair was in a military crew cut, lending to the very real possibility, as did his muscled frame, broad shoulders and clean-shaven face. His brown eyes looked as though they could pierce right through to a soul, causing the helpless victim of his gaze to spill all of their country's secrets.

At present, however, they looked burdened, as if he had a great load to bear.

'*Lyric. Right.*' Marcus forced himself to focus on the purpose of their visit. '*We should get to it.*'

Marcus led them to the sofa and saw that they were comfortably settled.

Jacqueline seemed to fit the look of a military wife. Elegant would be how Marcus would describe her. She seemed to be close to her husband's age – possibly late-50s. Beside her husband's dominant figure, her slim frame had regally come to his shoulder. Jacqueline's reddish-blond hair was a tribute to her daughter's looks and was caught up in a formal chignon. Her daughter's light blue eyes looked back at Marcus, open and friendly. That she was Lyric's mother was clearly evident. She was merely a more mature version of Lyric.

The two were dressed in what one would expect of the upper class.

William wore khaki slacks and a white polo shirt with nary a wrinkle and brown dress shoes.

Jacqueline had on a periwinkle pantsuit over a crisp, white blouse and a strand of pearls at her throat, finished by low, black heels.

Marcus settled in a chair, sitting on the edge of his seat, resting his forearms on his knees, hands clasped. "Thank you so much for coming," he began. "As I said over the phone, this will be much better in person."

"Please tell us what you know," Jacqueline burst out, the suspense too much. "We've missed our little girl so much!"

Marcus' palms were slick with sweat. He rubbed them on his jeans. "If it's alright, I'll just start at the beginning. The day I first met her."

William broke his stoic posture and leaned forward eagerly. Gesturing with a raised hand, he spoke. "Please proceed."

Licking his lips, Marcus began, speaking slowly at first, trying to collect his thoughts.

"Lyric came to me in late May of last year. I had put out an ad looking for a roommate. I was clear in stating that I was a Christian so there would be no misunderstanding for those that applied. Never did I imagine a *girl* would apply! In fact, she was the only one."

Marcus paused, knowing he would have to share Lyric's back story so they would understand why he had Lyric living with him. So they would understand it was for her protection. So they would understand it was innocent...at first. That what happened later was unforeseen.

How hard was this going to be for them to hear?

Marcus took a deep breath, preparing to shatter their world. "I had open interviews for potential roommates. I had set aside a day to have interested applicants come here to meet me. I had a series of questions I asked each one. Well, Lyric showed up that day and she – " he stopped. How could he possibly explain the state she was in to her parents? But it was that very reason that led him to make the decision he did, changing their lives forever. Her parents deserved to know.

He faltered. "Well, uh, she showed up, looking – there's no easy way to say this."

"What? *Please*! We've waited so long to hear news – *any* news – of our daughter," Mrs. Bell begged Marcus.

"Well..." Marcus hesitated. Slowly, he began again. "She was, uh, battered and bruised."

Both parents gasped aloud.

"Who did – ? How did – ? *Why?*" Mr. Bell spluttered, his face red with anger.

Trying to stay on course, Marcus decided the best approach was to be matter-of-fact. "She had a horrible black eye. It looked a few days old, in coloring, but it was quite atrocious to look at."

Lowering his voice in intimacy, Marcus relayed, "I don't mind telling you, Mr. and Mrs. Bell, that I was livid at whoever it was who had done that to her – to *any* woman. At the time, I didn't know who it was, but I suddenly felt very protective of her. Like she was my sister.

"It was an act of God, literally, that kept me from following her home and confronting whoever had done that. And I can honestly say, I am *not* usually a violent person. It was nearly impossible for me to even have her leave, not certain she'd make an escape from whomever this monster was."

"Marcus," Jacqueline breathed. "Surely you saved her life! We will forever be grateful to you."

Marcus held up his hand, knowing what was still to come. "Please, I deserve no gratitude. I only acted in a way I would hope someone would treat my sister – if I had one."

There were a few moments of silence as the Bells absorbed the news of their daughter.

Tentatively, Marcus broke the quiet, needing to tell all. "Lyric told me you two are Christians?"

"Yes, we are," Mr. Bell answered.

"I must apologize, then, for allowing her to live with me. At the time, I was acting out of concern for her safety and well-being. I honestly felt compelled by God to extend the offer to her."

"No apology necessary," William was quick to offer the young man who had probably saved his daughter's life. "I trust you did not take advantage of her."

"No, sir, I did not." Marcus paused, then colored. "At least, not in the way you may think."

In that moment of Marcus' complete, vulnerable honesty, Jacqueline Bell fully and completely warmed to the young man. Eyes on Marcus, she eagerly leaned forward, unconsciously mimicking her husband's earlier action. "I sense there's more to this story."

"Yes, ma'am."

"Well, then, tell us."

"It was about a month to six weeks after Lyric moved in that she made a startling announcement. The reason, in fact, that compelled her to make the decision to leave her abusive boyfriend, Austin. She was pregnant."

The two Bells exchanged gaping glances.

"We're grandparents?!" Jacqueline exulted.

Momentarily distracted, Marcus pulled out his wallet and opened it. He extracted a few pictures. Handing one to Jacqueline, he explained, "This one is a picture they took at the hospital. He's only a few hours old here."

William Bell visibly softened as he stared at the picture of his grandson. Sitting next to his wife, it was clear they were both in awe.

"He's adorable!" Jacqueline exclaimed.

Marcus handed them another picture. "This was taken at the end of April. He was barely three months old."

They ogled the picture greedily.

"Look at his baby blues," William marveled. "So like his mother."

Marcus produced a third picture. "And this was taken at the beginning of August. He had just turned six months the week before."

This was the last picture he had of Lucas and treasured it most. Not because it was the last photo taken of Lucas, but because it depicted Lucas and Lyric, cheek-to-cheek, their matching blue eyes sparkling, full of joy.

"Oh, look at those kissable, squeezable cheeks!" Jacqueline laughed. "And look at all of that blond hair. He looks just like Lyric did at that age – he looks just like Lyric!"

Jacqueline swiped at tears edging her lower lashes. "And she looks good – so – well!"

Turning to Marcus, sincerely she told him, "Thank you for taking such obviously good care of her."

Marcus glanced away guiltily.

"And they've left?" William questioned softly, noticing Marcus' glance.

"Yes, well, um, that's actually my fault, you see. Um...well, I'll continue, if you would like."

"Yes, please, go ahead," William urged.

Jacqueline started handing the photos back. Marcus waved her off. "You keep those." He knew she needed them more than he did. Even the last one.

"Are you sure?"

"Yes." Marcus stood. "If you'll excuse me for a minute?"

Will answered. "Sure."

Marcus quickly went to his bedroom and grabbed the framed photo on his nightstand. Bringing it back to the living room, he told Jacqueline, "I have this." He handed it to her

It had been taken at his parents' house. It had started out as a candid of Lyric and Lucas. Out of silliness, Marcus had leaned over toward Lucas, clearly in the picture, meant to tease his mom. He had fully expected her to shoo him out of the way. Instead, she had said, "Oh! What a cute picture."

At that moment, Lucas had turned his head toward Marcus and put a chubby little hand on his cheek, both grinning at each other, while Lyric had looked on with a smile, and Lynne had snapped the picture.

"My mom took it. See, after several months of living here, Lyric decided to start attending church with me. I go to the same one I grew up in, so my family met her and fell instantly in love with her."

'*As did you,*' Jacqueline silently added, noting the smitten look on Marcus' face as he spoke of Lyric. She felt she now had a pretty good idea of where all of this was headed.

"You got her back to church?" William was in shock.

"Not really," Marcus mumbled, embarrassed. "I suspect it was more God's doing. I just happened to be the vessel He used."

Jacqueline looked wistful. "I'm so glad she found family."

"My mom and sister-in-law, Rachel, even threw her a baby shower. It was the Saturday after Thanksgiving last year." Now it was Marcus' turn to be wistful.

Shaking himself, he continued. "I have an older brother, Levi. He and Rachel have four kids, two of each. One of each being a twin. And my parents are still married, too."

Now came the hard part, as far as Marcus was concerned.

"So...as time went on, we did encounter a couple of problems with Austin. They were more like nuisances, really, but I set him straight. Without *too* much violence," Marcus half-smiled. His heart was beating hard in anticipation of telling the rest of the story.

Softly, Will broke in with tears in his eyes. "Thank you for standing up for my little girl, since I couldn't."

Again, Marcus shied away from the praise. "I was only protecting her. Especially with the baby due and all."

Marcus flashed a grin, sidetracked again. "I got to be there when he was born. In the room and everything!"

Eyeing Lyric's dad, he quickly amended, "But I didn't *see* everything." William smiled, amused.

"What's his name?" Jacqueline asked then.

"Oh! I'm sorry! I thought I had said. It's Lucas James."

"I love that name. Lucas James." Quietly musing, Jacqueline wondered aloud, "I wish I knew how she came to choose it."

"Oh, I know that one," Marcus confessed sheepishly. "It's because of me."

Both parents fixed him with an inquisitive gaze.

"Oh?" Jacqueline asked.

"Yes, well, um…she chose Lucas because it sounded sort of similar to Marcus…the ending, anyway. And James is also my middle name."

"She must care for you a great deal."

"Yes, ma'am."

"And you must care for her a great deal."

"Yes, ma'am." Talking over the sudden lump in his throat, he boldly declared, "I love her."

Impulsively reaching forward and laying a hand on his arm, Jacqueline spoke directly, but kindly. "That is quite obvious, young man."

Marcus risked a glance at Mr. Bell and saw a small smile playing about his lips.

"And where is she?" Jacqueline carefully probed, knowing this was the crux of their whole reason for being there.

Shame-faced, Marcus admitted, "I don't know. My feelings for her progressed, turning to love. It was then, I think, that I began scaring her, forcing her to face her own feelings for me. She kept repeating that I was too good for her. That she didn't deserve me. That because of her past, she could only deserve someone like Austin." Marcus became pleading. "Mr. and Mrs. Bell, please believe me when I say I tried *hard* to convince her otherwise. I told her often that simply wasn't true. Yet, she didn't believe me and she also felt as if she owed me something." Marcus looked a little chagrined. "My mom had to explain that one to me.

"Since I had 'rescued' her, taken her in, helped care for Lucas, she felt she had nothing to give me in return." Marcus became desperate then. "She *did*, though! She gave me herself, in love, by letting me in. And, incredibly, she shared Lucas with me! She gave me so much, she just didn't realize it. She couldn't see it. She is *everything* I never knew I've always wanted!"

Jacqueline's eyes had welled up and spilled over. At Marcus' last declaration, she chuckled. "Do you write for Hallmark, Mr. Coulter?"

Will joined in then, too. Marcus echoed the mirth, wiping his moist eyes in embarrassment.

"On Lucas' six-month birthday, we kissed. Or, rather, *I* kissed *her.*" Marcus warily gauged Mr. Bell's reaction.

It wasn't hostile, so he proceeded. "I know now that I scared her. I scared myself a little, to be honest. Every day would have been a battle to overcome temptation.

"The morning after it happened, I told Lyric what I had to do and why. She *seemed* to understand. I started immediately to make arrangements and find another apartment. A couple of days before I was set to move out, she was gone. Just a note left behind, that was it." Marcus willed himself to hold together. The thought of Lyric leaving him still elicited tears.

By sheer grit, he continued. "I have to tell you, I did ask her to marry me. More than once, actually. It was more a topic of conversation, really, rather than the proper proposal it should have been."

Looking fully at William Bell, Lyric's father, he apologized. "I'm sorry I kissed your daughter. And I'm sorry I didn't obtain your permission to ask her to marry me. Sir, if I ever have the privilege to do it again, properly, may I please have your daughter's hand in marriage?"

It took William Bell a few attempts to clear his throat before answering. "Well, you have certainly proved you're worthy...son."

Chapter 22
Ay me! Sad hours seem long
William Shakespeare

Jacqueline jumped in then. "Maybe we should share a bit about Lyric's past."

Shocked, Marcus wondered at Mrs. Bell's sudden openness. Sure, he felt a bit more intimate with them, having shared what he knew of Lyric. He hadn't expected the act to be reciprocated. They certainly didn't owe *him* any explanations.

Jacqueline began. "We had tried for over a dozen years to conceive. Back then, there weren't as many options to try as there seem to be today. We got to the point where our hopes of ever getting pregnant were pretty much dashed."

Marcus listened and watched Mrs. Bell closely. Her emotions seemed just under the surface. Yet, she did well at keeping them at bay.

"We finally decided to look into adoption, when I found out I was pregnant with Lyric."

Turning to focus directly on Marcus now, she asked, "Remember how I asked about Lucas' name? How I was interested in how it was chosen?"

"Yes," Marcus dutifully answered, knowing there was more to come.

"I've always loved names. The history behind them. How people come to choose the names they do.

"My own name is special because I was named after my grandmother – my mother's mother.

"Anyway, when we found out God, indeed, was blessing us with our own child, it felt as though He was smiling down on us from heaven. My favorite verse quickly became Zephaniah 3:17."

Closing her eyes, a look of pure serenity washed over her face, as she recited, "The Lord your God is with you, the Mighty Warrior who saves. He will take great delight in you; in His love He will no longer rebuke you, but will rejoice over you with singing."

Opening her eyes, Jacqueline positively grinned. "In that verse, I knew the name we would bestow on our daughter. Lyric. Lyric Jacqueline, for my grandmother, the godly matriarch of our family, and for God's blessing."

Marcus sat, transfixed by Jacqueline's recitation and story of Lyric's legacy.

"We raised her to love God," William broke in then. "Or, so we thought.

"As a young girl, she learned verses and loved Sunday School. She talked of God often and seemed guided by the Bible in her decisions. She was baptized shortly after she turned twelve."

It was Jacqueline's turn to talk. "It was her freshman year of high school when we first noticed a change. She had a particular friend, Jenny, whose family was atheist. We didn't relish the thought of the ungodly influence, but Lyric seemed so sure of her faith in God, even at that young age, we thought that, perhaps, Lyric could positively influence Jenny. We did, however, caution Lyric about her friendship, explaining that, while she could be a good friend to Jenny, her *closest* friends should be other Christians.

"Unfortunately, she allowed herself to get caught up in the alternative lifestyle of not just questioning God, but everything, in general.

"At first, we thought it was merely a rebellious stage. It wasn't until it was too late that we realized it was more serious.

"And then, one day, we woke up to find she was gone. A note was left, but it didn't convey much."

Jacqueline delicately wiped her eyes with a napkin at the painful memory that was the last they had of their daughter.

The gloomy atmosphere prompted Marcus to try to interject some encouragement.

Quietly he stated, "Her upbringing wasn't forgotten, Mr. and Mrs. Bell. She chose to respond to my ad *because* I am a Christian. And she had started going to church with me. Before I ruined everything with that kiss, I think she was getting close to wanting to follow God again."

Marcus hung his head, so didn't see the spark of hope that lit their eyes.

"I regret scaring her off," Marcus murmured more to himself, full of shame. "I am truly sorry for taking advantage of her in that way."

"Well, son," William began, "putting that aside, it seems as though you were the best thing to have happened to her in New York. For that, as my wife said earlier, we will always be grateful to you. Furthermore, it is exceedingly obvious that you love her. I have no doubt, if given the chance, you will marry her. Don't give up hope. We didn't, and you happened along."

Marcus couldn't quite meet Mr. Bell's eyes. The despair seemed suddenly too great to bear.

"We'll find her," William was adamant.

Marcus peeked up. "I have been trying, sir. I have a friend working on it. He's somewhat of a computer expert. He's tracked her to Canada – Montreal or Toronto, he thinks. That's all that's known at this point. My mom and sister-in-law have cautioned me about pursuing her, even if she is found."

Smiling wryly, Jacqueline agreed. "Sounds like Lyric. When she has her mind set on something, or she's convinced herself of something, if you try to deter her or talk her out of it, she will only resist more and resent you for it. Your mother and sister-in-law sound like very wise women."

"They are," Marcus smiled.

"For the time being, we'll have to be patient awhile longer. I wouldn't be surprised if she showed up back here someday, seeking forgiveness. I suspect she would have tried that with Will and me if we hadn't been so hard on her.

"I'd wager she's in love with you, too, though. That's why she left; to give you a chance to change your mind about her. She probably didn't know it when she left, but she probably does now."

The Bells and Marcus chatted a bit longer and then exchanged information, promising to keep in touch, regardless of what happened with Lyric.

At the door, Jacqueline grabbed Marcus' hand and squeezed it. "Again, thank you *so much*, Marcus, for relieving our minds concerning Lyric. Despite whether or not she wants to see us again, I sincerely hope she comes back to you. I know you'll take good care of her and Lucas."

She hugged Marcus then. Pulling back, she had tears in her eyes. "And thank you for the pictures."

After he closed the door to the Bells, he reached for the phone to call Andrew.

"Hey, man, it's Marcus," he greeted when Andrew picked up.

"Hey, Marcus! I was just gonna call you." Without preamble, he went right on to say, "Listen, I've found Lyric!"

Marcus gripped the phone tighter. "You did? Where is she?"

"Toronto."

"Toronto, *Canada?*"

"Yep. I *told* you it was either there or Montreal. I have her address and everything!"

Marcus was silent, deliberating. His mom and Rachel's words, joined by Mrs. Bell's, flew through his mind. "I think…I may…leave her alone. Knowing *where* she is, is enough…for now."

"Ok…" Andrew answered uncertainly.

"I've been given some advice from my mom and Rachel…and Lyric's mom. I will try to be patient and wait to see if she comes to me."

"Lyric's mom?" Andrew gasped at the new development.

"Oh, yeah. I found her parents! In fact, they just left, right before I called you."

"Well…wow!" Andrew breathed.

"Yeah," Marcus agreed.

"Okay, man, well, give me a holler if you change your mind and want her information."

"'Kay, thanks, man. Will do."

Now all Marcus had to do was resist going to get Lyric and simply hope and pray that she would come back to him.

`````````````````````````````````````````````````````````````````````````````

Lyric stood at the window in her tiny apartment daydreaming…again.
`````````````````````````````````````````````````````````````````````````````

It was common now for her to gaze toward the lake. She always imagined traveling back home by boat and landing securely in Marcus' arms.

Lately, she'd felt as though she was running out of time. As if she knew, somewhere deep down, that she couldn't stay away from Marcus much longer.

Originally, she had wanted to stay there forever. Before she had left New York, she imagined herself starting over in Canada. Starting a new life, making new friends...maybe even falling in love. The thing was...she had already fallen in love. In New York. And she wasn't struggling as hard to get out of it as she had thought she would.

Things had not been so rosy. She was constantly anxious about Lucas. The girl she hired from a nanny agency had proven competent and trustworthy. But she had nothing on Miss Mary.

And Lyric had no time, nor inclination, to make friends. Sure, she was friendly with her co-workers, but as soon as her shift ended, she couldn't wait to get home to Lucas. She never went anywhere or did anything outside of work. Invitations from work friends to go out had been issued, but she declined them all. They seemed to understand and didn't take it as a personal affront when she didn't join them. The desire simply wasn't there.

That was during the days. Then, there were the nights. She was lonely. And the long nights when Lucas was fussy because of teething or myriad other reasons, made her miss Marcus. Not only because he would have relieved her, but because he had a calming presence. In the midst of baby wails, he seemed to know what to say and how to act to alleviate her fears concerning Lucas.

And now, if only to herself, she could admit that being away from Marcus made it abundantly clear that she loved him. Deep down, she knew she would find no one in Toronto – or *anywhere*, for that matter – worth comparing to Marcus. Yes, she was in love with him, but knowing that made it more difficult to decide what to do. Should she stay in Toronto or risk rejection, yet again, from Marcus? Despite the kiss they'd shared, Lyric didn't know about his feelings for her *now*. Maybe her absence had given Marcus time to cool toward her and rethink what had transpired between them.

Tears suddenly stung her eyes, surprising herself. Where were these tears coming from? It was her own fault for leaving. She had no one to blame but herself. Who knows how things might have turned out if she had stayed? Marcus had everything all planned out and she had to go and ruin it.

The same thing had happened with her parents. She longed to see them again. She missed them and she would most likely be welcomed home. It was only her stubborn pride that kept her away...from them *and* Marcus.

It was nearing Christmas and she didn't relish the thought of being alone.

Canada celebrated Thanksgiving in October, so it hadn't felt much like she was missing out on the holiday. Thanksgiving hadn't felt like Thanksgiving in *October*, not to mention the fact that in some parts of Canada, it wasn't even celebrated. And in the parts that it was, it wasn't as big of a deal as it was in America, and was viewed more like a holiday like Labor Day...merely an excuse to get away for the weekend, since it was on a Monday. And on the day in November, when it would have been celebrated in the States, it had felt like any other day to her. It had been easy to forget about.

Now, however, as Christmas approached, it also invoked memories of her last Thanksgiving in the States. Rachel and Lynne had thrown a beautiful baby shower in anticipation of Lucas. And then, a couple weeks later, they had celebrated her birthday. And then there had been Christmas and her foolish kiss. Nostalgia hit hard, making her homesick.

"Alright, Lord," she prayed aloud, startling herself in the silence. "I need a sign. Should I go home and see if Marcus will take me back, or should I stay here and make a go of it?"

Praying had lately been a daily occurrence. Usually, it was beseeching God to please, please, please let Lucas go back to sleep. Still, Lyric had a feeling it was leading her to something monumental. A breakthrough, of sorts. She had even started looking for a church. That, in itself, was significant.

Lucas started stirring from his nap. She heard him on the baby monitor she had received as a gift.

She went into the bedroom and was greeted with one of his biggest smiles.

For a moment, Lyric wished Lucas could look like Marcus. Instead, she had to settle with being grateful he favored her features rather than Austin's. The last thing she needed was a daily reminder of him. Despite her past regrets, she would never wish Lucas away. He was her entire life.

"What do you think?" she asked her gurgling ten-month-old as she picked him up. "Should we stay here or go home for Christmas?"

Lucas' answer was a slobbery grin, showcasing two bottom teeth and matching top teeth.

"I miss Marcus," she continued, conversationally.

Again, he merely grinned.

After she changed his diaper, she wandered with him back into the miniscule living room.

"Perhaps that's my answer, after all."

` ` ` `

It was the middle of December and Marcus felt himself to be falling into a depression. Sure, he could *function* well enough while at school and at work – he'd even managed to pull off good grades. While at home, however, when left to his own devices, he spent his time brooding.

How long would Lyric stay away? Would she *ever* come home? What was he doing *here*, rather than there, *really?* He knew his mom and Rachel meant well, but were they right?

So many questions! He longed to be able to simply fall asleep and awaken to find Lyric home, after all. That she had never left in the first place. And that he could hold and play with Lucas anytime he wanted.

He talked to Lyric's parents weekly. They called or he did, both parties desperate for some tie, no matter how tenuous, to Lyric.

Chapter 23

Promise me you'll never forget me because if I thought you would I'd never leave
Winnie the Pooh

Lyric had done the hard part, making a decision. Now she had to have the wherewithal to stick to it. That was proving to be a much harder task. Deciding to stay in Toronto had seemed like a good idea. She wouldn't have to deal with rejection from Marcus by staying in Toronto. She wouldn't have to deal with the almost-certain censure from the other Coulters if she stayed in Toronto. She wouldn't have to go job or house hunting again, if she stayed in Toronto. In short, she wouldn't have to admit wounded pride…if she stayed in Toronto.

Why hurt herself further by going back to New York? She wasn't sure of Marcus' forgiveness – if her leaving was the last straw for him. Although, she knew she should know better. She knew he would most likely forgive her, but *most likely* wasn't certainty. She didn't know if she could take that kind of rejection from Marcus, the *one* person who meant the most to her. His good opinion of her meant the world and she knew she had most certainly ruined it.

And yet, day after day, all she could think about was to go to Marcus and beg him for forgiveness and for a second chance. She knew she deserved neither.

It was a week before Christmas and Lyric's doubts about deciding to stay were gathering fuel. She continued telling herself it was only because of the holiday that she felt that way. Any other time of the year and she would have thought differently.

Her temporary work visa wouldn't expire for awhile, but she also knew she would need to think about re-applying for one if she planned on staying permanently. And, eventually, she would have to apply for citizenship.

All of the jumbled thoughts in her head finally made her decide to think of it no more until after the holidays. If she still missed Marcus and home, she told herself, she could call him and feel him out. Maybe that would be the sign she continued to pray for.

It lasted all of two days.

Lyric was at work on her break, when Jeri, a co-worker, came in the break room.

"Your break's almost over. Boss Lady wanted me to tell ya."

"Okay."

The employees all referred to Liz, their boss, as Boss Lady. To outsiders, it may sound derogatory. In fact, it was a term of endearment.

Sitting down, Jeri slid a foot out of one of her black loafers and began rubbing it.

She was a couple years older than Lyric, at twenty-six, with light brown hair she always wore in a braid that hung to her waist. Her wide, open, friendly brown eyes matched her personality and made her a favorite with
the customers.

"So, what are your plans for Christmas? It's only five days away. You wanna come over?"

Lyric had been so preoccupied with not thinking of it, she hadn't planned much. She had gotten Lucas a couple of presents, but that was all the planning she had done. She didn't even have a tree. She simply hadn't felt very festive. Certainly not the way she had with the Coulters last year....

"Hey, you okay?" Jeri asked, noticing Lyric's sudden frown.

"Oh, I just haven't been in a very festive mood. I keep thinking about home," she admitted with a slight flush and short, self-conscious chuckle.

Lyric had told hardly anything about Marcus, New York, or any of it. And the tiny bits she had disclosed had been only to Jeri. All Jeri knew, though, was that Lyric wanted a fresh start away from New York.

What Jeri had surmised from the way Lyric talked and behaved, Lyric was trying to run away from her feelings and someone she loves and, most likely, loves her. Lyric had certainly talked about Marcus enough for Jeri to know who.

After a few moments' silence, Jeri broke it gently. "It's gonna be Lucas' first Christmas, Lyric. Maybe…maybe you should go home."

Misunderstanding, Lyric leaped to her feet. "No, no! I feel fine. Why would I go home? I'm not sick and I still have four hours left on my shift."

Jeri softly laughed. "No, I mean *home*, New York, where your heart obviously belongs."

Lyric could only gasp. Instantly she *knew!* "You're my answer!" she blurted out.

"What?" Jeri was confused.

"I was praying for a sign, a *clear* sign, as to whether I really should stay here or go – home. I prayed – and I am *not* usually a praying woman – but I needed some sort of sign, although I didn't know what it would be or what form it would take. I only prayed I would know it when I received it."

Jeri beamed. "Well, I'm glad I could help. Now, you better get back out there before Boss Lady comes looking for you."

Boss Lady! She had to tell Boss Lady!

Summoning her courage, Lyric went in search of Liz.

For the rest of her shift, Lyric could hardly concentrate. When she had told Liz, Liz had said she understood, but Lyric could tell she was disappointed. She hated disappointing Boss Lady.

What had absolutely blown her away was that God had actually given her an answer! And she had known it instantly, just as she had asked to know.

On her way home, she remembered to offer up a prayer of thanksgiving.

After Lyric got home and the nanny left, Lyric tiptoed into the bedroom to check on the already sleeping Lucas. It was nearly eleven o'clock.

Quietly, she changed into her pajamas and then got herself a cup of tea. Sitting down, she had intended to pick up her copy of *Northanger Abbey* for some quiet reading. Instead, she found herself reflecting.

Perhaps God cared for her after all. Perhaps He had been waiting this whole time for her to find Him again. And here He was, right where she had left Him several years ago, waiting for her return. She sat for quite a while in awed silence. *Why?* Why had He waited for *her?* What made her so special? What could she possibly possess that made her worth the attention of the Creator of the universe? What would make Him stay right where she left Him just…waiting. For *her?*

The questions led to feelings of discomfort, at first. She wasn't used to attention. And here God was, noticing her. Giving her the answer to the only question she dared even ask Him. And she knew how very undeserving she was. She had only even asked the question to defy God, fully expecting Him to ignore her request so she could point the finger of blame back at Him.

Soon her thoughts turned exceedingly grateful. She didn't deserve Marcus. She didn't deserve Lucas. And she most certainly didn't deserve God's love. Yet, she somehow suddenly knew she had it and couldn't help but vow, then and there, that He could have her life, too.

"Take it," she said aloud, desperately meaning the words. "I am too weary of trying to do things on my own. I am weary of building walls to keep people out. People that really only want to help me…and love me. And I am especially weary of fighting you and your will for my life. So…you win, God. Here I am." A keen sense of relief washed over her, knowing she wasn't alone in her decisions anymore. She had no idea what her future held, but she knew she didn't have to always have everything figured out. She now had Someone to do that for her.

⁁⁁⁁

Marcus couldn't believe he would spend Christmas being sad and lonely. He had never been sad at Christmas before. And he had most certainly never *felt* lonely at Christmas. Even during all of the Christmases he had spent single.

As usual, he had big plans for Christmas Eve; dinner at his parents' followed by the Candlelight Service at church.

Christmas Day would be spent at his parents' also. His mom always made a huge brunch and then, in the afternoon, they opened gifts while eating pie. The remainder of the day would be spent by the adults playing games and the kids playing with their new toys.

And yet, Marcus knew it wouldn't be the same. He would be miserable, made more acute because of his secret hope that Lyric would miraculously materialize days before Christmas, was proven untrue. Pure and simple, he *was* miserable. All he could think about was Lyric and Lucas and how they weren't there and how it would be Lucas' first Christmas. And how he'd miss Lucas' first Christmas. And there was nothing he could do about it. His resolve to leave Lyric alone wavered and he was tempted to beg Andrew for all of Lyric's information.

He missed Lyric. He *needed* her. He wanted her. He desired her. Truthfully, he'd had a hard time living day-to-day since she had left. She constantly consumed his thoughts. He worried and wondered about her and Lucas. He missed them terribly. In short, he loved them.

'''

Lyric kept praying she wouldn't be too late. If she was, she would simply take another train, a taxi; she would walk if she had to, to get to him.

Anxiously, she willed the train to *move*. It was nearing midnight and the train wouldn't be arriving at its final destination until the morning. After that, she'd have to take a taxi…if she *ever* got off this train!

The decision to leave that night had been purely impromptu. The night of her talk with Jeri at work and her decision to follow God had been December twentieth, five days before Christmas. She had told Boss Lady that night that her last day would be the twenty-third, being that the restaurant closed early on Christmas Eve and wasn't even open on Christmas.

Lyric had had just enough time to quickly pack essential belongings. She figured she could deal with her apartment and other belongings later…depending on how things worked out.

Now, as butterflies attacked her stomach, all that mattered to her was that she was on her way *home!*

'''

Marcus had to drag himself out of bed Christmas morning.

'Put your happy face on again for the nieces and nephews,' he reminded himself.

As he stepped in the shower and tried to let the hot spray relax him, he relived the previous evening.

He had done a pretty good job, he thought, of faking Christmas cheer for the sakes of Zachary, Hailey, Logan and Sydney. If it had only been his parents, Levi and Rachel, he wouldn't have tried so hard. They had understood. He could see it in their eyes, in the way they had looked at him, all pitying.

Before he had left last night, Levi had hugged him and told him in a low voice, "I'm sorry, bro."

In fact, the whole family missed Lyric. Even the kids asked after her and wondered when they could see "Baby Luke" again.

Lyric had been adamant that Lucas' name was Lucas, but she didn't mind the youngest Coulters calling him Luke. It was made very clear, however, that they were the only ones allowed to do so.

Marcus toweled off and sluggishly dressed for the day. He looked at his face in the mirror as he haphazardly gelled his hair and noticed the dark circles under his eyes and the frown lines. He frowned deeper.

"I look like a miser," he harrumphed aloud.

Sighing, he tried again. "Stop it. It's not the end of the world!"

Then why did it feel like it?

If he didn't hear from Lyric by New Year's Day, his first act of 2004 will be going after her. Andrew was more than willing to impart his knowledge. Marcus only had to say the word.

Marcus padded into the kitchen in stocking feet and opened the fridge. Grabbing a nearly empty carton of orange juice, he chugged it down. After throwing it away, he slumped into the living room and grabbed his shoes. Ready to go, he tried to muster a good attitude that would serve him for the festive day.

"Think happy thoughts," he mimicked Peter Pan, even as he heard a knock on the door.

His sort-of happy mood diminished. "It's Christmas Day!" he groused. "Who in the world *is* that?"

He flung the door open with more force than was necessary, and froze.

"Hello, Marcus," she greeted.

Without a word, Marcus crushed her to him, mindful of the baby in her arms.

Lyric's free right arm wrapped tightly around Marcus' waist.

Lucas' squirming finally tore the two apart.

Marcus chuckled. Bending down, he kissed Lucas' chubby cheek and told him, "Merry Christmas, little man!"

Lyric stooped down to grab the large duffle bag by her feet.

"I should be a gentleman and grab that, but can I hold Lucas instead?"

Lyric gladly relinquished her son. Honestly, it was a toss-up between which one was heavier.

Along with the duffle bag, she had a backpack strapped to her back, her purse was slung crosswise on her body and the diaper bag was flung over her right shoulder.

Too quick for her, Marcus picked up the duffle bag, too. Seeing her begin to protest, he smiled and winked and led her inside.

After Lyric had deposited all of her things on the floor, Marcus set Lucas down to toddle and explore as he caught Lyric up in another tight hug.

"I've missed you," he breathed into her ear.

Feeling little hands around his ankles, Marcus pulled slightly back and looked down. He scooped Lucas up and lightly bounced him in his arms. "And I've missed you, too."

Lyric took the small break to compose herself, discreetly swiping at her damp eyes. This felt so right. "Marcus, there's something I have to tell you."

Marcus noted her grin and knew it wouldn't be bad.

"Wanna sit?" he offered.

"Actually, it was a long train ride. I'm gonna stand for now."

Marcus remained standing, happily playing with Lucas.

Facing Marcus fully, Lyric announced, "I am following God." Cringing, she tried again. "Sorry. That sounded cheesy. I mean, I'm, uh…well, I gave my life – "

She was cut off as Marcus, putting Lucas down once more, had come over and gently kissed her.

Pulling slightly apart, Marcus cupped her face in both hands, staring intently into her eyes. Solemnly, "I am very proud of you, Lyric. This news is the best present I could *ever* imagine receiving for Christmas."

Equally solemn, she returned, "And all I want for Christmas is a daddy for Lucas."

Taking a deep breath and closing her eyes, she asked the one question she had been dreading and anticipating. "Will you be Lucas' daddy?"

Forcing her eyes open, she saw Marcus' shocked expression. Then a wide smile spread over his face. Whispering, he answered, "As long as it means I get to marry Lucas' mommy." In a mock serious tone, he teased, "Lucas shouldn't have unwed parents."

Lyric answered by throwing her arms around Marcus' neck and pulling his head down for a long kiss.

Finally they pulled slightly apart once again, but Lyric leaned her forehead against Marcus'.

"Is tomorrow too soon?" Marcus asked.

Lyric giggled and blushed. "Probably…but I bet the courthouse is open the day after."

Chapter 24
Be still in the presence of the Lord and wait patiently for Him to act
God (Psalm 37:7)

Christmas Day was spent with great rejoicing. The Coulters celebrated Lyric's return and her good news.

It was decided Marcus would spend the next two days at his parents' so Lucas and Lyric could stay at their apartment. The arrangements were only until they could wed at the courthouse.

Lyric was agreeing to the courthouse thing now because Marcus promised her a "proper wedding" later.

Secretly Marcus was glad they had a couple days. He had a surprise and he didn't want to wait until later, but needed the extra days to have everything arranged.

The day of their nuptials dawned bright, clear and covered in fresh snow.

Lyric took extra care in getting dressed. Kurt and Lynne had even bought Lucas a little tux to wear for the occasion.

The day after Christmas, Marcus and Lyric had gotten cheap rings to use, deciding to take great care in choosing their rings later for their wedding. They just wanted to be married and start their life together as husband and wife. There was no reason to not at least make it official. The party with their friends and other family could wait.

Lyric's only regret was going to be not having her dad to walk her down the aisle. Perhaps there would be time to reconcile...

When she had confessed this to Marcus, he had agreed. The thought made her cringe, however. It would be hard.

"Maybe before our wedding I'll try..."

The conversation flashed in her mind as she finished getting Lucas ready. Instead of ignoring it or pushing it away as she was used to, she prayed. *'Give me the courage to talk to my parents when this is all over and before our wedding. I'm ready to have them back in my life.'*

Finally ready to go, Lyric grabbed her things and hoisted up Lucas before heading out the door.

The weather was a definite hindrance but, nearly an hour later, Lyric finally made it to the courthouse. Entering and taking the escalator to the second floor, Lyric walked down the hallway and spotted Kurt and Lynne waiting with Marcus outside of the courtroom door. They would serve as witnesses.

Levi and Rachel were going to wait until the wedding to see Marcus and Lyric exchange vows. Finding a sitter for their kids had proved difficult and it would have been challenging corralling two toddlers and two very active children in a small courtroom.

Their appointed time was eleven o'clock and it was ten 'til already.

Lyric reached Marcus' side and he laced his fingers through hers, giving a squeeze.

Lucas was a happy baby and had taken well to getting re-acquainted with the Coulters – especially Marcus. Upon seeing him, Lucas let out a gurgle and stretched his arms out to Marcus.

Releasing Lyric's hand, Marcus took Lucas. "Hey, kiddo." Marcus couldn't believe he got to call him son. Snuggling him close, he breathed in the scent of his baby head and kissed it.

Lyric couldn't help but grin at the picture the two made.

Two people walked up then and joined the group. Distracted, Lyric looked away from Marcus and Lucas and glanced up to see who had joined just as the bailiff came out to call them in for their appointment. Lyric scarcely had time to register the newcomers and breathe, "Mom? Dad?" as they were ushered into the room.

As they filed in, Lyric turned to Marcus with questions on her lips. It was then that she witnessed a conspiratorial look pass between him and her parents. Questions pounded inside, but the judge was ready to begin so she knew they'd have to wait.

Marcus handed Lucas off to his mom while a beaming Jacqueline sidled over to coo and acquaint herself with her grandson. Lyric wished she had time to savor the moment of her mother meeting her grandson for the first time.

Instead, she followed Marcus to the front of the courtroom. For the next few minutes, Lyric's total attention was on Marcus and the vows they exchanged. Then came the signing and witnessing of the marriage certificate. And they were married.

Lyric was so happy, she beamed, even through her tears. She scarcely paid attention to the tears that made their way down her cheeks. She had Marcus. Forever. They were a family. And her parents were there, making her joy complete.

She glanced over at her parents then. Her dad had Lucas now. The two rushed forward with Lucas and they crushed both Marcus and Lyric to them. Jacqueline motioned toward Kurt and Lynne who joined the group, amid much laughter and happy tears.

Finally the group was forced to disband as the bailiff had to usher in the next waiting couple.

Standing back out in the hallway, Lyric turned to her parents and tried voicing the many questions fighting to be asked. In her confusion, they all came tumbling out. "How? ...Where? ...Who? ... *How?*"

Her mom laughed, a sound Lyric reveled in, and suggested, "Perhaps we all could go to lunch and we can explain."

Lynne stepped in. "Well then, introductions are in order. I'm Lynne, Marcus' mom and this is my husband, Kurt. I take it that you're Lyric's parents." Lynne shook Jacqueline's hand, then William's.

"Yes. I'm Jacqueline and this is William."

"Let's go down the street to that little café," Lynne suggested.

They all filed out of the courthouse and gingerly picked their way down the snowy sidewalk. Soon they were all reconvening in front of *The Court House Grill*, even though it was more of a café and over a block from the courthouse.

Soon orders were placed and, settled in, explanations could begin.

"I didn't even know Marcus had been in touch with you two," Lyric began. Obviously, Kurt and Lynne hadn't been in on it, either, since they had all just met.

"Neither did we," Kurt spoke up.

Marcus started explaining. "I had been having Andrew look for Lyric after she left." He threw Lyric a sheepish look. "As good as he is with computers, it still took him awhile before he found anything. In the meantime, I thought that maybe if I could find her parents, they could shed some light on the mystery that was Lyric."

Jacqueline took over then. "Will and I were surprised to hear from this stranger. It may seem odd, but we both felt a sense of peace about it. In this day and age, it does seem pretty risky going to a stranger's apartment– "

"You went to his apartment?" Lyric broke in, incredulous. "Wow!" She couldn't fathom why her parents would go to a stranger's apartment, even if said stranger knew her. One glance at them fondly gazing at her and she suddenly guessed at how they must have felt. Now that she was a parent, she could only imagine what it would have felt like, had it been her in her parents' shoes and she had been looking for Lucas. The torture she must have inflicted on them when she left....

Suddenly she jumped to her feet. First she tightly hugged her mom, then her dad, whispering, "I'm *so* sorry."

Will was a pretty tough character, but he had tears glistening in his eyes as he told his daughter, "You're forgiven, sweetheart."

After Lyric made her way back to her seat next to her new husband, Jacqueline reached over and clasped her hand. "We love you and always will," she promised her daughter.

After that, the rest of the meal was spent with Marcus, Jacqueline and Will filling everyone else in on their first meeting and how their friendship grew, hinging on one thing: their love for Lyric.

"We got the best present ever Christmas evening," Jacqueline told at the end.

Turning to Lyric, she said, "You had left Kurt and Lynne's, honey. Marcus called up and told us you were home! Then he told us you two were getting married and he wanted us to come. He wanted to surprise you. And he explained about the wedding for later and guessed you would want daddy to walk you down the aisle."

Watching her mom's animated face, hearing her chatter like a girl and calling him daddy, just like she used to, warmed Lyric's heart. Once again, she wondered how she got to have everything she had always wanted.

Then something her mom said sunk in. She turned to Marcus and asked, "How did you know? I hadn't told you about wishing I had my dad to walk me down the aisle until the next day when we went ring shopping."

Marcus slung an arm over her shoulder and squeezed. Bending down, he told her in a low voice, teasing, "Guys can have intuitions, too."

"Not most guys," Lyric smirked.

"True. But I can read you like an open book."

Lyric chuckled. "Books usually are when you read them."

"Alright, now for some serious business. When is this wedding and what can we do to help?" Jacqueline wanted to know.

A lively discussion of wedding plans quickly ensued. Their little party didn't break up until nearly two. Lucas was passed out on Lynne's shoulder.

Lyric suddenly didn't want to leave her parents. Despite the fact that everything indicated they were back in her life, she had the irrational fear that she would never see them again.

Timidly, she asked, "Mom? Dad? Would you mind taking me home?" She craved time alone with her parents. She hadn't had any since leaving home. And she wanted a chance to talk to them alone about – everything.

Hoping Marcus would understand, Lyric asked, "Do you think your parents could take you and Lucas…?"

Marcus clearly understood. "I love you, Lyric Coulter," he breathed in her ear as he sent her off with a hug and a kiss.

Outside, as they were parting ways, he told her, "I'll be waiting for you…at home," and grinned.

Once inside the car, she grew nervous, playing with her wedding band. As she waited for her parents to get settled in, she suddenly burst into tears.

Presently, her door was opened and her mom was sliding in next to her. She engulfed her daughter in her arms and Lyric felt like a little girl again.

Gulping in air, Lyric stuttered, "I'm so-so-so s-s-s-sorry, M-M-M-Mama…Daddyyyy! I'm s-s-s-sorry I l-l-l-left home!"

Jacqueline shushed and soothed, caressing Lyric's face and stroking her hair as she used to do when Lyric was upset. "It's alright, honey. Let it all out."

Quietly, Jacqueline instructed her husband, "It's okay, Will. Go ahead and drive. It'll take awhile to get through the traffic and snow."

Trying to calm down, Lyric moaned, "I understand what you two must've felt like when I left. I can't imagine anything happening to Lucas – I love him *so much!* I owe you and daddy much more than I've given."

William was glad Lyric couldn't see him. Hearing her call him daddy again made his eyes mist over.

Jacqueline was quick to reassure their daughter. "We're just so happy we were able to see you again! And that we were able to share in your special day. Now we can be a part of your life! The past is forgiven, okay? The only one hanging onto it is you. Let it go, sweetheart. We're not going anywhere. We were only waiting for you."

Her mom's words brought to mind the night of December twentieth when she was still in Canada. It was as if her mom was putting voice to everything Lyric had felt God was trying to say to her. And Lyric knew she still didn't deserve any of it…not Marcus…not Lucas…not her parents' acceptance and forgiveness. Most certainly not God's grace and mercy. Yet, He had decided she got to have it all anyway, deserving or not. Gratefulness welled deep inside.

Silently, William passed the box of tissues from the center console back to his wife.

After a long while, Lyric finally composed herself enough for normal conversation. "How much did Marcus tell you?"

"He told us everything." Jacqueline hugged her daughter. "Oh, honey, I'm so proud of you. We both are."

Clearing her throat, Lyric asked in a small voice, "So…what do you think…of Marcus?"

"You picked a good man, Lyric. That boy truly loves you."

"Well, *I* couldn't have chosen him. If God hadn't intervened, I would've picked wrong."

Jacqueline chuckled. "I suppose you've got that right."

From there, the conversation launched into catching up and the future all at once. It was a dizzying, confusing and wonderful time for Lyric with her parents.

Too soon, William pulled up to the apartment building. Marcus was waiting with Lucas under an awning, having just arrived himself.

"Do you guys want to come up?'

Jacqueline got out to let Lyric out and gave her another hug. "No, sweetheart, we'll visit another time."

William joined the two women on the sidewalk for good-byes. He gave Lyric his own hug. "You go enjoy your little family today and we'll be back soon."

Lyric joined Marcus and waved good-bye to her parents.

Together, they made their way upstairs.

After getting settled in, they cuddled on the couch.

"Thank you for today, Marcus." Lyric kissed him.

"You're welcome," he smiled.

"And thank you..." she had to pause to keep her voice from cracking with emotion. It had been a very emotional day. "...thank you for my parents. For getting in contact with them. For getting them here today. For making it possible for me to reconcile with them."

"Lyric...*you* did that part. Give yourself *some* credit. I only got in contact with them for you. It was up to you how you'd react to that. It was up to you to reconcile. I'm proud of you."

Contentedly sighing, she nuzzled into Marcus' side. "And now I get to have my daddy walk me down the aisle."

Closing her eyes to rest, Lyric quickly fell asleep, her breathing deep and even.

Laying his cheek on top of her head, Marcus closed his eyes and thanked God simply for the moment.

After having a month to settle in to their new life, Marcus and Lyric started focusing on their wedding.

"First things first, though," Marcus told her. "I need to make Lucas' adoption official. Before we decide one more thing about the wedding, I want to know that Lucas will be my son, even on paper."

They both had the same unspoken fear that Austin would show up one day and try to take Lucas, despite the fact that they hadn't heard from him since the weeks after Lucas' birth and he had showed up, creating problems. It was as if he had fallen off the face of the earth, which suited them just fine. If he ever showed up again, it would be to find he had no claim to Lucas, legal or otherwise.

The wedding was set for a Saturday in June of that year, 2004. That way, they had plenty of time to plan everything. Now, the colors were chosen: sage green and rose pink.

"And I will wear a cream dress," Lyric continued on in her conversational tone, in planning mode.

"Wait, what? Why cream?" Marcus wanted to know.

Blushing slightly, Lyric suddenly found it difficult to explain. "Er...um, I'm not...I'm not – *pure.* I wasn't when I married you, either. It wouldn't...feel right."

"Are you doing it for you...or because of me?"

"For me," she answered quickly. Too quickly. "And you," she amended quietly.

"Is this going to be our first fight as newlyweds?" Marcus teased. Turning serious, "You know I don't think of you that way – as impure."

"Why does it matter so much to you *what* color my dress is?"

"It only bothers me because it seems, once again, you are de-valuing your true worth, based on your past. Your past is gone, all mistakes erased by God...no, not *erased.* Made clean and new. Don't you see? You *are* pure now!"

"Well, it still feels like a lie," Lyric stubbornly insisted. "Like I'm trying to be something I'm not."

Marcus and Lyric had been squaring off across the living room. Now, Marcus crossed over to her.

Grabbing her around the waist, he nuzzled her neck and seductively suggested, "You know…your virtue would already have been in question, based on our wedding night…." he brushed his lips against her neck.

Trying not to be thoroughly seduced by her husband – she secretly thrilled at using the word – she rolled her eyes and gently pushed him away. "Okay," she breathed, trying to think clearly with some distance, "how about ivory?"

Marcus smiled crookedly. "Are you offering our first compromise as a newlywed couple?"

Not having to try so hard not to be distracted by her husband, she wound her arms around Marcus once more. Smiling up through her lashes flirtatiously, she answered, "I am."

Holding her tight, he breathed in her scent. "You're pretty irresistible yourself, so…done!"

Chapter 25

Don't marry the person you think you can live with; marry the individual you think you can't live without
James C. Dobson

Marcus fidgeted nervously. Ten minutes until the ceremony began.

They had decided to marry in Central Park. It was a beautiful early-summer day and perfect weather for an outdoor wedding.

Lyric had asked her mom and Camilla to stand with her as bridesmaid and –matron. Rachel served as matron-of-honor.

Marcus had chosen his dad and Andrew as groomsmen and Levi as his best man.

Nature provided all of the decoration they needed. There was only a white gazebo set up at the head of the aisle where Marcus and Lyric would exchange their vows and pledge their love, this time in front of friends and family.

An aisle was formed by a white runner with chairs set up on either side.

The reception would take place on the lawn that was beyond the gazebo.

Lyric and her party's dressing area was a white tent set up across a nearby footbridge; they were common throughout Central Park.

Inside the tent, Lyric fretted. She wasn't sure why she was so nervous now! It had been only six months since she had done nearly this very thing – promising herself to Marcus. The only difference now was the friends and family who were watching.

"Time to line up," Lynne announced. She was to walk down the aisle with Lucas, the ring bearer. Zachary and Logan were going to help their new cousin with ring bearer duties and would walk with their grandma, too. Zachary got to carry the actual pillow.

Hailey and Sydney were to serve as flower girls.

Too soon, Lyric found herself being propelled forward and then outside the white tent.

And there stood her dad. He tucked her arm into his and they waited for the rest of the wedding party, the guys having joined them outside of the tent, to go ahead of them over the footbridge and down the aisle.

At the end of the footbridge there were flowering shrubs. The beginning of the white runner aisle started just around the corner from the shrubs. Until turning the corner, the wedding party would be out of sight to the wedding guests.

Despite their nuptials at the courthouse, Marcus and Lyric had kept their wedding traditional. He would first see her in her wedding dress in all of her radiant glory as she walked down the aisle on her father's arm.

Holding her breath, Lyric simultaneously clutched her dad's arm with one hand and her bouquet of flowers with the other more tightly as they waited by the flowering shrubs.

Lyric glanced down at her ivory dress that fell to the ground in a pool of silk elegance, and smiled. She really did feel like a princess. Sleeveless, with a scoop neck and a string of her mother's pearls at her throat, matching earrings adorned her ears. Her strawberry-blonde waves were caught up in twists and woven throughout with pearls, a few chosen curls artfully escaping the arrangement.

All too soon, her cue was being played by the orchestra.

As tradition dictated, the groomsmen and bridesmaid and –matron had walked down the aisle first, followed by the best man and matron-of-honor, to Pachelbel's *Canon in D.*

Then Lynne had gone with Zachary and Logan, pushing Lucas. Hailey and Sydney were close behind, strewing red rose petals for Lyric.

As the music swelled from the key of D to start in on the *Bridal Chorus*, also known as *Here Comes the Bride,* Lyric gingerly took her first step forward from behind the flowers.

Marcus heard the change in music and strained to see Lyric. Trying to calm himself, he ordered himself to relax. *'You will see her soon enough, just as you've done every day for the past six months.'*

He knew better. He knew this day was different.

And suddenly, there she was. And he forgot how to breathe.

His first coherent thought was, *'She's so beautiful!'* It was so strong, it was on the tip of his tongue to say it aloud for everyone to hear.

Instead, he settled for murmuring to Levi, "Look at her! She's so beautiful!"

Levi grinned back. "Get ready, bro, she's almost here."

Sure enough, Lyric and William stepped up to the minister and Marcus.

"Who gives this woman?" the minister began.

"Her mother and I do," William barely choked out.

Carefully, William lifted Lyric's veil, kissed her cheek and smoothed the veil back down. He then placed Lyric's hand into Marcus' eager, waiting one, handing her off.

The simple, yet significant, act brought fresh tears to Lyric's eyes.

Turning back, she grabbed her dad's arm as he began to walk away. Stopping, William looked back. Lyric threw her arms around him. "Thank you, daddy," she whispered, tears tracking down her cheeks.

Cupping her cheek, he answered for her ears only. "I love you, baby girl."

Taking back Marcus' hand, they turned back to the minister as one, not noticing that there was nary a dry eye.

`````````````````````````````````````````````````````````````````````````````````
`````````````````````````````````````````````````````````````````````````````````

The reception was dwindling, most of the guests had left. All had been done; the bouquet toss, the garter fling, the cake cutting and shoving – sharing – and there had been plenty of dancing.

Marcus and Lyric had changed and were getting ready to leave, amidst the bubble blowers, in their decorated car.

Lyric found it a bit amusing, since they were only going to their apartment.

"Did your mom strap Lucas in already?" Lyric asked Marcus.

They had decided it would be easier to have Lynne get Lucas situated first, before they made their way through the bubble-blowing crowd. That way, they could simply drive away without a hitch.

Marcus smiled crookedly, averting her gaze. "I'm not sure."

A moment of panic seized Lyric. "Well, we need to be sure! He's tired and cranky and it would be best if he was ready to go."

Kissing her temple, Marcus murmured, "Don't worry about it."

Glancing at him questioningly, Lyric was going to inquire further but, instead, Marcus asked, "Ready?" Without waiting for a reply, he grabbed her hand and whisked her through the bubbles and well-wishers.

Opening her car door for her, Marcus helped Lyric in.

As Marcus hurried around to the driver's side, Lyric glanced to the back seat. It was empty. It didn't even have a car seat in it.

Marcus got in then and closed his door.

"Marcus," Lyric began panicking, "where is Lucas?"

"Your parents have him," he told her calmly, pulling away from the gathered crowd.

"What? Why?"

Turning to her, he flashed a grin. "We are going on a honeymoon!"

Her mouth opened with a gasp. "What? What about Lucas?"

"Your parents are going to watch him, with lots of visits from my parents, I'm sure."

Lyric was torn. On the one hand, she was excited about the prospect of real alone time with Marcus. On the other hand, she was anxious. "I didn't even get to say good-bye!"

"I know. That's why we are going to stop by the apartment first. Your parents agreed to take him there so we could say a private, *unhurried* good-bye. Our flight isn't until eleven tonight, so we have plenty of time."

Marcus could see she was still worried. One hand on the wheel, he took his other hand and cupped the back of her neck, caressing. "Lyric, you haven't been away from him, except for work, since the day he was born. He's eighteen months old! It's time for a break. We need our own time," he told her gently.

Lyric eyed him skeptically. She turned the idea around in her mind for a while, as Marcus navigated their black Toyota Corolla through New York City's streets. Coming to a conclusion, she finally broke into a grin, feeling a bit giddy at the prospect. "Okay."

Breathing a sigh of relief, Marcus echoed, "Okay."

Now that she knew Lucas would be well taken care of, Lyric thrilled to the thought of getting Marcus all to herself, without interruption.

Pulling up outside of their apartment building, Marcus parked and got out. Opening Lyric's door, he pulled her to him and kissed her breathless, making her blush.

"You are very beautiful, Mrs. Coulter," he told her as they disentangled.

Closing and locking the car, he encircled her waist with an arm and continued conversationally as they walked inside, "You looked positively stunning walking down that aisle."

Lyric flushed.

As they turned a corner on the stairs, Lyric stopped him. Standing before him, she told him sincerely, "Thank you for today. And for wanting to marry me – *again*." A girlish giggle escaped.

They continued on to their apartment. Reaching it, Marcus opened the door, calling out, "Mom, Dad, we're home!"

Lyric smiled at Marcus being so comfortable with her parents.

And then her mom was standing there with Lucas in her arms. Sleepily, Lucas reached for Lyric.

Lyric immediately took him and he snuggled against her, putting his little left hand on the side of her neck, his right hand tucked under his chin.

Suddenly, Lyric wasn't so sure she could leave him. Going to a chair, she looked back at her mom. "Mama...help," she moaned. "I can't do this. I can't leave him."

Sitting on the couch across from Lyric, Jacqueline said, "Don't worry about that now. You have time. I'll help you then. For now, enjoy your time with him."

Patting her knee, Jacqueline stood up and joined Marcus and William in the kitchen.

"Was this a bad idea? Should I have asked her first?" Marcus fretted.

"Absolutely not," Jacqueline assured him. "You are sweet for thinking of her and wanting to give her a honeymoon. If you had asked her, she probably would have wanted to bring Lucas along. She needs this, as do you...she simply doesn't know it yet."

Biting his bottom lip, he hesitantly looked through the kitchen to Lyric and Lucas in the living room. "I'm having a hard time wanting to leave now, too."

Will and Jacqueline shared a knowing chuckle.

William informed him, "That little boy has his grammy and grampy wrapped around his little finger. He'll be just fine."

"But will I?" Marcus wondered, miserable at the thought.

"Perhaps you should go join Lyric in saying good-bye to your son."

Marcus couldn't believe how incredibly good it felt to be able to use that word. Lucas' adoption had been made official only a week ago – he was legally Lucas' daddy. A *daddy!* Lyric had reassured him all along that he was already Lucas' daddy, legal or not. She had told him, "It takes a *real* man to be a daddy."

Slowly, Marcus shuffled into the living room, already dreading the good-bye.

Sensing his presence, Lucas stirred in Lyric's arms and lifted his head, giving Marcus a sleepy smile.

Marcus reached for Lucas. "Can I say good-bye, too?"

Lyric released her hold, but stayed close to her husband and son.

William and Jacqueline wandered into the room after a while, arms around each other's waist. Before interrupting, they watched the sweet and beautiful tableau in front of them.

Lightly clearing his throat, William spoke softly. "It's time, I'm afraid, or you'll miss your flight."

Lyric looked up with sad eyes. "He's asleep and when he wakes up, we won't be here."

Jacqueline went to crouch in front of her daughter. Gently, she told her, "I promised you I'd help when it was time. It's time. You'll see him in only ten days. It's not so long."

Marcus and Lyric rose. Resigned, Lyric had to give in. "Okay. We'll go tuck him in first."

Jacqueline lightly prodded. "Okay, but you'll need to leave soon. You still have the drive to the airport."

After a few minutes, Marcus and Lyric came out of Lucas' room clasping hands.

Jacqueline and William couldn't help but laugh at their tragic faces. "You two look as if you're going to a funeral, not on your honeymoon," Jacqueline teased.

Efficiently and effectively, Jacqueline urged Marcus and Lyric to the door.

Before leaving, however, Marcus and Lyric took turns giving Jacqueline and William hugs.

"Thank you for everything," Marcus began, "especially for agreeing to stay here with Lucas so he could be in familiar surroundings."

Then it was Lyric's turn. "Thank you for walking me down the aisle today, daddy."

Out of the sentimental wedding atmosphere, William ducked his head, uncomfortable. "It was my pleasure – and honor, honey. I gladly gave you to Marcus today…he's a good man."

Brought up short, Marcus answered in surprise, "Thank you, sir!"

Catching a glance at the clock, Jacqueline admonished, "Ach! Time to get a move on," and successfully shooed them out of the apartment and on to their honeymoon.

ˏˏ